THE
ELAGHIN
AFFAIR
and other stories

THE ELAGHIN AFFAIR

and other stories

IVAN BUNIN

*Selected and Translated
from the Original Russian by*
BERNARD GUILBERT GUERNEY

MINERVA PRESS

PREFATORY NOTE

〜 〜

BY WAY OF COMMENT on this collection, the present writer
would rather offer an appreciative *causerie,* referring the
reader curious for biographical detail to the autobiograph-
ical note prefacing the English version of *The Village,* and
adding that since the publication of that note the number
of Bunin's writings has been considerably added to, that he
has travelled still more extensively, and that one of his
journeys took place in 1933, when he went to Sweden to
receive the Nobel Prize for Literature. . . .

Bunin is, as far as I can perceive, a figure unique in Russian literature. And distinctly of the *aristoi,* in either Russian or universal letters. As a literary figure, in stature if
not in bulk, he strikes one, almost irresistibly, as a French
Academician—and one learns that, in the old Russia, he
was "one of the Twelve Honorary Academicians, who correspond to the French Immortals." One thinks of him not
as of a Slav, but as of a Gaul who has chosen impeccable
Russian as his medium. The obvious objection is that he
has not the Gallic verve—to which the equally obvious retort is that there have been French writers who were far
from being sprightly. On the other hand, if the time-worn
and thoroughly detestable cliché of "Slavic melancholy" be

aired in regard to Bunin, one has but to point out that, despite the ready and pathetic acceptance of this cliché, melancholy is *not* a literary manifestation exclusively Slavic.

Nor have I much patience with clichés concerning Bunin's "profoundly Russian" outlook on religion. To me, for one, such a phrase seems devoid of much meaning, even though he does treat of Russian superstition—beautifully, as in *Aglaia* and *The Third Cock-Crow;* harrowingly, as in *I Say Nothing* and *The Sacrifice.* If anything, he is imbued with Oriental mysticism: to perceive this, one has but to read *A Compatriot, Brethren, Death, Gautami, The Night of Denial.* And in *The Cicadas* (which is, as well, his confession of faith as a writer) one can see a belief in Buddhism and his origin in the paradisaical lands of the East. Best of all, however, his religious and artistic beliefs are summed up in his quotation from Saadi: "I strove 'to view the face of the earth and leave thereon the impress of my soul.' "

He is a greater cosmopolite that even Turgeniev was. He is, indubitably, a Russian stylist. He can write impeccably, in a style chill, hard, brilliant, like rock-crystal, best described in his own phrase, in *The Cicadas* poem in prose: ". . . wondrous blossoms, that seem to grow in crystal spirals." He wanted, we are told, to be a painter; and he is a painter, even in giving his reaction to sounds, as in the above quotation. Nor could I, offhand, mention any other writer as imagistic, as evocative of pictures. But, in addition to this style, he can write unerringly of peasants and the petty bourgeoisie of the Russia that was. Never is the speech of any stratum or substratum of the old Russian social structure incorrect, or false, or mixed. But in either style he is ever aloof, ever objective. It is really curious how few of his stories are told in the first person. . . .

Kuprin has been called the Poet of Life. Bunin could, I think, with equal justice be called the Poet of Death. (I do not believe his popularity would be either augmented or diminished by such an appellation.) He is more than half in love with death—and that not necessarily easeful death. Again, it is highly curious how many of his stories deal with death, directly or indirectly. He can extract the honey of bitter poetry even out of the brutal and brutish death of a peasant. . . . Yet the accusation of morbidity would hardly hold against him. Once more the reader is referred to *The Cicadas:* is there anywhere a more eager pæan to life? Or a more zestful savouring of earthly sights, sounds, smells—all sensuous experiences—than in *The Star of Love?* Death to Bunin is a part of, if not a sequel to, life: an obverse of a medal he yearns to decipher.

And, besides life and death, his particular province is love: but here, too, he prefers to pose peculiar situations, even as in his psychological studies. He may not have the fiendish insight of Dostoievski, but nobody writing today wields a scalpel more delicately than he has done in *Light Breathing, The Son, The Grammar of Love.* "After all, the creepiest thing in the world is the soul of man. . . ."

No estimate of Bunin as a literary figure can be complete unless his work as a poet be taken into account. Such a consideration is, unfortunately, impossible for the general reader because of both the barrier of a foreign language and the practical obstacles to the publishing of all poetry, but especially poetry in translation. Yet it is as a poet, in *On the Alps,* that Bunin has stated the alpha of his credo as artist in life and letters:

Upon the heights, upon a snowy peak,
I carved a sonnet with a blade of steel.
Day follows day. If any were to seek,
The snows may still my lonely track reveal.

Upon the heights, where heaven's blue turns bleak,
Where wintry rays in joyous riot reel,
The lone sun saw my dagger verse-wounds deal
On ice gem-green, and obdurate as teak.

And the thought gladdens me: Some poet will
Well understand me. Loud the mob may speak
In valleys, greeting—joy he will not feel!

Upon the heights, where heaven's blue turns bleak,
I carved, at eve, a sonnet with cold steel
Only for him who may attain the peak.—

and, in *An Inscription,* the omega:

An ancient chalice he found, on the shore of the sea,
    blue and surging—
In an ancient grave-mound, on a wild, sandy sea-marge.
Long he laboured, long putting together
The fragments the sepulchre had kept three thousand
    years a thing sacred;
And on the chalice at last he deciphered

PREFATORY NOTE

The utterance ancient of the graves and the sepulchres
    speechless:

*Eternal are only the sea—the shoreless sea—and the
    heavens;*
Eternal are only the sun, the earth, and earth's beauty;
*Eternal is only that which bindeth, with a band that the
    eye cannot compass,*
*The soul and the heart of the living with the dark soul
    of sepulchres.*

BERNARD GUILBERT GUERNEY

New York City
Autumn, 1934

CONTENTS

༄ ༄

THE
ELAGHIN
AFFAIR
and other stories

THE ELAGHIN AFFAIR

~ ~

A HORRIBLE AFFAIR, this—strange, enigmatic, unsolvable.
On the one hand it is very simple; but, on the other, very
intricate, resembling a dime novel—which was precisely
what everybody in our town called it—and, at the same
time, it might be utilized in the creation of a profound and
artistic work of literature. On the whole the counsel for the
defence spoke justly at the trial:

"In this case," said he at the opening of his speech,
"there seems to be no room for disagreement between the
prosecuting attorney and myself. Why, the defendant has
himself pleaded guilty, while both his crime and his personality, as well as the personality of his victim—whose
will he may seem to have violated, as it were—must appear
to well-nigh all those present in this court-room unworthy
of any special philosophizing, because of their apparently
sufficient inanity and drabness. But all this is not at all so;
all this is so only in appearance; there is plenty to disagree
over—the grounds for dispute and deliberations are very
numerous. . . ."

And further on he said:

"Let us suppose that my aim is to attain leniency, at least,
for the accused. Were this the case I would have but

3

little to say. No lawmaker has indicated by what, precisely, judges must be guided in cases such as ours; a great latitude has been left for the exercise of their understanding, conscience, and insight—which, in the upshot, are precisely the determining factors in deciding upon this or that framing of the law which fittingly punishes the act. And so my endeavour then would be to influence that understanding, that conscience; my endeavour would be to place in the very foreground all that is best in the accused, and all that mitigates his guilt. I would strive to awaken kindly emotions in the judges, and would do so all the more insistently inasmuch as the defendant denies but one element in his guilt—that of malice prepense.

"However, even if it were a case of such pleading, could I possibly avoid a dispute with the prosecutor, who has classified the prisoner at the bar as nothing more or less than a 'criminal lycanthrope'? In every trial it is possible to regard everything in different ways—everything may be shown in this light or that, or represented just as one wishes, in one way or another. And what do we see in this case of ours? Why, this—that there seems to be not a single trait, not a single detail in it, which the prosecution and I could regard alike, which we could be in agreement upon when it comes to telling about it or throwing light upon it! Every minute I am forced to say to the opposing counsel: 'Everything is so—and yet it isn't so!' But that is just the most important thing: at its very core everything 'isn't so' about this case! . . ."

Here is how this affair began:

It was the 19th of June of last year. The morning was young—between the hours of five and six—but it was al-

ready light in the dining-room of Likharev, captain of the
Life Guards Hussar regiment; it was also stuffy, dry, and
hot from the summer sun over the city. However, things
were still quiet—all the more so since the captain's quarters
were in one of the buildings of the Hussar barracks, located
outside the city. And, making the most of this quiet, as
well as of his youth, the captain was sleeping soundly. The
table was cluttered with bottles of liqueurs and half-
finished cups of coffee. Another officer, Count Koshitz, the
staff captain, was sleeping in the adjoining room, the parlour; while still farther off, in the study, slumbered Cornet
Sevski. The morning, in a word, was quite a usual one, and
the scene simply set; but, as is generally the case when in
the midst of what is usual there happens something unusual, that which happened so suddenly in the quarters of
Captain Likharev during the early morning of the 19th of
June was all the more horrible, amazing, and somehow
seemingly more improbable. Unexpectedly, amid the complete stillness of the morning, the bell jangled in the entry;
then came the cautious, light, barefoot patter of the orderly
running to open the door; after which an intentionally
raised voice rang out:

"Is the captain at home?"

And it was with a noisiness just as intentional that the
visitor entered, flinging open the door into the dining-room
with particular familiarity, clattering with his boots and
clinking his spurs with particular audacity. The captain
lifted a bewildered and sleep-laden face. Standing before
him was one of his messmates, Cornet Elaghin—a diminutive, puny, carroty, and freckled fellow, bandy-legged and
unusually spindly-shanked, booted with that dandyism

which, as he was fond of saying, was his "chief" weakness. He quickly shed his summer uniform top-coat and, having chucked it on a chair, said loudly: "There y'are—here are my shoulder-straps!" And after that he made his way to the divan placed against the opposite wall, slumped upon it on the flat of his back, and flung his hands behind his head.

"Hold on, hold on!" muttered the captain, following him with goggling eyes. "Where are you coming from—and what's the matter with you?"

"I've killed Manya," said Elaghin.

"Are you drunk? What Manya?" asked the captain.

"Maria Sosnovskaya, the actress."

The captain let his feet drop to the floor.

"Come, now, what are you up to—are you fooling?"

"Alas, not at all, to my regret—or, perhaps, to my good fortune."

"Who's there? What's up?" the count called out from the drawing-room.

Elaghin stretched himself and, with a light kick, threw the door leading into the drawing-room ajar.

"Stop yelling," said he. "It's I, Elaghin. I've shot Manya."

"What's that?" asked the count—and, after an instant's silence, burst into sudden laughter. "Oho, so that's it!" he shouted gaily. "Well, what the devil—it won't count against you this once! It's a good thing you woke us up, or else we'd surely have overslept. We were cutting up again yesterday until three in the morning."

"I give you my word I killed her," Elaghin repeated insistently.

"You're lying, fellow, you're lying," the host began shouting as he reached for his socks. "Why, you had me all scared, thinking something had really happened. . . . Ephraim, serve the tea!"

Elaghin reached down into a trouser-pocket, pulled out a small key, and, having deftly tossed it over his shoulder onto the table, said:

"There, go and have a look for yourselves."

During the trial the procureur had a great deal to say about the cynicism and horror of certain incidents comprising the Elaghin drama, and more than once did he stress the above incident as well. He forgot that on this morning it was only during the first minute that Captain Likharev had failed to notice Elaghin's "supernatural" pallor, as he expressed it, and that "not human" something in his eyes; but after that the captain was "simply overwhelmed by both the one and the other. . . ."

II

And so this is what took place on the morning of the 19th of June of last year:

Half an hour later Count Koshitz and Cornet Sevski were already standing at the entrance of the house where Sosnovskaya had lived. Now they were no longer in a mood for jesting.

They had all but made their cabby founder his horse; they had leapt headlong from their light carriage, had thrust the key into the keyhole repeatedly, and had rung the bell desperately—but the key did not fit, and all was silence on the other side of the door. Losing patience, they hastened into the courtyard and started a search for the caretaker. The caretaker hurried into the kitchen through the back entrance and, upon his return, reported that, according to what the maid had said, Sosnovskaya had not passed the night at home—she had gone away early in the evening, taking some sort of parcel along with her.

The two officers were taken aback—what was to be done in such a case? After due deliberation and shrugging of shoulders they got back into their carriage and went off to the police station, taking the caretaker with them. From there they rang up Captain Likharev.

The captain yelled furiously into the transmitter:

"This damned fool—he's got me almost bawling like a baby over him—forgot to say that you shouldn't have gone to her rooms at all, but to their so-and-so secret love-nest—" and he gave the address. "Did you get that?"—and he repeated it. "Something in the nature of a Parisian *garçonnière* or bachelor apartment, with the entrance directly from the street."

They galloped off to the new address.

The caretaker sat with the driver; the police sergeant, with restrained independence, took a seat in the carriage, opposite the officers. It was hot; the streets were crowded and noisy, and it was hard to believe that on such a sunny and lively morning someone could be lying dead somewhere, and the mind was nonplussed at the thought that that someone had been done to death by the twenty-two-year-old Alec Elaghin. How could he ever have found the heart to do it? What had he killed her for? Why, and how, had he killed her? It was impossible to understand anything; the questions remained without any answer.

When they finally stopped in front of an old and uninviting two-storey house on a street in the old quarter of the town, the two officers "fell in spirits altogether," to use their words. Could it be possible that *this* was here, and could it be possible that *this* had to be seen—even though they were drawn to see it, and drawn irresistibly? The police sergeant, on the other hand, immediately felt himself stern, alert, and self-assured.

"The key, if you please," said he crisply and firmly, and the officers hastened to surrender the key to him with the same timidity that the caretaker would have evinced.

In the central arch of the house were iron gates; beyond the gates could be glimpsed a small patio with a sapling, the verdure of which was somehow preternaturally vivid —or seemed so against the dark-grey stone walls. And to the right of the gates was that same mysterious door, issuing directly on the street, which they had to open. And now the police sergeant, assuming a frown, thrust in the key, and the door opened—and Count Koshitz and Cornet Sevski beheld something that looked like an utterly dark corridor. The police officer, having guessed, as though by scent, where he had to seek for the switch, stretched out his hand, scraped it over the wall, and lit up a dark and sombre place, in the dark recesses of which, between two armchairs, stood a small table bearing plates that held remnants of game and fruit.

Yet still more sombre was that which met their eyes when they penetrated farther. On the right side of the corridor there proved to be a small entrance into an adjoining room, likewise utterly dark. It was sepulchrally illumined by a small lantern of opalescent glass, hanging close to the ceiling, under black silk draped like an enormous

9

parasol. Some black fabric also draped, from floor to ceiling, the walls of this room—a room devoid of even a single window and, save for the door, without any outlet.

Here, also in the farther recess of the room, stood a large, low Turkish divan—and lying upon it, whitely gleaming, clad only in a night-gown, with eyes and lips half-open, with head drooping on her bosom, with her extremities stretched out and her feet slightly apart, was a very young woman of rare beauty.

III

The beauty of the deceased was rare in that it satisfied to a rare degree those exacting demands which fashionable painters, for example, set themselves when portraying comely women. Here was everything requisite—a superb form, a superb body-tone, a foot tiny and without a single blemish, a childlike, simple-hearted charm about the lips, small and regular features, marvellous hair. And all this was by now dead; all had begun to petrify, to fade, and her beauty made the dead woman still more awesome. Her hair was in perfect order—her coiffure would have graced any ball. Her head was lying on a slightly raised cushion of the divan, while her chin rested lightly on her bosom, which position bestowed upon her fixed, half-open eyes and her entire face an apparently somewhat puzzled expression. And all this was strangely illumined by a small opalescent lantern hanging near the ceiling, at the bottom of an enormous, parasol-shaped black drapery, resembling some bird of prey that had spread its webbed wings over the dead woman.

On the whole the scene overwhelmed even the police sergeant. Next, hesitatingly, they all began a closer inspection.

The superb bare arms of the dead woman were extended straight along her body. Upon her breast, on the lace of her night-gown, were lying two visiting-cards of Elaghin's, while at her feet lay a Hussar sabre, looking exceedingly crude by the side of their feminine nakedness. The count was about to pick it up in order to take it out of the scabbard, labouring under the absurd notion that there might be traces of blood on the blade. The police sergeant held him back from committing any such unlawful act.

"Ah, of course, of course," the count mumbled in a whisper. "One must not handle anything yet, of course. I'm struck by the fact that I don't see any blood anywhere, or, in general, any traces of a crime. . . . A case of poisoning, evidently?"

"Have patience," said the police officer sententiously. "Let's wait for the coroner and the doctor. But, beyond a doubt, it does look like poisoning as much as anything else—"

And, really, things did have that look. There was no blood anywhere—neither on the floor, nor on the divan, nor on the body, nor on the dead woman's night-gown. Thrown over the arm-chair near the divan were a pair of step-ins and a *peignoir;* under these was a tiny chemise—blue, with a pearly sheen—a skirt of excellent dark-grey material, and an opera-cloak of grey silk. All these had been tossed down pell-mell, but they, too, were free from any blood-stain—there was not a single drop. The poison theory was also further confirmed by the things which were found on a wall-ledge above the divan: on this ledge, amid champagne bottles and corks, candle-ends and hairpins, and amid scribbled and torn scraps of paper, stood an unfinished tumbler of porter and a small medicine vial, on the long, white, tongue-like tag of which, staring blackly and ominously, was the inscription: *OP. PULV.*

But just at the moment when the police sergeant, Count Koshitz, and Cornet Sevski were by turns examining this tag, they heard out in the street the noise of the carriage with the doctor and the coroner driving up, and in a few minutes it turned out that Elaghin had been telling the truth: Sosnovskaya had really been killed with a revolver. There were no blood-stains on the night-gown. But then a dark-purple spot was revealed under the gown, in the region of the heart—and, in the centre of this spot, a small, round wound with scorched edges; dark, watery blood was oozing out of the wound, but this blood had not stained anything, since the wound had been covered with a handkerchief crumpled into a wad.

What else did the expert post-mortem examination establish? Not a great deal: that the dead woman's right lung showed traces of tuberculosis; that the shot had been fired point-blank, and that death had come instantaneously, even though the late Sosnovskaya had still been able to utter a short phrase after the shot; that there had been no struggle between the slayer and his victim; that she had drunk champagne, and that she had taken a small quantity of opium with porter, but not sufficient to poison her; and, finally, that on this fatal night she had had sexual relations with a man. . . .

But why had this man killed her, and what for? In answering these questions Elaghin stubbornly persisted that

it was because both of them—he as well as Sosnovskaya—
were in a "tragic situation"; that they could see no other
way out of it except death; and that in killing his mistress
he had merely carried out her own behest. However, all
this seemed to be entirely contradicted by the notes the
woman had written just before her death. For had there
not been found on her breast two of Elaghin's visiting-
cards, closely written in her hand in Polish—and that, it
must be said by the way, quite wretchedly spelled? One
card was addressed to General Konovitzin, chairman of the
Board of Directors of her theatre, and ran:

Dear Friend:
    I thank you for your noble friendship of several
years. . . . I send you my last regards, and beg of
you to pay to my mother all the sums due me for my
recent appearances. . . .

The other read:

This man has acted justly in killing me. . . . Mother
—my poor, unfortunate darling! I am not asking for
forgiveness, inasmuch as I am dying not of my own
will. . . . Mother! We shall see each other again . . .
there, above. . . . I feel that this is the last moment. . . .

On just such other cards did Sosnovskaya write her other
ante-mortem notes as well. These were strewn over the wall-
ledge, in painstakingly torn pieces. When assembled and
pasted together they read as follows:

13

This man demands my death and his own. . . . I am not fated to come out alive. . . .

And so my last hour has struck. . . . My God, forsake me not!— My last thought I dedicate to my mother— and to my art, which I hold sacred—

An abyss . . . abyss. . . . This man is my fate. . . . My God, save me, succour me. . . .

And, finally, came the most enigmatic one:

Quand même pour toujours—

All these notes—those that were found quite intact on the dead woman's bosom, as well as those that had been found in fragments on the wall-ledge—apparently contradicted Elaghin's assertions. But, to be precise, only *apparently*. Why had not those two cards been torn up which had been lying on Sosnovskaya's breast, and one of which bore such fatal words for Elaghin as: "I am dying not of my own will"? Elaghin had not only not torn them up and carried them off with him, but had even put them in the most conspicuous place himself—for who else but he could have done so? Had he not torn them up in his hurry, perhaps? In his hurry he might, of course, have forgotten to do so. But if he had been in a hurry, how could he have put on the dead woman's bosom notes so fraught with danger for him? And then, in general, had he been at all flustered? No; he had put the dead woman to rights, had, after having first protected the wound with a handkerchief, readjusted her night-gown, and then had been dressing and putting himself in order. . . . No, the prosecuting attorney had been right at this point: all this had not been done in a hurry.

IV

The prosecuting attorney said:

"There are two classes of criminals. First, criminals by accident, whose misdeeds are the fruit of an unfortunate conflux of circumstances and of that exasperation which is scientifically designated as a 'raptus of insanity.' And, secondly, criminals who act as they do through malicious and premeditated intent—these are the congenital enemies of society and of the social order; these are the lycanthropes, the criminal wolves. In which division shall we number the man on the prisoner's bench? In the second, of course. He is, indubitably, a criminal wolf; he has committed his crime because he has become bestialized by his idle and unbridled mode of living. . . ."

This tirade was an unusually strange one (even though it did voice the almost universal opinion in our city concerning the Elaghin case), and all the more strange because all through the trial Elaghin sat with his head leaning on his hand, which also served to screen his face from the public, and answered all questions quietly, abruptly, and with a certain heart-rending timidity and sadness. And yet, at the same time, the prosecuting attorney was also right— the criminal sitting on the prisoner's bench was by no means an ordinary one, and not at all one stricken by a "raptus of insanity."

The prosecuting attorney posed two questions: in the

15

first place, of course, whether the crime had been committed in a state of aberration—that is, of excitement; and, in the second, whether Elaghin's had been merely an involuntary complicity in the slaying? And he answered both questions with complete assurance: "No, and no!"

"No!" he had said in answer to his first question. "There cannot even be any idea of any aberration whatsoever—and that, first and foremost, because no state of mental excitement can continue for several hours at a stretch. Then, too, what could have brought on Elaghin's aberration?"

To settle the last question the prosecutor put a great number of minute questions to himself—and immediately rejected them, or even held them up to ridicule and scorn. Said he:

"Hadn't Elaghin been drinking more than usual, perhaps, on this fatal day? No; he generally drank a great deal —but on this day no more than usual.

"Was the accused a man sound of health, and is he so at present? I join in the opinion of the medical men who have had him under observation: he is quite sound, but utterly unused to curbing himself.

"Wasn't the aberration brought on, perhaps, by the impossibility of his marrying the woman he loved—that is, if it be admitted that he really did love her? No—inasmuch as we know that the accused did not entertain the idea of any such marriage or undertake any steps whatsoever to bring it about."

And he said further:

"Wasn't his aberration brought on, perhaps, by Sosnovskaya's proposed departure for abroad? No, inasmuch as he had long known about such a departure. But, in that case, might not his aberration have been brought on by the idea of breaking off with Sosnovskaya—a breaking-off consequent upon her departure? Again no—for they had discussed this breaking-off a thousand times prior to this night. And, if that be the case, what *did*, finally, bring on his madness? Their talks about death? The strange setting of the room—its witch's spell, so to say, its depressiveness, even as, in general, the depressiveness of this entire unwholesome, eerie night? But, as far as talks about death are concerned, surely they could not possibly have been a novelty to Elaghin! Such conversations had been carried on between him and his inamorata incessantly, and, of course, he had become utterly fed up with them ever so long ago. As for the unholy obsession of the room—why, it's mirth-provoking even to speak of it! Surely such a spell was *quite* modified by objects quite prosaic: by the supper, by the scraps of that supper on the table, by the bottles, and even—if you will pardon me—by the chamber-pot. . . . Elaghin ate, drank, answered the calls of nature, went into the other room—now after wine, now after a knife to sharpen a pencil. . . ."

And the prosecuting attorney concluded as follows:

"As for whether the murder committed by Elaghin was a fulfilment of the dead woman's will: really, we do not have to deliberate long over this question. For the determination of that point we can take the uncorroborated assertions of Elaghin that Sosnovskaya herself had begged him to kill her—or we can take Sosnovskaya's own note, so utterly fatal to him: 'I am dying not of my own will. . . .' "

V

A good deal could have been objected to in the details of the prosecutor's speech. "The accused is quite sound. . . ." But where is one to draw the line between health and ill health? "He undertook no steps whatsoever to bring the marriage about." But then, in the first place, he did not undertake any such steps only because he was thoroughly and firmly convinced of their futility; and, in the second place, are love and marriage so very closely bound together? And would Elaghin have found peace and, in general, a complete and satisfactory denouement for the drama of his love by espousing Sosnovskaya? Really, is it not well known that there is about every strong love, and, in general, about every love that is not altogether humdrum, a peculiar tendency apparently to shun wedlock, somehow?

Yet all these, I repeat, are but details. For basically the prosecuting attorney was right—there had been no aberration.

He said:

"The medical experts have arrived at the conclusion that Elaghin had been 'rather in a calm state' than in an aberrant one; whereas I maintain that his state had been not merely calm, but amazingly calm. We are convinced of this by an inspection of the tidied-up room where the crime had been committed and where Elaghin had still remained for a long time after his crime. Then we have the evidence of the witness Yaroshenko, who had seen with what calmness Elaghin left this apartment and how meticulously, how unhurriedly he turned the key in the street-door. Also, there is Elaghin's behaviour at Captain Likharev's. What, for instance, did Elaghin say to Cornet Sevski, who pleaded with him 'to come to his senses,' to recollect if Sosnovskaya had not shot herself? Elaghin had said: 'No, brother—I remember everything *very well*'—and immediately proceeded to describe just how he had fired the shot. The witness Budberg was 'even unpleasantly struck by Elaghin— after his confession he had drunk tea with utter sang-froid!'

"As for the witness Foht, *he* had been struck still more. 'I hope, sir,' Elaghin had said ironically to Staff-Captain Foht, 'that you will excuse me from drill duty today.'— 'This was so frightful,' says Foht, 'that Cornet Sevski could not restrain himself and broke into sobs.' True, there was a moment when Elaghin, too, broke into sobs; this was when the captain had come back from the commander of the regiment, to whom he had gone for instructions concerning Elaghin, and when Elaghin had gathered from the faces of Likharev and Foht that he, Elaghin, was in reality no longer an officer. Only at that very moment did he break into sobs," the prosecuting attorney concluded. "Only at that moment!"

The last phrase is likewise a very strange one. Who does not know how frequently such an awakening from the stupor of misfortune occurs suddenly brought about by something utterly insignificant, something which may meet one's eye by chance and in a moment reminds a man of all his former happy life—and of all the hopelessness, all the horror of his present situation? And yet Elaghin had been reminded of all this not at all by something insignificant, casual. Why, he was an officer born, you might say—ten generations of his ancestors had been in the army. And now he was no longer an officer. And, as if that were not enough, he was one no longer because the woman whom he loved truly more than he did his own life was no longer in this world—and because he, he himself, had done this monstrous deed.

However, these, too, are but details. For the main thing is that there really had been no "raptus of insanity." But, in that case, what had there been? The prosecuting attorney admitted that "in this shady affair everything must first of all resolve itself into a consideration of the characters of Elaghin and Sosnovskaya, and into a clearing up of their relations." And he firmly declared:

"We have here the coming together of two individualities having nothing in common."

Was that really so? It is precisely therein that the whole question consists: Was that really so?

VI

Concerning Elaghin I would say, first of all, that he is two-and-twenty—a fatal age, a dreadful period which determines what a man's whole future is to be. Usually during this period a man is living through what is medically known as puberty, or sexual maturing, and, in terms of life, one's first love, which is almost always looked upon merely poetically and, on the whole, quite frivolously. Frequently this "first love" is accompanied by dramas, by tragedies; but nobody at all ever gives a thought to the fact that it is precisely at this time that men and women are living through something far more profound, more complex, than the agitation and torment which are ordinarily styled the "adoration of a beloved being." They are living, without themselves being aware of it, through the weird blossoming, the excruciating revelation, the first sacred mass, of sex.

And so, had I been Elaghin's counsel, I should have asked the judges to direct their attention to his age precisely from this point of view, and also to the fact that the man sitting before us was not at all an ordinary one in that respect. "A young Hussar, a locoed wastrel, burning the candle of his life at both ends," the prosecutor was saying, echoing the general opinion. And, in proof of the correctness of his words, he cited the story of one of the witnesses, the actor Lissovski—of how Elaghin had once arrived at the theatre in the daytime, as the cast was gathering for rehearsal; and how Sosnovskaya, upon catching sight of him, had jumped aside and hid behind Lissovski's back and quickly said to him: "Screen me from him, Uncle!"—"Screen her I did," Lissovski told his story, and this Hussar youngster, full to the gills with wine, suddenly stopped short, as if he were locoed. He stands there, with his legs wide apart, and gapes in perplexity—where could Sosnovskaya have gone to?"

There you have it, precisely—a locoed fellow. But the only thing is—locoed by what? Come, could it really have been by his "idle and unbridled mode of living"?

Elaghin came from a genteel and well-to-do family. He had been at a very early age deprived of his mother (who, mark you, had been of quite an exultant nature). From his father, a man morose and stern, he was estranged, first of all, by that fear in which he, Elaghin, had both grown and reached maturity. The prosecutor, with a cruel effrontery, depicted not only the moral but also the physical image of Elaghin. And it was he who said:

"Such, gentlemen, was our hero in his picturesque raiment of a Hussar. But look at him now! Now nothing any longer prettifies him; before us is a squat and stoop-shouldered young man with a little moustache like an albino's, and with an extremely indeterminate, vacuous expression on his face. In his skimpy black frock-coat he reminds one but very little of Othello. . . . In other words the accused is, in my opinion, an individual with sharply defined degenerate peculiarities; extremely timorous in certain cases, as, for instance, in his attitude toward his father, and extremely arrogant in others, without taking any obstacles into consideration—that is, when he feels himself free from his father's eye, and, in general, hopes to go unpunished. . . ."

Well, there was a great deal of truth in this blunt characterization. But I, as I listened to it, failed to understand, first of all, how anyone could regard lightly all those frightfully intricate and tragic things which frequently mark persons of sharply defined hereditary taint; and, secondly, I saw in that which was true about the characterization only a very small moiety of truth, after all. Yes, Elaghin had grown up in fear and trembling before his father. But fear and trembling do not constitute cowardice, and this holds particularly true when it is one's parents who inspire the fear and trembling, and, to boot, in a man who is endowed with an intensified sensitiveness of all that heredity which binds him to all his sires, grandsires, and great-grandsires. —Yes, Elaghin's outward appearance is not the classical appearance of a Hussar; but in this as well I see one of the proofs of the extraordinariness of his nature. "Look more closely," I would have said to the prosecutor, "at this carroty, stoop-shouldered, and spindly-shanked fellow, and you will perceive, well-nigh with fear, how far removed from insignificance is this freckled face with its small and greenish eyes, whose gaze avoids yours. And, after that, turn your attention to his stamina—the stamina of a degenerate: on the day of the murder he had been drilling (from early morning, as a matter of course), and at breakfast had drunk six ponies of vodka, a bottle of champagne, two ponies of cognac—and, with all that, had remained almost perfectly sober!"

VII

In great contradistinction to the generally prevalent low opinion concerning Elaghin was the testimony of many of his messmates. All of these gave the finest reports about him. Here, for instance, is the squadron commander's opinion of Elaghin:

"Upon entering the regiment Elaghin had placed himself on a remarkably fine footing with the officers, and, when it came to the rank and file, was always exceedingly kind, considerate, and just. His character, to my way of thinking, had but one marked trait—that of nervousness. This, however, found its expression not in anything disagreeable, but merely in frequent and rapid transitions from gaiety to melancholy, from talkativeness to taciturnity, from self-assurance to utter despondency about his merits, and, in general, about his whole destiny. . . ."

Next we have the opinion of Captain Likharev:

"Elaghin had always been a kind and good comrade, only he had his peculiarities—now he would be modest and shyly secretive, then he would get into a certain devil-may-care mood, a mood of bravado. After coming to me with his confession of murdering Sosnovskaya, and after Sevski and Koshitz had gone off to the old quarter of the town, he had kept on, by turns, now weeping passionately, now laughing sardonically and riotously. And when he was arrested and was being carried off to be locked up, he consulted us, with a wild smile, as to what tailor he ought to order his civilian clothes from. . . ."

Then there is Count Koshitz's opinion:

"Elaghin was, on the whole, a fellow of gay and gentle disposition—nervous, impressionable, even inclined to exaltation. He was especially affected by the drama and by music—the latter often brought him to tears; and, besides, he himself had unusual musical ability. . . ."

All the other witnesses as well voiced almost the same views:

"A fellow exceedingly susceptible to infatuations, but apparently always expecting something genuine, something out of the ordinary. . . ."—"At our little friendly sprees he was, for the most part, gay, and something of a charming pest: he'd call for more champagne than anybody else, treating all comers to it."—"Having entered into a liaison with Sosnovskaya, and trying his utmost to conceal from everybody his feelings toward her, he became very much changed. He was frequently brooding, sad; he used to say that he was becoming confirmed in his intention of doing away with himself. . . ."

Such are the reports concerning Elaghin, emanating from

persons who had lived on terms of the greatest intimacy with him. Whence, then (I reflected as I sat through the trial), had the prosecuting attorney taken such black pigments for his portrait of Elaghin? Or has he some other reports? No, he has not. There remains, therefore, only the supposition that he had been induced to use these black pigments by the generally prevalent notions of the *jeunesse dorée,* and by what he had learned from the only letter of Elaghin's at the disposal of the court, written to a friend of his in Kishenev. In this letter Elaghin spoke with great freedom concerning his life: "I've attained, brother, to some sort of indifference: nothing—nothing!—matters. If things are right today—well, glory be to God for that! As for what the morrow may bring—I should worry! Morning bringeth counsel, and all that sort of thing. I have got me one fine reputation—that of the first drunkard and ninny throughout the whole town, almost. . . ."

Such a self-appraisal seemed to go hand in hand with the eloquence of the prosecutor, who contended that "for the sake of animal enjoyment Elaghin had placed in the pillory of public judgment the woman who had given him her all, and had deprived her not only of her life but even of the last honour—that of Christian interment—" But *did* these two appraisals really go hand in hand? The prosecuting attorney had taken from this letter only several lines. For in full it ran as follows:

My dear Sergei:
    I've received your letter, and, although I've taken my time about answering it, such a delay couldn't be helped. Probably, when you read my letter, you'll be

thinking: "These pot-hooks look as if they had been made by a fly that had just crawled out of an ink-well!" Oh, well, handwriting is (so they say), if not a mirror of one's character, at least an expression of it, to a certain degree. I'm still the same mooncalf I've always been—or, if you like, even a worse one, since two years of independent life and *a thing or two besides* have left their impress upon me. There is a thing or two, brother, which Solomon the Wise himself could not convey. And for that reason don't be surprised if one fine day you find out that I went root-a-toot and bumped myself off. I've attained, brother, to some sort of indifference: nothing—nothing!—matters. If things are right today—well, glory be to God for that! As for what the morrow may bring—I should worry! Morning bringeth counsel, and all that sort of thing. I have got me one fine reputation—that of the first drunkard and ninny throughout the whole town, almost. And yet, at the same time (would you believe it?), at times I feel within my soul such strength, and torment, and yearning for everything that is good, that is lofty—in general, a yearning for the Devil alone knows what; all I know is that it creates a nagging ache in one's breast.

You'll say that these are still growing pains. How is it, then, that others of my own age do not feel anything of the sort? I've become fearfully nervous. Sometimes, on a winter night, with a blizzard raging and with a hard frost, I jump out of bed, get on horseback, and go flying through the streets, startling even the police, who have got over being startled by anything. And, mark you, at such times I'm as sober as a judge, and not just getting over a terrific jag. I long to seize some ever-elusive melody which, apparently, I have heard somewhere—and yet it never, never comes! Oh, well, I'll confess it to you: I've fallen in love, and that with a woman who is not in the least— not the very least!—like all the others with which this town swarms.—However, enough of this. Write me, please. You know my address. Remember how you used to put it?—"Cornet Elaghin, Russia—"

It is amazing: how could anybody, after having read merely this letter and nothing else, say that "We have here the coming together of two individualities having nothing in common"?

VIII

Sosnovskaya was a pure-blooded Pole. She was older than Elaghin, being eight-and-twenty. Her father had been an insignificant government clerk who had ended his life by suicide when she was only three. Her mother had long remained a widow and then had married again (again a petty government clerk) and had soon become a widow again. As you see, Sosnovskaya's family was rather medi- ocre. Whence, then, came all those strange psychic traits by which Sosnovskaya was distinguished, and whence that passion for the stage which, as we know, was so early re- vealed in her? All this, I think, was not at all due to the up- bringing she received in her family and in the private boarding-school where she had studied. And, apropos, it must be said that she had studied exceedingly well and, in

27

her spare time, had read a great deal. And, in reading, she
had at times jotted down excerpts from the books of
thoughts and utterances that were to her liking—of course,
as always in such cases, connecting them with herself in
one way or another. And, as a general thing, she was forever making certain notations, keeping something in the
nature of a diary—if only one may call a diary those scraps
of paper which she sometimes did not so much as touch for
months on end, and upon which she poured out at hap-
hazard her dreams and her views of life—or else simply
used for keeping track of her accounts with her laundress,
her dressmaker, and of other things of that sort. But just
what was it that she excerpted from her reading?

"Not to be born is the foremost happiness of all; the
second is to return into non-existence as quickly as possible." A marvellous thought!

The world is wearisome—deathly wearisome—whereas
my soul is striving toward something out of the ordinary. . . .

"Men comprehend only those sufferings from which
they die."—De Musset

No, I shan't marry—ever! I vow I never shall, by
God and Death. . . .

There is naught but Love and Death. But where, in all
Creation, a man whom I could fall in love with? There
is none such—there cannot be! Yet how can I die—I
who love Life like a woman possessed?

There is naught in Heaven or on Earth more fearful, attractive, and enigmatic than Love. . . .

Mother, for instance, says that I ought to marry for money. I—*I!*—to marry for money! What an unearthly word *Love* is; how much hell and charm there is in it—even though I have never loved!

The whole world regards me with millions of carnivorous eyes: it reminds me of my visits to the menagerie when I was a little girl. . . .

"It is not worth while to be a human being. Nor an angel, for that matter. Even the angels murmured and rose up against God. It is only worth while to be either God or a nonentity."—Krassinski

"Who can boast of having penetrated into her soul, when all the efforts of her life are directed toward concealing the depths of her soul?"—De Musset

Having finished boarding-school, Sosnovskaya had immediately informed her mother of her decision to dedicate herself to art. Her mother, a good Roman Catholic, would not at first, of course, even hear of her daughter's becoming an actress. However, her daughter was not at all the sort to submit to anybody whatsoever and had even before succeeded in instilling into her mother that her life, the life of Maria Sosnovskaya, could not possibly be humdrum and inglorious.

At eighteen she had gone to Lvov and had rapidly realized her dreams: not only had she got on the stage without any difficulties, but in a short while had become prominent on it. In a short time she had attained celebrity both before the public and in the theatrical world—a celebrity so considerable that after her third year on the stage she had received an invitation to play in our city. However, in Lvov, too, she had been jotting down in her little note-book much the same things as before:

"Everybody talks about her, everybody weeps and laughs over her—but who knows her?"—De Musset

Were it not for my mother, I would kill myself. This is my constant longing. . . .

Whenever I chance to go beyond the city, and behold the sky, so splendidly beautiful and so bottomless, I don't know what comes over me. I want to scream, to sing, to declaim, to weep . . . to fall in love and to die. . . .

I shall choose a splendidly beautiful death. I shall rent a little bit of a room and order it draped with some funereal material. There will have to be music playing somewhere on the other side of the wall, and I shall lie down in an unpretentious white gown and surround myself with innumerable flowers—and it will be the scent of these very flowers that shall kill me. Oh, how wonder-inspiring that will be!

And, further on, we have:

They all, all demand my body and not my soul.

Were I rich I would go all around the world and make love all over the terrestrial globe.

"Does man know what he wants? Does he feel certain of that which he thinks?"—Krassinski

And, finally:

The scoundrel!

Who was this scoundrel who, of course, had done that which it is not so very hard to surmise? All that is known is that he had existed—and could not but have existed. "Even at the time she was in Lvov," said the witness Zauhse, a fellow-trouper of Sosnovskaya's in that town, "she would undress rather than dress whenever she had to go on to act, and when she received her friends and admirers at home, she did so in a transparent *peignoir* and with her feet bare. Their beauty threw everybody, but the novices especially, into rapturous amazement, whereupon she used to say: 'Don't you be astonished—they're all my own—' and would show her legs up to above her knees. At the same time she never ceased from reiterating to me (often with tears) that there was nobody deserving of her love, and that her sole hope was in death."

And lo, on the scene had appeared this "scoundrel," with whom she took trips to Constantinople, Venice, Paris, and whom she visited in Cracow and Berlin. This had been some Galician landowner or other, a man exceedingly rich.

The witness Volsky, who had known Sosnovskaya from her very childhood, said concerning him (and her):

"I've always considered Sosnovskaya a woman of a very low moral plane. She did not know how to conduct herself as befitted an *artiste* and one who came from our locality. All she liked was money—money and men. It was cynical, the way she sold herself, while still almost a little girl, to that old boar from Galicia."

It was about this very "boar" that Sosnovskaya had told Elaghin in the conversation she had had with him just before her death. Letting a word drop here and there, she complained to him:

"I grew up in loneliness; there was no one to look after me. . . . I was altogether a stranger in my family—and even in the whole world. . . . A certain woman (may all her offspring be accursed!) was making me depraved— pure, trusting little girl that I was. . . . And in Lvov I came to love a certain man, sincerely, like a father, who turned out to be such a scoundrel—such a scoundrel!— that I cannot even recall him without horror. And it was he who taught me to use hashish, to drink wine; he used to take me to Constantinople, where he had a whole harem. He used to loll in this harem of his, eying his naked odalisques, and compelled me to strip as well—the vile, low-down fellow! . . ."

IX

In our town Sosnovskaya soon became a "byword on all tongues."

"While still in Lvov," testified the witness Meshkov, "she had suggested to many a man that he die for one

32

night with her, and was forever repeating that she was seeking a heart capable of love. She was seeking very persistently for this loving heart, but she herself was constantly saying: 'My chief aim is to live and to make use of life. A vintner must try all wines—and not become intoxicated with any single one. And just so must a woman act with men.' And act accordingly she did," said Meshkov. "I am not at all certain whether she tasted all the wines, but I do know that she surrounded herself with an enormous lot of them. However, it may be that she did this, just as she did everything else, in order to create a hubbub around her, to acquire *claqueurs* for her appearances. 'Money,' she used to say, 'is so much rubbish. I'm greedy, at times miserly, as much so as any woman of the bourgeoisie; but, somehow, I don't give money a thought. The main thing is fame; everything else will come!' And, in my opinion, she was forever harping on death also with this object of making people talk about her. . . ."

The same sort of thing that had taken place in Lvov continued in our town as well. And the notes she wrote were almost of the same tenor as before:

God, what ennui, what anguish! If only an earthquake or an eclipse would come along!

Somehow, one evening, I happened to be in a churchyard. It was so splendid there! It seemed to me . . . but no, I am not able to describe this emotion. I felt like remaining the whole night . . . declaiming over the graves . . . and then dying of exhaustion. On the following day I played better than ever before. . . .

And again:

> Yesterday I visited the churchyard at ten in the eve-
> ning. What a depressing spectacle! The moon poured
> its beams upon the headstones and crosses. It seemed
> to me that I was surrounded by the dead in their thou-
> sands. Yet I felt so happy, so joyous! Mine was an
> exceedingly fine mood. . . .

And after she had come to know Elaghin and had heard
from him of the death of a corporal in his regiment, she
had demanded that Elaghin take her to the chapel where
the dead man was lying, and had jotted down that the
sight of the dead man and the chapel in the light of the
moon had made a "staggeringly rapturous impression"
upon her.

The thirst for fame, for being noticed by her fellow-
mortals, had at this time become simply a frenzy with
her. Yes, she *was* exceedingly good-looking. Her beauty
was not, on the whole, of an original cast, and yet there
was about it some sort of a peculiar, rare, unusual charm,
some sort of mixture of simple-heartedness and innocence
with feral cunning, and also an admixture of constant play-
acting and sincerity. Look at her portraits. Note attentively her gaze, a gaze peculiarly her own, a gaze always
somewhat from under her brows, with her rosebud lips
constantly open just a wee bit; a gaze pensive, but most
frequently of all endearing, enticing, holding forth a promise of something—as if consenting to something secret,
something depraved.

And she knew how to make use of her beauty. On the

stage she not only snared her adorers through her especial ability, when actually treading the boards, to make herself blossom forth through all her charms, through the sounds of her voice and the loveliness of her movements, by means of her laughter and her tears, but she also snared them by appearing, most frequently of all, in roles that afforded her an opportunity to exhibit her body. And when at home, she wore seductive Oriental and Greek costumes, in which she would receive her multifarious guests.

One of her rooms she had set aside specially for suicide, as she herself put it. Here one could find not only revolvers and dirks, but also swords, scimitar- and creese-shaped, as well as vials with all sorts of poisons. And she made death her constant and favourite subject of conversation. But that did not suffice: frequently, while conversing about all the numerous and diverse devices for doing away with oneself, she would snatch a loaded revolver off the wall and, cocking the trigger and putting the muzzle up to her temple, would say:

"Kiss me, quick, or I'll shoot this very minute!"

Or else she would take a capsule of strychnine in her mouth and announce that unless her visitor fell on his knees instanter and kissed her bare foot she would swallow this capsule. And she did and said all this in such a way that her visitor blanched with fear and took his departure doubly bewitched by her, going forth and spreading throughout the town precisely those universally agitating rumours which she so desired.

"On the whole, she was hardly ever her own self," the witness Zalesski, who had known her very intimately and very long, testified at the trial. "Play-acting, teasing—

these formed her constant occupation. She was a great
hand at driving a man to frenzy with tender, enigmatic
glances, smiles fraught with great meaning, or with the
sad sigh of a defenceless child. And that's just the way she
behaved with Elaghin. Now she would set him in a blaze
—now she would douse him with a bucket of cold water.—
Did she want to die? Why, she was as fond of life as any
carnivorous animal; she was inordinately afraid of death.
There was, in general, a great deal of the joy of life and
of gaiety in her make-up. I remember how Elaghin had
once sent her the skin of a polar bear. She had a great
number of visitors just when it arrived, but she became
perfectly oblivious of them that very instant, that's how
enraptured she was with this rug. She spread it upon the
floor, and, paying no attention to anybody, began to turn
somersaults on it, to perform feats which would have
aroused the envy of any professional acrobat. . . . She
was an enchanting woman!"

However, the same Zalesski told of how she had suffered
from fits of despair and ennui. Doctor Seroshevski, who
had known her for ten years and had treated her even before her departure for Lvov (she had had incipient con-
sumption), likewise testified that of late she had been suffering excruciatingly from serious nervous derangement,
loss of memory, and hallucinations, so that he felt apprehensive about her mental faculties. It was because of this
same derangement that she was under the care of another
physician, by the name of Schumacher, whom she was constantly assuring that she would not die a natural death and
from whom she had once borrowed a couple of volumes
of Schopenhauer, "which she had read very attentively,

and, most surprising of all, had understood splendidly, as it later turned out." And still another physician, Doctor Niedzelski, gave the following evidence:

"She was a strange woman! Whenever she had guests, she was, for the most part, very jolly, very coquettish; but there were times when she would suddenly lapse into silence for no reason on earth, rolling up her eyes and letting her head sink on the table. . . . Or else she'd begin throwing and smashing tumblers and wineglasses against the floor. . . . On such occasions one always had to request her, as quickly as possible: 'There, keep it up, keep it up!'—and she would immediately desist from this pastime."

And it was this very woman whom Cornet Alexander Elaghin eventually encountered.

X

How had this encounter taken place? How had the intimacy between them been born, and what were their feelings, their attitudes, toward each other? Elaghin himself told about this on two occasions: the first time, briefly and fragmentarily, to the coroner, a few hours after the murder; the second time, at the interrogations which took place three weeks after the first.

"Yes," he had said, "I am guilty of having taken Sosnovskaya's life, *but by her own will.* . . .

"I became acquainted with her a year and a half ago in the box-office of her theatre, through Lieutenant Budberg. I came to love her ardently, and thought that she shared my feelings. But it wasn't always that I felt certain of this. At times it even seemed to me that she loved me more than

I did her, but at other times things seemed quite otherwise. Besides that, she was constantly surrounded by admirers, and playing the coquette, whereas I suffered all the
cruel pangs of jealousy. However, in the upshot, it wasn't
this at all that constituted our tragic situation, but something else that I'm unable to express. In any event I swear
that it was not out of jealousy I killed her. . . .

"As I say, I became acquainted with her in February of
last year, at the theatre, near the box-office. I called on her
shortly after that, but up to October I did not visit her
more than twice a month, and then always in the daytime.
In October I confessed my love for her, and she allowed me
to kiss her. A week after that she and I and a friend of
mine named Voloshin took a trip to a suburban restaurant
for supper; but she and I returned from there alone, and,
although she was feeling gay, kindly, and somewhat tipsy,
I felt such timidity before her that I was afraid even to
kiss her hand.

"Some time after that she asked me for a volume of
Pushkin, and, having finished his *Egyptian Nights,* she
said: 'But would *you* have spirit enough to give up your
life for a single night with the woman you loved?'—and
when I made haste to answer that I would, she smiled
enigmatically. I was already very much in love with her
and clearly perceived and felt that, for me, this love was
a fatal one. As our intimacy increased, I grew bolder: I
began to speak to her of my love more and more often;
I used to say that I felt myself perishing—if only because
my father would never permit me to marry her, or because,
as a theatrical star, she would find it impossible to live
with me out of wedlock, since Polish society would never

have forgiven her anything like an unconcealed liaison with a Russian officer. And she, for her part, complained against her fate, against her strange soul; she avoided, however, any direct response to my confessions of love, to my unvoiced questions as to whether she loved me; rather, she seemed to hold out hope for me, as it were, through these complaints of hers and their intimacy.

"Then, since January of this year, I began to call on her every day. I sent her bouquets to the theatre, I sent flowers to her home, I made her presents. . . . I gave her a couple of mandolins, a polar-bear rug, an elaborate diamond ring, and a bracelet, also of diamonds. I had also decided to give her a brooch in the form of a skull. She adored emblems of death, and more than once had said to me that she wished to have just such a brooch from me, with an inscription in French: *Quand même pour toujours!*

"On the twenty-sixth of March of this year I received an invitation to supper from her. After the supper she yielded herself to me for the first time—in what she called her Japanese room. And it was also in this very room that our further assignations took place—she would send her maid off to bed after supper. And then, later on, she gave me a key to her bedroom, the outside door of which led directly to the staircase. . . . To commemorate the twenty-sixth of March we ordered wedding rings for ourselves, on the inside of which rings were engraved, by her wish, our initials and the date of our intimacy. . . .

"During one of our excursions beyond the city, in a village, we walked up to a cross standing near a Roman Catholic church, and I made a vow of my eternal love for her in front of this cross, saying that she was my wife in the sight of God, and that I would be true to her to my very grave. She stood there, sad and thoughtful, and kept silent. Then she said, simply and firmly: 'And I love you, too. *Quand même pour toujours. . . .*'

"One day, at the beginning of May, as I was having supper at her place, she took out some opium in powder form and said: 'How easy it is to die! One has but to add a sprinkling of this to one's food, and all is over!' And, having put the powder into a goblet of champagne, she brought the drink up to her mouth. I snatched it out of her hand, dashed the wine into the fireplace, and smashed the goblet against one of my spurs. On the following day she told me: 'Yesterday's tragedy turned out to be a comedy!' And she added: 'Well, what can I do? I can't get up nerve enough to do it myself, while you, too, cannot, dare not do it—what a disgrace!'

"And after that we began to see each other at rarer intervals: she said that she could no longer receive me at home evenings. Why?—I was going crazy and suffering dreadfully. But, besides that, she changed toward me—she became cold and mocking; at times she received me as if we were barely acquainted, and was forever taunting me because of my lack of firmness. . . . And then, suddenly, everything changed once more. She began dropping in on me to take me along driving, she started making playful advances to me—perhaps because I, too, had begun to adopt a cold reserve in my treatment of her. . . . Finally she told me to rent another apartment for our love trysts, —but this apartment would have to be on some little-frequented street, in some sombre old house; it would have to be perfectly dark, this apartment, and I would have to decorate it as she would tell me. . . . You know just how this apartment was decorated. . . .

"And so, on the sixteenth of June, I dropped in at her place about four in the afternoon and told her that the apartment was ready, and handed over one of the keys to her. She smiled and, returning the key to me, answered: 'We'll talk of this later.' Just then there was a ring at the door—a certain Shkliarevich had come. I hastily put away the key in my pocket and began speaking of this and that. But, as Shkliarevich and I were going away, she said to him in the entry, loudly: 'Come Monday,' whereas to me she whispered: 'Come tomorrow, at four'—and she whispered this in such a way that my head began to swim. . . .

"The next day I was at her place on the stroke of four. What,' then, was my astonishment when the cook, who opened the door, informed me that Sosnovskaya was not able to receive me—and with that she handed me a letter from her! She wrote that she was not feeling well and that she was going to her mother's country place, that it was 'too late now.' Utterly beside myself I dropped into the first refreshment place I came to and dashed off a dreadful note to her, asking her what she meant by 'too late,' and sent this note off by messenger. But the messenger brought it back to me; it turned out that she was not at home.

"Thereupon I decided that she wanted to break off with me once and for all, and so, on getting home, I wrote her another letter, sharply reproaching her for the whole game she was carrying on with me and requesting her to return to me her wedding ring, which was probably nothing but a joke to her, but was to me the dearest thing in life, that which was to go into the grave with me; by this I wanted to say that everything was at an end between us and to make her understand that death was all that was left for me. Together with this letter I returned to her her photograph, all her letters to me, and all the things of hers which I treasured so—gloves, hairpins, a toque. . . . My orderly came back and told me that she was not at home and that he had left my letter and package with the caretaker. . . .

"In the evening I went to the circus, where I ran into Shkliarevich, whom I was barely acquainted with. Dreading to be alone, however, I drank champagne with him. Suddenly Shkliarevich said to me: 'I say, I can see what you're going through, and I know the why and wherefore. Believe me, she's not worth it. We've all gone through the same thing; she's led all of us around by our noses. . . .' I felt like snatching out my sabre and splitting his head open, but I was in such a state that I not only did not do anything of the kind, and did not cut such talk short, but, in secret, even rejoiced at it—rejoiced over the chance of having found a sympathizer in anybody at all. And I don't know what came over me. I didn't drop a single word to him, nor did I say a word concerning Sosnovskaya; but I did bring him to the old quarter of the town and show him the apartment which I had so lovingly picked out for our trysts. I felt so bitter, so humiliated because I had been tricked thus in the matter of this apartment. . . .

"From there I made my cabby drive like blazes to Neviarovski's restaurant. It was drizzling, and the cabby flew along, but even this drizzle and the lights ahead hurt me and terrified me. At one o'clock in the morning I came home from the restaurant with Shkliarevich and had already begun to undress when my orderly handed me a note:

Sosnovskaya was waiting for me in the street; she begged me to come down immediately.

"She had come in a carriage with her maid, and told me that she had become so frightened on my account that she had been unable to come alone, even, and had therefore taken the maid along. I bade my orderly see the maid home, while I myself took a seat in Sosnovskaya's carriage and we went off to the old quarter of the town. On the way I upbraided her, accusing her of playing a game with me. She kept silent and, gazing ahead of her, from time to time wiped away her tears. She seemed calm, however. And since she could almost always communicate her mood to me, I began to calm down in my turn.

"When we arrived, she brightened up altogether: the rooms were very much to her liking. I took her hand, begged forgiveness for all my reproaches, also begging her to give me back her photograph—I mean the one I had sent back to her in my exasperation. We had frequent quarrels, and, in the upshot, I always felt myself at fault and always begged forgiveness.

"At three in the morning I escorted her home. On the way our talk again took a sharp turn. She sat staring straight ahead of her. I could not see her face—I was conscious only of the odour of her perfume and the icy, malicious sound of her voice. 'You're no man,' she was saying, 'you haven't any backbone at all! I can, whenever I wish, either drive you crazy or calm you down. Were I a man, I'd make mincemeat of such a woman as myself!' Whereupon I yelled at her: 'If that's so, take your ring back!'—and I put it on her finger by force. She turned to me, and, smiling in confusion, said: 'Come tomorrow.' I answered

43

that I would not come, under any circumstances. Awkwardly, timidly she fell to imploring me, saying: 'No, you will come, you will . . . to our new apartment.' And she added decisively: 'No, I'm imploring you to come! I'm going abroad soon and want to see you for the last time; but, mainly, I must tell you something very important.' And bursting into tears once more, she concluded: 'The only thing that amazes me is that you claim you love me, that you cannot live without me and will shoot yourself— yet you don't want to see me for the last time. . . .' Whereupon I said, trying to be restrained, that if such were the case, I would inform her on the morrow at what hour I would be free. When we parted at the entrance to her house, in the rain, my heart was rending from pity and love for her. On getting back home I was surprised and disgusted to find Shkliarevich sleeping there. . . .

"Monday morning, the eighteenth of June, I sent her a note, saying that I would be free from noon on. She answered: 'At six; the new place.' "

XI

Sosnovskaya's maid, Antonina Kovanco, and her cook, Vanda Linevich, testified that on Saturday, the 16th, their mistress, as she had been lighting a spirit-lamp to heat the curling-iron for her bangs, had through absentmindedness thrown the match on the front of her light *peignoir*, and the *peignoir* had blazed up, while Sosnovskaya screamed out wildly, tearing and throwing it off herself. She had become so frightened that she took to her bed, sent for the doctor, and kept on repeating:

"There, you'll see: that signifies a great misfortune. . . ."

The charming, unhappy woman! This incident of the *peignoir,* and her childlike terror, agitate and touch me extraordinarily. This trifling detail somehow amazingly connects and illuminates for me all that is fragmentary and contradictory in what we had always heard about her, and what had been dinned into our ears, both in society and all through the trial, ever since she had met her end. But, mainly, it awakens within me, amazingly, a lively sense of the real Sosnovskaya.

In general, I would say once more: Amazing is the poverty of human judgment! It was as though all had agreed to utter nothing but vulgar banalities. "Come, now, what was there to make such a fuss about here? He was a Hussar, a jealous and besotted wastrel, burning the candle of his life at both ends; she was a play-actress, a stroller, who had got all tangled up in her shiftless and immoral life. . . ."

"Private dining-rooms; wine; cocottes; debauchery," people summed him up. "The clanking of his sabre made him deaf to all the loftier feelings. . . ."

Loftier feelings, wine, indeed! But what *is* wine, and especially for such a nature as Elaghin's?—"At times I feel within my soul such torment, and yearning for everything that is good, that is lofty—in general, a yearning for the Devil alone knows what; all I know is that it creates a nagging ache in one's breast. . . . I long to seize some ever-elusive melody, which, apparently, I have heard somewhere—and yet it never, never comes! . . ." But when one is tipsy, one breathes more easily and expansively; when one is tipsy, the elusive refrain sounds more clearly and nearer at hand. . . .

"She did not love him," they said of her, "she was merely afraid of him; why, he was forever making threats to her that he would kill himself—that is, that he not only would burden her soul with his death, but would also make her the sorry heroine of a great scandal. We have testimony to the effect that 'she even experienced a certain aversion for him.' She had belonged to him just the same, you say? But then, does that really alter matters? Whom hadn't she belonged to! However, Elaghin had wanted to turn into a drama one of those numerous comedies of love which she was so fond of performing. . . ."

And people also said:

"She was terrified by that frightful, inordinate jealousy which he began to evince more and more. On one occasion, while he was present, the actor Strakuhn happened to be one of her guests. Elaghin had at first sat on calmly, merely paling from jealousy. But suddenly he got up and went into an adjoining room. She darted after him and, catching sight of a revolver in his hand, fell on her knees before him, imploring him to take pity on himself and her. And probably not a few such scenes had been played out. Isn't it comprehensible, after this, that she would at last resolve to rid herself of him, to set out for a trip abroad, for which trip she had already made all preparations on the very eve of her death? He had brought her a key to the apartment in the old quarter of the town—an apartment she had thought of only to have a pretext for not receiving him in her own place up to her departure. This key she had not accepted. He began importuning her to accept it. She had declared that now it was 'too late'—as much as to say: 'It's no use my taking the key now—I'm going away.'

But he dashed off such a vehement letter to her that, upon receiving it, she galloped off to him at the dead of night, beside herself from fear that she might find him already dead. . . ."

Let us admit that everything is so—even though all these reasonings contradict Elaghin's confession utterly. But still, why was Elaghin so "fearfully," so "inordinately" jealous, and why had he wanted to turn the comedy into a drama? What did he want to do all that for? Why had he not simply shot her during one of his attacks of jealousy? Why had there been "no struggle between the slayer and his victim"? And, furthermore: "She had at times even experienced a certain aversion for him. . . . She had occasionally, in the presence of strangers, made mock of him, had bestowed humiliating nicknames upon him, had called him a 'bowlegged puppy,' for instance. . . ."

But even as far back as her Lvov notes there is an entry concerning the aversion she had experienced toward some unknown: "So he still loves me! But what about me? What are my feelings toward him?—Both love and aversion!" She used to insult Elaghin, you say? Well, on one occasion, having quarrelled with him (quarrels were a quite frequent occurrence with this couple), she had called in the maid and, having chucked her "betrothal" ring on the floor, had shouted: "Take this nasty rubbish for yourself!" Ah, yes—but what had she done just before this? She had run into the kitchen just before and had said to her maid: "I'm going to call you in right away and fling this ring on the floor and tell you to take it for yourself. But remember, I'll only be putting on an act. You must give it back to me this very day, because with this ring I've betrothed myself to him, to this booby—and it is the dearest thing in the world to me."

It was not at all in vain that they called her a "woman of light conduct." Hers was wholly one of those natures with sharply expressed, unsatisfied, insatiable sexuality—a sexuality which it is even impossible to satiate. As a consequence of what? But then, how do I know what it is a consequence of? And notice what always occurs: it is precisely men of that fearfully complex type which is, in a greater or lesser degree, atavistic—persons who are by their very being hypersensitive not only as far as women are concerned, but, generally, in all their consciousness of the world—it is such men who are drawn by all the forces of their souls and bodies to precisely such women. Why? Because of their low taste, because of their dissoluteness, or simply because of the accessibility of such women? Of course no—a thousand times no! No, if only because such men do, after all, excellently perceive and feel to what an extent a liaison or propinquity with such women is always agonizing, and, at times, downright destructive. They feel, they perceive, they know all this, yet nevertheless are drawn most of all to them, to precisely these women; are irresistibly drawn to their agony and even their destruction. Why?

"Of course, she had been merely putting on an act when she was writing her little farewell notes, making herself believe that her last hour had really come. And no diaries whatsoever convince one to the contrary—which diaries, it must be said by the way, are quite banal and naïve; nor, for that matter, do we find any of her churchyard visits convincing—"

No one denies the naïveté of her diaries and the theatri-

cality of her churchyard jaunts, just as no one denies that
she was fond of hinting at her resemblance to Marie Bashkirtseva and Marie Vetser. But then, why had she chosen
precisely such a sort of diary and not some other, and why
had she wanted to be akin to precisely such women? She
had everything: beauty, youth, fame, money, hundreds of
admirers; and all these she had availed herself of with
passion and intoxication, and yet her life was one continuous yearning, a ceaseless craving to get away from this
baneful earthly vale, where everything is never, never the
thing sought for, longed for. For what reason? This: that
she had hypnotized herself through having play-acted all
this for so long. But why had she play-acted precisely thus
and not in some other way? Was it because all this sort
of thing is so customary among women who have dedicated
themselves (as they express it) to art? But—why should
all this be so customary? Why?

XII

On Sunday morning the tap-bell in Sosnovskaya's bedroom began ringing a little before eight o'clock; she had
awakened and had called her maid considerably before the
usual time. The maid had carried in a tray with a cup of
chocolate and then parted the curtains. Her mistress was
sitting up in bed, and, as her wont was, watched her pensively and absent-mindedly from under her eyebrows and
with lips half-open; then she said:

"But d'you know, Tonia, that I fell asleep yesterday immediately after the doctor left? Oh, Mother o' God, how
frightened I was! But no sooner had the doctor come than
I began to feel so well, so calm. In the night-time I woke

up, got on my knees in bed, and prayed for a whole hour.
. . . Just think: what would I have looked like if I had
been burned all over? My eyes would have been just a
couple of burst blisters, my lips would have puffed up. I'd
have been just a fright to look at. . . . My whole face
would have been covered over with cotton wool. . . ."

She would not touch the chocolate for a long time and
all the while sat brooding over something. Then she drank
off the chocolate and, having taken her bath, sat down at
her tiny escritoire in her little bath-robe and with her hair
down, and wrote several letters on black-bordered station-
ery—she had ordered it long before. After dressing and
breakfasting she went away. She visited her mother in the
country and returned only at midnight, together with
Strakuhn, the actor, who had "always been one of the
family" to her.

"They were both jolly when they arrived," the maid told
her story. "I met them in the entry and at once called her
aside and handed her the letter and the things which
Elaghin had sent in her absence. She whispered to me about
the things: 'Hide 'em, quick, so Strakuhn won't see 'em.'
Then she hastily opened the letter, and at once turned pale,
lost her head, and began shoutin', no longer payin' any attention to Strakuhn, who was sittin' in the drawin'-room:
'For God's sake, run as fast as ever you can for a carriage!'
I ran out an' got one an' found her all ready on the front
steps when I come back. We dashed along at full speed,
an' all the way she kept crossin' herself and repeatin': 'Oh,
Mother o' God! If only I might find him alive!' "

On Monday, bright and early in the morning, she went
off to the river to bathe. On this day she had invited to din-

ner Strakuhn and a certain Englishwoman who generally came to her almost every day to give her lessons in English, and almost never did. After dinner the Englishwoman left, while Strakuhn stayed on for another hour and a half. He smoked, lying on a divan, with his head on the lap of his hostess, "who had on nothing but a loose, light dressing-gown, and little Japanese slippers, without any stockings." Finally Strakuhn left, and, as she was bidding him good-bye, she begged him to come "this very evening, at ten."

"Won't that be rather too often?" Strakuhn had asked, laughing, as he looked for his cane in the entry.

"Oh, no—please come!" she had said. "But if I should happen to be out, don't you be angry at me, now, Luci"—using the familiar diminutive of his first name, Lucian.

And after that, for a long while, she was engaged in burning certain letters and papers in the fireplace. She hummed, and jested with the maid:

"I'm going to burn everything now, since I wasn't burned up myself! Ah, but it would have been fine if I'd been burned up! Only altogether, so's there would be nothing but ashes left of me! . . ."

Then she said: "Tell Vanda to have supper ready by ten tonight. Well, I'm going now."

She left about six, taking along with her "somethin' that was all wrapped up in paper and that looked like a revolver."

She set out for the old quarter of the town, but on the way ordered her carriage to turn aside so that she might call on Leshchinskaya, her dressmaker, who was mending and altering the *peignoir* which had caught fire Saturday when she had it on. And, according to Leshchinskaya's

words, the actress "had been in a gay and charming mood."
After she had looked over the *peignoir* and it had been
wrapped up in paper together with the parcel she had
taken with her from home, she had sat on for a long time
in the work-room among the apprentice girls, repeating all
the while: "Oh, Mother o' God, how late I am—it's time
I was going, my little angels!"—and still would not leave.
At last she resolutely got up and with a sigh, but gaily, said:

"Good-bye, Pani Leshchinskaya! Good-bye, my little
sisters, my little angels! Thanks for chatting with me. It's
such a pleasure for me to sit in your feminine circle, you
darlings—for it's always men and men with me!"

And, once more nodding her head with a smile from the
threshold, she walked out.

Why had she taken the revolver along with her? This
weapon belonged to Elaghin, but she kept it in her place,
being apprehensive that he might shoot himself. "But now
she intended to return it to its proper owner, inasmuch as
in a few days she was going abroad for a long period," the
prosecuting attorney had said, and added: "Thus she set
out for the fatal assignation—yet not knowing that it was
fatal. At seven she was in the ground-floor apartment of
that house in the old quarter of the town—and then the
door of this flat closed, to open again only on the morning
of the nineteenth of June. What had taken place there in
the night? There is none to tell us this save Elaghin. Let us
hear him once more, then. . . ."

XIII

And once more, amid deep silence, all of us who formed
the dense throng in the court-room listened to those pages

of the indictment which the prosecuting attorney deemed it necessary to refresh our memory with, and with which Elaghin's story concluded:

" 'Monday morning, the nineteenth of June, I sent her a note, saying that I would be free from noon on. She answered: "At six; the new place." At a quarter to six I was there, bringing with me some cold delicacies, two bottles of champagne and two of porter, two small glasses, and a flacon of eau-de-Cologne. But I had to wait a long while —she came only at seven.

" 'On entering she gave me an absent-minded peck, then passed on into the second room and threw the parcel she had brought down on the divan. "Leave the room," she said to me in French, "I want to undress." I went into the outer room and again sat alone for a long while. I was fully sober and fearfully depressed, vaguely sensing that everything was at an end, that everything was coming to an end. . . . The setting itself was a strange one: I was sitting under artificial light, as if it were night, and yet at the same time I knew and felt that out of doors, beyond the walls of these bottled-up dark rooms, it was still daylight, and that the summer evening was beautiful. . . . She did not call me for a long time, nor do I know what she was doing. It was perfectly quiet on the other side of her door. Finally she called out: "You may come in now. . . ."

" 'She was lying on the divan in nothing but her *peignoir*, without stockings or slippers, and did not say anything, merely staring from under her brows at the ceiling—at the lantern. The parcel she had brought was now unwrapped and I caught sight of my own revolver. I asked: "What ever did you bring that thing for?" She waited a space before answering: "Oh, just so,— As you know, I'm going away. . . . You'd better keep it here, and not in your place. . . ." A frightful thought flashed through my head: "No, she's not doing this without some reason!"—but I didn't say anything. . . .

" 'And the conversation which began between us after this was constrained and cold for a considerable time. In secret I was frightfully agitated; I was constantly striving to conjecture something, constantly expecting to get my thoughts together at any moment and finally to tell her something important and decisive. For I understood that this was, perhaps, our last time together, or, in any event, a parting for a long period—and yet I still couldn't say anything, feeling my complete impotence. She said: "Smoke, if you like." "But you don't like my smoking," I answered. "No, *now* nothing matters," said she. "And do let me have some champagne!" I became as elated at this as if it were my salvation. In a few minutes we had finished the whole bottle. I sat down near her and started kissing her hands, saying that I would not survive her departure. She rumpled my hair and uttered, as if her thoughts were elsewhere: "Yes, yes. . . . What a misfortune it is that I cannot be your wife! . . . Everything and everybody is against us; only God alone, perhaps, is on our side. I love your soul; I love your *fantasy*." What she meant to express by this last word I do not know. I looked up at the drape on the ceiling and said: "Look—you and I are here as in a crypt. And how quiet it is!"

" 'She merely smiled back sadly for answer.

" 'About ten o'clock she said she felt hungry. We passed into the front room. But she ate little, and so did I; for the most part we drank. Suddenly she looked at the cold things I had brought and exclaimed: "Silly-billy, what a lot of stuff you've bought again! Don't you dare do it the next time!" "But when is the next time going to be?" I asked. She looked at me oddly, then let her head drop and rolled up her eyes. "Jesus, Mary!" she uttered in a whisper. "What are we to do? Oh, I want you, madly! Let's go, quick!"

" 'After some time I glanced at my watch; it was already past one. "Oh, how late it is!" said she. "I simply *must* go home, this very minute!" However, she didn't even get up, and added: "D'you know, I feel that I must get away as quickly as possible, yet I can't stir from the spot. I feel that I shan't leave this place. You're my doom, my fate—the will of God! . . ." All this was something I could not understand. Probably she wanted to say something in keeping with what she wrote later: 'I am dying not of my own will.' You think that by this phrase she expressed her defencelessness before me. But, in my opinion, she wanted to say something else: that our ill-starred encounter was her doom, the will of God; that she was dying, not of her own will, but by God's. However, I did not attribute any particular significance to her words at the time—I had long since grown used to her eccentricities. Then she said, suddenly: "Have you a pencil?" I wondered once more. Why should she want a pencil? But I hastened to give it to her—I had one in my memo-book. She also asked me for one of my cards. When she began writing something on it, I said: "I say, it's rather awkward to be writing notes on a fellow's visiting-card!" "No, these are simply notes for no one but myself," she answered. "Leave me now—I want to think a little and take a nap." And, having placed the card on her breast, she closed her eyes. Everything became so quiet that I fell into some sort of coma. . . .

" 'Not less than half an hour must have passed thus. Suddenly she opened her eyes and said, coldly: "I forgot: I came to give you back your ring. You yourself wanted to end everything yesterday." And, raising herself a little, she chucked the ring on the wall-ledge. "Why, do you really love me?" she all but shrieked. "I can't understand how you can calmly allow me to go on living! I'm a woman —I haven't any firmness. It isn't that I fear death—it's torment that I fear; but you could, with a single shot, put an end to me, and then, with another, kill yourself." And at that point I comprehended more fully, with fearful clarity, all the horror, all the despair of our situation, and that it was on the verge of some solution at last. But as to killing her—no, I felt that I could not do that. I felt something else: that the decisive moment for me had arrived. I took the revolver and cocked the trigger. "What, you're going to kill only yourself?" she cried out, jumping up. "No, I swear before Jesus—not for anything!"—and she snatched the revolver out of my hand. . . .

" 'And again that excruciating silence fell. I remained sitting; she was lying down. And suddenly, indistinctly, she said something to herself in Polish, and then spoke to me: "Let me have my ring!" I handed it to her. "And your own!" said she. I hastened to comply with this request as well. She put on her own, and, having commanded me to put mine on, too, she began to speak: "I've always loved you, and I love you now. I've driven you mad and have tortured you to the very end—but such is my nature, and such is our destiny. Hand me my skirt, and bring me some porter." I handed her the skirt and went after the porter.

" 'And when I returned, I noticed that there was a small vial with opium near her. "Listen," said she firmly, "now is the end of all play-acting. Could you live without me?" I answered that I could not. "That is true," said she, "I've taken all your soul, all your thoughts. You wouldn't waver about killing yourself? And, if that's the case, take me with you as well. I couldn't live without you any more than you could without me. And after you kill me, you can die with the realization that, at last, I am all yours—and that for all time. And now listen to what my life has been. . . ." And, lying down once more, after a moment's silence and calming down somewhat, she began telling me her whole life, from her very childhood. . . . I remember almost nothing of her story. . . .

XIV

" '. . . Neither do I remember which one of us was the first to start writing (I broke my small pencil in halves). We began to write in silence, and remained silent all the time we were writing. I wrote first of all to my father, I think. . . . You ask me why I reproached him with "not desiring my happiness," when I had not so much as attempted, even once, to ask his consent to my marrying her? I don't know— Why, he wouldn't have given me his consent anyway. . . . Then I wrote to my fellow-officers, bidding them farewell. . . . Then whom else did I write to? Yes—to the commander of my regiment, requesting that I be given a decent funeral. You say that means I must have felt certain I would do away with myself? Of course! But still, how is it I didn't do so? I don't know.

"'As for her, she wrote slowly, I remember, often stopping and deliberating over something; she'd write a word and then stare at the wall from under her eyebrows. . . . She herself tore up the notes, and not I. She'd write, tear up what she'd written, and then throw the pieces anywhere at all. . . . It seems to me that even in the grave it will not be so frightful as when, at that late hour, in that silence, under that lantern, we were writing all those unnecessary notes. . . . It was her will that we should write them. . . . In general, I submitted without a word to everything she commanded me to do on that night, up to the very last moment. . . .

"'Suddenly she said: "Enough! 'If it were done . . . then 'twere well it were done quickly!'"" Was she consciously quoting? I cannot tell. "Let me have a little porter, then," she said. "Mother o' God, bless me!" I poured out a glass of porter for her, and she, raising herself a little, resolutely threw a pinch of powder into the glass. Having drunk off more than half, she ordered me to finish the rest. I drank it. But she began to beat about and, snatching at my hands, fell to imploring: "And now kill me, kill me! Kill me for the sake of our love!"

"'Just how did I do it? I put my left arm around her, I think—yes, of course, it was my left arm—and clung with my lips to hers. She was saying: "Farewell, farewell—or no, let it be an *Ave*, and that for all time now! . . . If we have not succeeded here, then we may meet with better fortune up there, above. . . ." I pressed her to me and held my finger on the trigger of the revolver— I remember my whole body jerking. . . . And then the finger jerked, by itself, somehow. . . . But she had time to say, in Polish: "Alexander, my beloved!"

" 'What hour was this at? About three, I think. What else did I do for two hours after that? Why, you forget that it took me about an hour to walk to Likharev's. As for the rest of that time, I spent it in sitting near her; and then I began putting everything in order, although I myself couldn't tell you for what reason. . . .

" 'Why didn't I shoot myself? Why, I forgot to, somehow. When I saw her dead, I forgot everything in this world. I just sat there and could do nothing but look at her. Then, in the same wild unconsciousness, I began putting her to rights and tidying up the room. I would be incapable of not keeping my word, which I had given her, that I would kill myself after her; but a complete apathy seized hold of me. . . . Just as apathetically do I regard the fact of my being alive now. But I cannot become reconciled to being thought an executioner, apparently. No— no! Perhaps I am guilty before the law of man, guilty before God—but never before her!' "

XV

By ten years of penal servitude must Elaghin expiate his guilt before the law of man.

But before God—and before her?

God's judgment is not known. But what would she have said, were it in our power to make her arise from her grave? And who would then dare to come between them?

THE BRIDE

~ ~

Upon the yellowed visiting-card with its patrician
coronet the young doorman of the Hotel Versailles somehow managed to read only the first name and the patronymic, both decidedly Polish: Casimir Stanislavovich;
these were followed by something still more complicated
and harder of pronunciation. After turning the card this
way and that the doorman glanced at the passport which
had been handed to him by the new arrival at the same
time with the card, and shrugged his shoulders (none of
those who came to the Versailles presented visiting-cards),
chucked both passport and card into the drawer of a little
table, and again fell to admiring himself in the small
silvery-milky mirror hanging above this table, puffing up
his thick hair with a comb. He had on well-polished boots
and was dressed in an overcoat that was tight at the waist
and then fell in wide folds to the knees; the gold braid on
his stiff cap was smudged with grease—the hotel was an
execrable one.

Casimir Stanislavovich had left Kiev for Moscow on
the 8th of April—Good Friday—after receiving a tele-
gram from someone, which consisted of but two words:
"The tenth." Funds appeared from somewhere or other;

he took a seat in a second-class car, drab, poorly lit, yet certainly affording him a sense of luxury and comfort. The train was heated during the journey, and this warmth in the car, the smell of the radiator, and its strained knocking, like that of little hammers, might have recalled other times to Casimir Stanislavovich.

Occasionally it seemed that winter had come back; a white—an exceedingly white—blizzard was covering with snow-drifts the bristles of tawny stubble in the fields, and the great leaden-hued pools where wild ducks swam. But this blizzard would fitfully and frequently cease, and thaw; the fields would become clearly visible. One felt that there was a great deal of light behind the clouds, while at the stations the platforms appeared black and the rooks cawed among the denuded poplars. Casimir Stanislavovich got off at every important station to visit the buffet; he would come back to his compartment laden with newspapers, but did not read them; instead he sat plunged in the smoke of his cigarettes, which gave off heat and sparks as they burned, and said not so much as a word to his fellow-travellers; Odessa Jews who played cards throughout the whole journey.

He had on a light overcoat with gaping, sagging pockets, a very old *crêpe* opera-hat, and footgear that was new, but coarse and evidently picked up at some flea-market. His hands (the characteristic hands of a habitual drunkard and of a basement-dweller of long standing) shook whenever he struck a match. Everything else as well bore testimony to his poverty and dipsomania: the absence of shirt-cuffs, his soiled linen collar, his ancient cravat, his inflamed and hopelessly time-worn face, and his eyes, vividly blue and watering. His side-whiskers, dyed with a poor brown dye, had an unnatural look. He had an air of fatigue and disdain.

The train arrived at Moscow the next day, not at all on schedule—it was all of seven hours late. The weather was uncertain. Although the weather was uncertain, it was an improvement on that of Kiev and not quite so wet, with something in the air that stirred one's senses. Casimir Stanislavovich hired a cab without bargaining and gave orders to be driven directly to the Versailles.

"Brother," said he, unexpectedly breaking his silence, "I've known this hotel ever since my student days."

Just as soon as his small hamper, tied with a stout rope, was brought into his room, he left the Versailles.

Evening was coming on. The air was warm; the black trees on the boulevards were putting on a green hue; there was a great number of people, of carriages, everywhere. It is a lonely thing for a man who has lived through his life, who has ruined it, to be in a populous, strange city on an evening in spring. Casimir Stanislavovich covered the whole length of the Tverskoi Boulevard on foot; he beheld anew, in the distance, the cast-iron figure of Pushkin, deep in thought, the gold and the lilac domes of the Strastnoi convent. . . . For an hour or so he sat in the Café Philipov, sipping chocolate and looking over the tattered comic periodicals. Then he set out for a cinema, the fiery, double-sided sign of which showed afar off on Tverskaya Street in the bluish twilight. From the cinema he took a cab to a restaurant on one of the boulevards—likewise a place familiar to him since his student days. His cabby was an old man, bent almost in a bow, sad, morose, deeply sunk in himself, in his old age, in his muddled thoughts; all the way he insufferably and persistently encouraged his indolent nag with all his being, muttering something to her all the time and occasionally upbraiding her venomously; finally he got his fare to the destination, whereupon he cast his heavy burden from his shoulders for a space and sighed deeply as he accepted his hire.

"Why, I hadn't made out what you said; I thought you was wantin' to go to the Braga," he let drop, as if he were actually dissatisfied, although the Praga, where he now was, meant a longer haul, and with that he slowly turned his horse around.

"I remember the Braga as well, old-timer," answered Casimir Stanislavovich. "But you surely must have been driving over Moscow for a long time!"

"Drivin', says you?" the old man echoed him. "It's goin' on fifty-two years that I've been drivin'. . . ."

"Well, then, maybe you've carried me as well," remarked Casimir Stanislavovich.

"Mebbe I did," the old man answered dryly. "There's lots of folks in this world; there ain't no rememberin' all of you. . . ."

Of the former restaurant, as Casimir Stanislavovich had known it, there was only the name left. Now this was a large restaurant of the first rank, even though flashy. Above the entrance blazed an electric globe which shed a certain unpleasant heliotrope light upon the second-rate cabbies with first-class pretensions, brazen and merciless to their trotting horses, which were wind-broken and gaunt and roared deeply on the run. In the damp entry stood big flower-pots of laurel, of tropical plants—the sort which travel on wheeled platforms from funerals to weddings and then back again. In the coat-room several men dashed up to Casimir Stanislavovich at the same time, and every man jack of them had the same thick shock of hair as the doorman of the Versailles.

The big green-tinted hall, with its multiplicity of broad mirrors and with a raspberry-coloured holy lamp warmly glimmering in one corner, was still empty, and only a few of the electric bulbs were on. Casimir Stanislavovich sat alone for a long time, with nothing to do. One could feel that the long evening had not yet grown dark beyond the windows with their drawn white shades; the clicking of horse-hoofs on the roadway floated in from outside; a little fountain in the centre of the hall plashed monotonously over an aquarium where little fungus-eaten gold-fish, lit up through the water from somewhere below, were lazily stirring. A bus-boy in white set the table and brought bread and a small carafe of vodka. Casimir Stanislavovich began on the vodka without any appetizers, compressing it in his mouth before swallowing, and, after swallowing, clenched his teeth, and, as though with aversion and by way of an antidote, sniffed the black bread. Suddenly, and actually frightening him, an orchestrion crashed forth and began to blare, filling the hall with a medley of Russian songs, now exaggeratedly tempestuous, devil-may-care, now inordinately tender, long-drawn-out, of soulful sadness. . . . And the eyes of Casimir Stanislavovich turned red and became veiled over with tears to the sound of this sweet and snuffling moaning.

Next a grey, curly-haired, dark-eyed Georgian brought him a half-raw, odoriferous *shashlik* on a formidable iron pike, with a certain debauched and skilful daintiness sliced the meat off onto his plate, and, to make the Asiatic simplicity of the thing more pronounced, sprinkled the dish with chopped onion, salt, and rusty-looking barberry powder, the while the orchestrion thundered through the empty hall a cake-walk that hypnotically egged one on to spasmodic squirms and hops. . . .

After this, Casimir Stanislavovich was served with Roquefort, red wine, coffee, Narzan mineral water, and liqueurs.—The orchestrion had long since fallen silent. In its place a German orchestra of females in white dresses had long been playing on the platform. The hall, now all lit up and becoming more and more crowded, grew warm, became dim from tobacco-smoke and densely permeated with the smell of the viands. The waiters swept through the room like whirlwinds; intoxicated diners demanded cigars, which shortly nauseated them; the *maîtres d'hôtel* were profligate with their solicitude, which at the same time was accompanied by an intensified watchfulness over their personal dignity; within the mirrors, within their turbidly watery abysses, there was reflected, with ever-growing disorderliness, something enormous, noisy, involved. Casimir Stanislavovich left the heated hall several times, going out into the cool corridors, into the cold lavatory—the latter, queerly enough, smelt of the sea. He walked as if on air, and, each time he came back to his seat, called anew for wine.

Toward two in the morning, shutting his eyes and snuffling the night freshness into his drugged head, he was flying in a fine, high, light carriage with pneumatic tires and a first-class driver, beyond the city, to a house of joy. He saw in the distance endless chains of nocturnal lights, running away somewhere downhill and then climbing uphill anew; but he saw them just as if it were not he but some other who was seeing them.

In the house of joy he all but had a fist-fight with some stout gentleman or other who, as he advanced upon Casimir Stanislavovich, shouted that he, this stout gentleman, was known to all thinking Russia. After that, with all his clothes on, Casimir Stanislavovich was lying on a wide bed covered with a quilted bed-spread of satin, in a small room half-lit by a light-blue lantern suspended close to the ceiling. This room smelt cloyingly of scented soap, and there were dresses hanging from a hook let into the door; near the bed was a vase of fruit, and the girl whose duty it was to entertain Casimir Stanislavovich was eating a pear— in silence, greedily, with gusto, slicing it off with a fruit-knife—while a girl friend of hers, with bare, stout arms, in nothing but a chemise which made her look like a little girl, was rapidly writing a letter on the dressing-table, paying no attention whatsoever to the casual lovers. She wrote— and wept. What about? There are lots of folks in this world; one can't find out everything. . . .

On the 10th of April Casimir Stanislavovich awoke late. Judging by the frightened way in which he opened his eyes, one could gather that, for an instant, he had been overwhelmed by the thought that he was in Moscow, and by what had taken place yesterday. He had come back not earlier than between five and six in the morning. As he had been going up the steps of the Versailles, he swayed; however, he had gone unerringly to his room, down the long, stinking tunnel of the corridor, with but one small lamp

66

sleepily smoking near the very beginning. Outside of each room stood boots and shoes—all of them belonging to people who were strangers, unknown to one another and inimical to one another. Suddenly one of the doors opened, inspiring Casimir Stanislavovich almost with horror. On its threshold appeared an old man in a dressing-robe, who looked like a ham actor playing the titular role in *The Memoirs of a Madman,* and Casimir Stanislavovich caught a glimpse of a green-shaded lamp in an exceedingly cluttered room: the den of a lonely old lodger. The room had holy images in one corner, and countless cigarette-tube cartons piled on top of one another almost up to the very ceiling in proximity to the images.—Could it possibly be that same half-demented compiler of the Lives of the Saints and Martyrs, the same crack-pot hagiologist who had lived in the Versailles three-and-twenty years ago? . . .

Casimir Stanislavovich's dark room was dreadfully stuffy with some sort of acrid and odoriferous dryness. The darkness was faintly pierced by the light coming through the transom. He went behind a partition, took the opera-hat off his exceedingly scandent, bandolined hair, and chucked his overcoat over the head of his unmade bed.—No sooner did he lie down than everything started going in circles under him, then was plunged into abysmal depths, and he instantaneously fell asleep. In his sleep he was constantly conscious of the stench of the metal wash-stand which was near his very face; but what he saw was a day in spring—trees in blossom—the great hall of a big manor-house, and a vast throng in awesome expectation of the arrival, at any moment, of a high church-dignitary. And this expectancy tormented and haunted him all night long. . . .

Now in the corridors of the Versailles one could hear
call-bells, and running steps, and people calling to one another. On the other side of the partition, through the dusty
panes of the double-frames, the sun was shining, and it
was hot. Casimir Stanislavovich took off his jacket, rang
the bell, and began to wash. A hall-boy came on the run—
a keen-eyed urchin whose hair was like the down on a fox's
belly. He had on a long-skirted coat and a pink blouse
buttoning on a diagonal over the right shoulder.

"A twist-loaf, a samovar, and a lemon," said Casimir
Stanislavovich, without looking at him.

"D'you want to order tea and sugar?" the hall-boy asked
with a briskness that was typical of Moscow.

And a minute later he came flying back, balancing a boiling samovar on the palm of one hand, held even with the
shoulder; in another moment he had spread a white cloth
over the round table in front of the divan and had placed
thereon a tray with a tumbler and a battered slop-basin
of brass, and then let the legs of the samovar bang on the
tray.—Casimir Stanislavovich, while the tea was infusing,
mechanically opened the Moscow *Gazette* which the hall-
boy had thrust under the samovar. His eye was caught by
an item about a man picked up somewhere in an unconscious state. "The victim was taken to a hospital," he read,
and chucked the paper aside.

He felt very wobbly and bad. Getting up, he opened
the window; it looked out on a courtyard, and he felt a
breath of freshness and of the city; there were borne to
him the studiedly canorous cries of the hucksters, the clang-
ing of horse-trams droning by beyond the house across the
way, the blended rattling of carriages, the musical boom-

ing of church-bells. . . . The city had long since been living its noisy, enormous life on this bright spring day, which was almost summery.

Having squeezed almost the whole lemon into his tumbler of tea and avidly drunk off this turbid, sour liquid, Casimir Stanislavovich again withdrew behind the partition. The Versailles had quieted down. Everything was pleasant and peaceful; his glance glided indolently over the office notice on the wall: "Any guest staying three hours will be charged for a full day"; a mouse was noisily scurrying in a chest of drawers, rolling about a piece of sugar left by some transient guest. . . . Thus, in a half-doze, Casimir Stanislavovich lay behind the partition until such time as the sun disappeared from the room and there was drawn through the window a different freshness—the freshness that heralds the evening.

Thereupon he painstakingly put himself in order: he untied his hamper, changed his linen, got out a handkerchief (very cheap, but fresh), whisked off with a brush his shiny frock-coat, his opera-hat, and his overcoat, took out of the torn pocket of the last a smudged Kiev newspaper dated January 15, and tossed it into a corner.—Having dressed, and combed his side-whiskers with a comb which dyed them at the same time, he took stock of his resources —he had four roubles and seven ten-kopeck pieces in his purse—and went out.

Precisely at six o'clock he was near a very squat, ancient little church on the Molchanovka. Behind the church paling a spreading tree was bursting into small green leaves; children were at play there—one thin little girl, who was skipping rope, had one of her black stockings constantly

falling; wet-nurses, tricked out in Russian national costumes, sat on a bench, with sleeping infants in baby-
carriages before them. The whole tree was a-crackle with
sparrows; the air was soft, for all the world like that of
summer—there was a smell of dust, even, just as in summer—and the sky beyond the houses was tenderly aureate
above the sunset, and one felt that, anew, there were joy,
youth, and happiness somewhere in the world.

The hanging chandelier was already lit in the church,
and the lectern was in its place, with a small rug spread in
front of it. Casimir Stanislavovich carefully doffed his
opera-hat, trying not to disarrange his hair, and entered the
church hesitatingly—it was thirty years by now since he
had set foot in any church. He found a place for himself
in a withdrawn nook, yet so situated that he would be able
to see the bride and groom. He examined the frescoed
arches, lifted his eyes to the cupola; and his every move-
ment, his every sigh, found a sonorous echo in the stillness.
The church was gleaming with gold, was expectantly and
intermittently making its candles splutter. And now, crossing themselves, but fully accustomed and quite at their
ease, those who were to officiate at the holy services, and
the choristers, began to enter; then came crones, children,
the wedding guests in gala attire, and the preoccupied
ushers.

But when a stir was heard near the porch, and a carriage
drove up with crunching wheels, and all turned toward the
entrance, and *Come, my dove!* thundered forth in greeting,
Casimir Stanislavovich turned deathly pale from the beating of his heart, and involuntarily made as if to move forward. And near, very near him, even grazing him with her

bridal veil and enveloping him with the scent of her lilies-of-the-valley, there passed by him one who was not even aware of his being in the world; she passed by with her lovely head bowed, all in flowers and diaphanous gauze, all snowy white and immaculate, happy and timorous, like a princess going to her first communion. . . .

Casimir Stanislavovich hardly perceived the bridegroom who met her: rather squat, broad-shouldered, with his yellow hair cut badger-style and terminating in a short, flat cow-lick on the crown of his head. And throughout the whole wedding ceremony there was nothing before his eyes but her bowed head in its flowers and bridal veil, and a tiny hand tremblingly holding a burning candle with a white ribbon entwined around it and tied in a bow. . . .

At ten o'clock in the evening he was back in his room. His whole overcoat had become permeated with the odour, with the air of spring: after he had come out of the church and, near the porch, had caught a glimpse of the interior of the bridal carriage, upholstered in white satin, and the reflection of the sunset in its plate-glass window, and a final flash, behind this glass, of her who was being carried off from him forever—after all this he had long wandered through some side-streets or other, occasionally emerging on the Novinski Boulevard.—Now he slowly took off his overcoat with hands that trembled, and placed on the table a small paper bag with two cucumbers that, for no earthly reason, he had purchased off a huckster's tray. They gave off an odour of spring even through the paper, and, springlike, an April crescent, riding high in the yet undarkened sky, was letting its liquid silver stream in through one of the upper window-panes.

Casimir Stanislavovich lit a candle, lighting up dismally his desolate, chance haven, and sat down on the divan. He sat thus for a very long time. He did not ring, did not ask for anything, and locked himself in. All this appeared suspicious to the hall-boy, who had seen him enter his room with dragging feet, had seen him taking the key from the outside of the door to lock himself in. Several times the hall-boy tiptoed his way to the keyhole and peeped in: Casimir Stanislavovich was sitting on the divan, all shaking, and wiping his face with a handkerchief; he was weeping so bitterly, so copiously, that the brown dye was coming off his side-whiskers and smearing his cheeks.

In the night he tore the cord off the window-shade, and, blinded by his tears, began tying it to a clothes-hook. But the expiring candle flickered eerily; dark waves of dread floated and quivered through the locked room. . . . No, he had not the strength to die by his own hand!

In the morning he drove off to the railway station some three hours before the departure of his train. At the station he wove slowly in and out among the passengers, with his tear-reddened eyes cast down; unexpectedly he would halt now before one, now before another, and in a voice low, even, expressionless, yet sufficiently rapid, would say:

"For God's sake . . . I'm in a desperate fix. . . . I must have enough for a ticket to Briansk. . . . If only a few coppers—"

And some, trying not to look at his opera-hat, at the napless velvet of his overcoat collar, and at his ghastly face, with its side-whiskers now faded to a violet hue, would give him something, hastily and shamefacedly.

But later he became fused with the crowd which was

making a rush for the exit leading to the train platform, and in that crowd he vanished, while in the Versailles, in the room which had been his, as it were, for two days, the servants were carrying out the slop-pail of the wash-stand, throwing the windows wide open to the April sun, and, roughly moving the chairs about, were sweeping and throwing the rubbish out. And, together with the rubbish, they swept out his torn note, forgotten by him with the cucumbers and then fallen under the table, under the slipping table-cloth:

"I request that no one be blamed for my death. I had been at the wedding of my only daughter, who—"

THE MORDVINIAN SARAFAN

~ ~

R EALLY, WHY AM I GOING TO SEE HER; why am I going to
this strange woman, who is pregnant, to boot? Why have
I struck up one more superfluous acquaintance, and why am
I keeping it up? This does not require much reflection, of
course; it is a foolish visit, no matter how you regard it—
silly, false, and somehow unpleasant, on the whole. We had
chanced to meet again in Leontiev Park, and again there
was her joyous smile, a minute's desultory, constrained
talk, and then a warm hand-clasp and the request:

"*Do* drop in some day at the candlelight hour! I'll be *so*
glad to see you! Drop in whenever you think of it; I'm
always at home. Drop in tomorrow—I'll show you my
new sarafan with the Mordvinian embroidery. . . ."

And so I am going again, and even, for some reason,
hurrying.

A raw March wind is blowing in my face. A black spring
night is hanging over Moscow. Ahead of me is the clean-
cut glow of the street-lamps. Far, far above, against the
black-blue sky, is the faint white of puffy clouds, lit from
below by the glow of the city. On the right church cupolas,
their gilt mysteriously glimmering, melt away into these
clouds. And from everywhere comes the reddish peering of

the countless eyes of houses, which, in the darkness, seem enormous.

Of course she had again been expecting me all day and making preparations; had gone to buy fruit and pastry; had put on her best things. . . . She had, in general, apparently imagined that her life had suddenly acquired a certain joyous interest, that there had been found a certain "sensitive" man who would at last appreciate her soul, which went unappreciated by her husband.—At the thought of all this one feels so ashamed that there is a desire to turn and run back.

However, here is the entrance. The vestibule is so-so, but poorly illuminated and none too predisposing to visitors. The doorman is young, with atrocious manners, and wears a long coat, tight-waisted and long-skirted. No sooner had he caught the slight noise I had made on entering than he raised, from within, the little red curtain over the small window of his door and peered out inquisitively. Downing my embarrassment I pass him with an independent air and, without pausing, mount the narrow staircase, covered with threadbare carpeting. "The Devil!" I puff. "How high up she lives, and how ridiculous this whole business is!" But no matter—I've already rung. There are hurrying steps on the other side of the door, and it is opened—and that not by a maid, but by the hostess herself.

Again the joyous (and, as always, for some reason wondering) smile, an instant of mutual confusion, and then the hurried phrases, evidently prepared beforehand:

"Ah, how charming of you to keep your promise and to wander in at the candlelight hour! Why, I'm all, all alone; I've even let the servants off—for the cinema is

really a mania with them, you know. . . . There, divest
yourself of your things and let's go in to tea. . . ."

How fond she was of that "candlelight hour"! And, to
top that, "divest yourself," and the tactless kiss on my
temple when I kissed her hand, and the announcement about
the absence of the servants. I already feel unbearably
ashamed; however, I enter the drawing-room briskly, as
if nothing were the matter, nonchalantly wiping my eye-
glasses with a handkerchief. And, as I rub them, I am
thinking: "Yes, her hair is arranged very fetchingly, evidently by a hairdresser (I was right, then: she *was* expecting me); and then there's that dress of marsh-green velvet,
leaving her full breasts somewhat open, and that string of
pearls nestling between them, and those stockings of grey
silk, and her tiny satin slippers—"

"Do sit down, my dear Peter; I'll be with you in just a
minute. . . ."

And she quickly steps out. She is very much excited and
(the truth must be told) very far from bad-looking. Some
sort of peculiar good looks, belonging to pregnancy, a
miraculous blossoming forth of the whole body. The lips
are already slightly inflamed, somewhat swollen; but then,
how magnificently dark and shining her eyes are!

With a sigh I let my whole carcass slump on the divan.
The setting is, of course, the usual one: a black piano, with
the keyboard open; above it is a portrait of Beethoven,
awesome, with high cheek-bones; near the piano is a great
lamp on a high stand and under an enormous rose-coloured
shade; before the divan is a small table, with a spirit-
lamp for the tea-pot, and pastry, fruit, and small fruit-
knives of gold, while dolls are sprawled out on all the easy-

chairs in distorted and helpless poses—a country wife in a yellow-red sarafan; a bonny lad in a flame-coloured blouse, a sleeveless jacket of velveteen, and a round little hat with peacock feathers; a Marquise in a white wig of cotton wool; a Harlequin; a Columbine—

"Well, and here am I!"

She puts the tea-pot on the spirit-lamp, applies a light, gathers up the toys from the chairs, and, with a smile, dumps the whole motley crew on my knees.

"My new *chefs-d'œuvre*. Admire and criticize."

I dutifully admire them; to lend an air of interest, attentiveness, and impartiality to the thing, I invent petty objections, mixing them well with flattery. She pours the tea— "You prefer it rather strong, don't you?"—and with a smile hands me my cup, with her little finger sticking out. And the conversation is on—if one may call it such, since, as usual, it is only she who speaks. What about? About the same things as always, of course. At first about the toys, which I cannot bear, but which I continue examining even during the conversation, since they are "her passion, the only things wherewith she can divert her soul, which was really created only for art." Then the talk turns to her husband, whom up to now I had not seen even once, and of whom she says, with false gaiety: "He sleeps until ten, goes off to work, dines, sleeps again, and again goes off!"— and, finally, she speaks of her first baby, which died. She speaks only of herself. About me there is never a word, even such as mere politeness might prompt: up to now she has not learned, nor evinced the least intention to learn, who I am, where I work, whether I am married or single. . . .

77

She is especially excited today. Both excited and, it seems, very gay. She talks on without cease, with unusual expressiveness, and is so exacting of attention that I soon begin to grow dazed, cataleptic, and merely keep on smiling, inanely and absent-mindedly. Suddenly she jumps up— "Ah, I've forgotten the most important thing!"—disappears for an instant in an adjoining room, and returns with an exulting smile:

"Voilà! And every switch done with my own hands! Pretty, isn't it?"

In her hands she has something strange and fearful: a long, loose robe of coarse, peasant-spun linen, with appliqués and embroidery on the shoulders, the bosom, and the hem, in dark-brown and indigo-blue silks. She shows it to me this way and that; she holds it up against herself, against her full breasts and her abdomen, which is beginning to round out, and regards me as she does so, both questioningly and joyously. I get up and, again assuming attentiveness, examine the garment and go into raptures over it, and yet, at the same time, things have already become simply unbearable: there is something sombre, ancient, and somehow sepulchral about this robe; it evokes within me some eerie and exceedingly unpleasant feeling, linked up with her pregnancy and tragic gaiety. She will probably die in giving birth. . . .

Tossing the sarafan on top of the piano, she seats herself by my side, and, without taking her widened eyes off me, begins to talk of her feelings toward her prospective child. They are extraordinary, inexpressible, are these feelings. She "senses, with terror and rapture, a new life within her, and is already filled with a love such that every other love

78

compared with it, and especially love for a man, is but blasphemy, vulgar banality." If God were to take this love from her, she would do away with herself, without a moment's reflection; this she has already firmly resolved upon. . . . Or else she will go into a convent. This convent idea is an old, long-cherished idea of hers. Oh, if it weren't for her being married, and having children, she wouldn't delay entering a convent for even a day! If only because there was nobody and nothing to delay for, nobody and nothing to sacrifice herself for!

"Tell me, my dear fellow, who is there?" she asks ardently, fixing me with her eyes. "Should I, perhaps, delay and make sacrifices for him who hardly even suspects that I have my own personal life, my own personal joys and sorrows, which I have no one in the whole wide world to share with?"

Without taking her eyes off me she attempts to laugh; why, really, her husband seems hardly human, but rather some wild creature, to judge by his propensity for sleeping at the least chance given him!—Now she leans back, now bends forward, placing a hand upon my knee; and I become conscious of all her emanations—the odours of her breath, her hair, her body, her dress. Her cheeks are now flaming; her eyes are downright magnificent; her movements are abrupt, and there are small precious stones sparkling on her bosom, on her fingers, in her ears. But I—I am all the time looking at her abdomen, showing roundly under the velvet of her dress, at the way she crosses her legs, giving a generous view of each grey stocking, which is loosely put on. . . .

And suddenly comprehending that there had finally arrived that precise moment the secret hope of which had both led me to her and had stayed with me all evening, I take her hand and, murmuring: "Enough, dear—calm yourself!" draw her to me. And she suddenly bites her lower lip, quickly puts her handkerchief to her mouth, quickly changes her easy-chair for a seat next to me on the divan, and, with tears, lets her head sink on my breast. . . .

I am returning home about two in the morning. There is not a soul out on the streets; the wind has shifted, is blowing harder, and one can sniff the sea in it. An occasional drop of rain strikes my face. The clouds overhead no longer show white; a dense darkness is hanging over Moscow. And I stride ahead rapidly; I feel as if I were drunk.

"I must cut and run, run—no later than tomorrow!"— this thought will not leave me, filling my head. "To Kiev— to Warsaw—to Crimea—wherever my eyes may lead!"

A CREEPY STORY

〰 〰

In the park, denuded of its leafage, made hideous by
wintry death, and blackly gaping before the house, was
the darkness and desolateness of a night in March, and new-
born, white snow, as soft as swan's-down, was powdering
the old, grey snow.

They (all we know is that there were two of them) had
been sitting in the park since the coming of evening, waiting for the dead of night.

And the house was watchfully peering with its many lit
windows into the dark park; she, this old Frenchwoman in
chestnut-hued wig and eyes as goggling as a lobster's, living
absolutely alone in the upper rooms of the house during the
owners' visit to the city—she felt the sinister presence of
those who were watching her. She put the lights on in all
the rooms—and the rooms were many, and all large; she
decided not to sleep all night, and all the time kept on passing from room to room, throughout the house, all empty
and a-glitter with lamps and candelabra.

The strangest thing of all was that instead of going into
the basement, where the cook and the laundress lived, or
to the servants' quarters, where all the other domestics were
sleeping—instead of calling someone to her—she, already

fully aware of her doom, merely kept on passing from room to room, and even got the notion into her head of jotting down brief notes. She wrote:

12.15—I keep on walking and walking! I feel I am lost. There is somebody in the garden. I even know that there are two of them. . . .

It has just struck one—downstairs, on the big clock in the vestibule. The hour struck awesomely and solemnly. . . . *One of them* is very short, with legs as bandy as those of a dachshund. But I am going to stay awake all night; I am going to defend my-self. . . .

She played a cake-walk on the grand piano; she made many attempts to play, and played tempestuously, with despairing gaiety, and always broke off short:

I am playing a cake-walk [she wrote] as if I were mad. My terror attains to ecstasy—I cannot play even one piece to the end. . . .

After that she picked over the books in a case in the study; she looked at them and then threw them on the floor, leaving all the doors of the case open. She was picking out something to read and at last took a volume of Reclus's *Geography*.

She left one more note on her employer's desk:

My God! But why must *I* be the victim? I am going to defend myself; I won't give myself up alive.

With the volume of Reclus in her hands she lay down on the morocco-upholstered divan in the study, and, after opening the book and reading it for some time, and even making some pencilled notations, she had suddenly fallen asleep.

And it was on this very divan that they found her in the morning with her throat slit from ear to ear, minus her wig, her skull absolutely bald, her lobster-eyes wild, fixed, astounded.

The panes in the double French window in the drawing-room, serving as a door to the garden balcony, had been forced in and extracted. The wind blew into the drawing-room, bringing with it a chill exhalation, a mist, from the hoary park. And the whole house was ablaze with lights that showed yellow in the pallid light of a raw and whitely murky day.

Who had slit her throat? And wherefore?

It was *they*, those two who had been lurking in the garden, who had slit her throat. But wherefore? That no one knows; they did not carry off, did not as much as touch, the least thing.

There really had been two of them. This was proved by the wet, muddy prints left by their feet on the parquet floor. And the footprints of one of them were not altogether ordinary—spread far apart, club-footed. . . . Beyond a doubt he had crooked legs.

There had been two of them. But who were they? No one knows. They were never found—never caught.

After all, the creepiest thing in the world is the soul of man.

And especially that soul which, having done its frightful

deed, having sated its fiendish lust, remains forever unknown, uncaptured, undivined.

Where are they now, these two? And yet it may very
well be that they are alive up to this very day; that they
are working at something, somewhere; that they are walking about, eating, drinking, chatting, laughing, and smoking. . . .

TEMIR AKSAK KHAN

⌒ ⌒

A-a-a, Temir Aksak Khan!" an ululating, passionately
and hopelessly yearning voice wildly wails in the tiny village coffee-house.

The spring night is dark and raw; the black wall of the
mountain precipices is hardly distinguishable. Near the
coffee-house, which clings to a cliff, out in the chalky mud
of the paved road, stands an open automobile, and from its
frightful, blinding eyes stretch forward, out into the darkness, two long, prostrate pillars of hazy light. From afar,
from below, sounds the surge of the unseen sea; a moist,
disquieting wind, coming from all directions, blows out of
the dark.

Tobacco-fumes fill the interior of the coffee-house; it is
dimly lit by a small tin lamp hanging from the ceiling
and is warmed by a heap of red-hot embers smouldering
on a hearth in one corner. The beggar who had abruptly
begun his song concerning Temir Aksak Khan with a pierc-
ingly nasal plaint, an excruciating scream, is squatting on
the clay-daubed floor. He is a centenarian ape, in a sheepskin jacket and a shaggy ram's-wool cap, turned rusty red
by rains, by the sun, by time. On his knees lies something in
the nature of a rude lyre, fashioned of wood. He is bend-

ing over—his auditors cannot see his face; all they can see are his ears, sticking out from under his cap. Snatching harsh sounds out of his lyre at rare intervals, he wails in unbearable, despairing woe.

Near the hearth, on a tabouret, sits the keeper of the coffee-house: a womanishly corpulent, comely Tatar. He had at first kept on gnawing sunflower seeds absent-mindedly and had smiled, somewhat condescendingly and mockingly. Then he had simply become cataleptic, with eyebrows raised and with a smile which was suffering and bewildered.

On the bench under the small window sat a hajji, smoking; tall, with gaunt shoulder-blades, grey-bearded, in a black robe and with a turban of white, the latter wonderfully emphasizing the swarthiness of his pock-marked, austere face. Now he has forgotten his chibouk; he has thrown his head back against the wall, has closed his eyes. One leg, bent at the knee, in a striped woollen stocking, is resting on the bench; the other hangs down, the slippered foot barely touching the floor.

And at a little table near the hajji sit those passers-by who had been moved by a whim to halt their automobile near the village coffee-house and to drink a tiny cup apiece of execrable coffee: a large-sized gentleman in a derby hat, in a British waterproof; and a handsome young lady, now pale because of her attentiveness and agitation. She is of the South; she understands the Tatar tongue, understands the words of the song. . . . "A-a-a, Temir Aksak Khan!"

There was not in all the universe a Khan more mighty and renowned than Temir Aksak Khan. All the sublunar world was in trepidation before him, and the most splendidly beautiful women and maidens on earth were ready to die for the happiness of being, if for but an instant, his slaves. But before his end Temir Aksak Khan sat in the dust, on the cobbles of the bazaar, and kissed the tatters of the cripples and the beggars passing by, saying unto them:

"Take the soul out of me, ye cripples and ye beggars, for there is in it no longer even the desire to desire!"

And when the Lord at last had taken pity upon him and had freed him from vain, earthly glory and vain, earthly delights, soon did all his domains crumble; into desolation fell his cities and his palaces; and the dust of sands swept over their ruins under the skies eternally blue, like to precious glaze, and under the sun, eternally blazing, like to the fire of Gehenna. . . . *A-a-a, Temir Aksak Khan! Where are thy days and thy works? Thy battles and thy victories—where? Where are those women, young, tender, jealous, who loved thee; where are those eyes that, upon thy couch, shone like to black suns?*

All are silent; all are vanquished by the song. But, strangely enough, that desperate sorrow, that bitter reproach to someone, which makes the song so heartbreaking, is sweeter than the loftiest, the most passionate joy.

The transient gentleman is gazing intently at the table, and puffs hard at his cigar until it glows. The lady with him has opened her eyes wide, and tears are coursing down her cheeks.

A few minutes later both step over the threshold of the coffee-house. The beggar has ended his song and has fallen to rending, to munching the tough, flat round of bread the host has given him. But the song still seems to sound, to go on and on; it still seems that there is no end to it, nor that there ever will be.

The lady, as she was leaving, had thrust a whole gold piece upon the beggar; but she is thinking, uneasily, that this is not enough; she wants to go back and give him another gold coin—no; two, or three, or a kiss upon his calloused hand, in the presence of all. Her eyes are still smarting from her tears, but her emotion is such that she feels as if never in her life had she been happier than at this minute, after the song proclaiming that all, all is vanity and sorrow underneath the sun; never happier than on this dark and humid night with the distant surge of the unseen sea, with the odour of the spring rain and of the wet bark of trees, with the restless wind that penetrates to the very depths of one's soul.

The chauffeur, who had been half-lying on his seat, hurriedly hops out, resembling some animal in his fur coat, that seems for all the world to be turned inside out; he bends over into the beams from the head-lights, does something to the machine, and it suddenly comes to life, starting to thrum, to quiver from impatience. The gentleman helps the lady in, sits down beside her, covers her knees with a plaid; she thanks him, absent-mindedly. . . . The automobile darts over the down grade of the road, gets up speed for climbing, thrusting its light-pillars against some shrubbery or other, and once more brushes them off to one side, drops them into the darkness of a new descent. . . . On the heights, over the outlines of the barely seen, seemingly Cyclopæan mountains, stars twinkle amid the tenuous clouds; far ahead a bend of the bay barely, barely shows the white of its surf; the wind, softly and powerfully, beats upon one's face. . . .

O Temir Aksak Khan (proclaimed the song), there was not on this sublunar plane any more doughty, more happy, or more renowned than thou: swarthy-visaged, fiery-eyed, radiant and beneficent as the Angel Gabriel; wise and magnificent as King Suleiman! More vivid and more green than the verdure of Paradise was the silk of thy turban, and with a seven-hued, starry fire did its plume of diamonds play and quiver; and for the happiness of touching, with the slightest touch of their lips, thy hand, slim and dark, the most splendidly beautiful queens and concubines on earth were ready to die. But, having drunk the cup of earthly delights to the dregs, in the dust of the bazaar didst thou sit, Temir Aksak Khan, grasping at, kissing, the rags of cripples passing by, imploring them:

"Take my suffering soul out of me, O ye maimed!"

And ages have sped over thy forgotten grave, and sands have swept over the ruins of thy mosques and thy mansions, under the sky eternally blue and the sun pitilessly joyous; and the wild rose has shot up through the few tiles of azure faience still left on thy sepulchre, so that, with every new spring, there might languish upon it, anew and anew, the hearts of the nightingales, straining their throats in songs excruciatingly passionate, yearning for happiness unutterable. . . . *A-a-a, Temir Aksak Khan, where is it, that bitter wisdom of thine? Where are all the torments of thy soul, which with tears and with gall hath spewed forth the honey of earthly seductions?*

The mountains have gone, have receded; the sea is rushing by the side of the paved road, breaking in foam, with the noise and odour of watery freshness, against the white gravel of the shore, that resembles endless heaps of bones. Far ahead, amid the dark, low-lying stretches, are scattered lights, red and white; the roseate glow of the city, like that of a distant conflagration, is unmoving; and the night over it, and over the sea-bay, is black and soft, like soot.

THE SCREAM

~ ~

ONCE, IN THE EARLY SPRING, we were sailing from Port
Said to Batoum.

Bubonic plague was raging in Stamboul, and, since our
freighter had no business to transact there, we decided to
avoid the Golden Horn and to wait for daylight at the
Kovaki, near the entrance to the Black Sea: no ships are
permitted to sail out of the Bosporus at night. And so
two quarantine guards, both of them Turks, were dispatched
with us from the Dardanelles, so that, upon our arrival at
the Kovaki, they might certify as to our not having made
a stop at the Golden Horn.

We weighed anchor from the Dardanelles at four. Five
is the sailors' supper hour. Before supper they are supposed
to get a pannikin of spirits apiece. But, it being Maundy
Thursday, some of the sailors considered it a sin to drink
anything strong on such a day. However, not to have the
spirits go entirely to waste, they proffered it to the Turks,
just for the fun of the thing. The drink knocked them off
their feet, since they were not accustomed to liquor, and
they fell asleep—one, well grown, stalwart, on the poop,
over the very propeller; the other, a small fellow, on a
hatch-cover between the poop and the engine-room. And

just before dozing off, this small fellow kept on muttering, not only in Turkish and Greek but even in Russian:

"Th' Rooshian, him all ri'—th' Arab, him no all ri'!"

He told how he, a man simple and poor, had had a wife who was such a beauty that he had never called her by her name, even, but always said "Djanim—My Heart"; but she had died long ago, having borne him a son. His son, too, was handsome, tender and respectful, like any girl,— but he'd been carried off to Stamboul, had been sent off to war, to Arabia. "But you never return from Arabia!" he was saying. And, leaping up, he would emit a loud sound as if he were firing off a carbine, fall on his back, imitating someone killed outright, and then turn up his bandy legs in their striped woollen stockings. His trousers, which narrowed very much toward the bottom, were all in patches; the coat of his uniform was very short, and all in tatters; his fez was dirty, his ram-like eyes were turbid, his moustache drooping, his chin long unshaved, and his face, burned by the sun and wind, was all in wrinkles. And the sailors laughed loudly and spoke with pity:

"The liquor, now, maties—just see what liquor will do to a man!"

When I went to bed in the evening, I left orders to be called just as soon as the lighthouse was sighted. About two in the morning my orderly knocked on the door of my cabin and said in a low voice:

"We're approaching."

"Right-o!" I answered. "Is it very cold?"

"Three above."

"Foggy?"

"All clear."

I found my overcoat and cap in the dark and stepped out. A single light burned dully and dismally in the main cabin. A light breeze was blowing in through the open door, beyond which the moonlit night showed bluely, and the feathery, small fronds of a dwarf Japanese palm standing in a pot near the fireplace barely quivered, crisply rustling. Amid the silence reigning everywhere the only clearly distinguishable sounds were this rustling and the slow ticktock of a wall clock. But the barely audible tinkling of the liqueur-glasses suspended from the ceiling of the bar, and that faint quivering which made the whole steamer tremble and which proceeded from the engine working in the depths of the steamer, dully and evenly, like an enormous heart—these did not disturb the silence. I walked over to the port side and became lost in contemplation of Stamboul, now approaching—of its scattered nocturnal lights, opalescently glowing behind a whitish, rare mist— of its spectre, fantastic and grandiose, mysteriously wan against the bluish background of the moonlit night.

Next I mounted to the bridge. Looking straight ahead, near the telegraph, stood the captain and the mate on watch, in caps and pea-jackets. They did not turn around as I took my place behind them near the pilot-house, where, in the murk, the helmsman was standing as if turned to stone, with his hands on the spokes of the steering-wheel and his eyes glued to the compass, lit up by an electric lamp, shaded and hanging low. These men, likewise under the spell of the night and of Stamboul, called to each other, with precision, but slowly, in a low voice.

"Port easy," the captain would command phlegmatically, without turning around.

"Port easy it is, sir," the helmsman would respond in a drawling, hoarse alto. But he, too, responded phlegmatically, as though half-asleep, in keeping with the midnight stillness. Evenly, slowly, the sighs of the engine came reverberatingly from the depths of the ship, and slowly there passed and unrolled before us the faery realm of the great city.

"Hold her to it," the captain was saying, in an ordinary and cautious tone.

"Ho—old her it is, sir!" the helmsman responded, his voice taking four tones higher.

I enter the pilot-house.—A dead calm prevails. There is a full, bright moon motionless to starboard, almost behind us, over the misty silhouettes of the Prince Islands. An enormous golden streak gleams lengthwise between them, underneath that shadow which always lies upon the horizon beyond the glimmer of the moon. A glimmer, as of greenish glass, arises and expires, playing upon the shagreen, oily billows near the ship's very side.

But everything in the distance—not only the hilly shores, but the Golden Horn slowly opening before us, and the wan spectres of Scutari, Stamboul, Galata, Pera—everything is misted over with an opalescent whitish yashmak, as soft, as diaphanous, as precious gossamers of Brusa. And behind this yashmak, like countless eyes, mysterious and splendidly beautiful, opalescently and unmovingly shine countless lights, far and near: of gold, and small, thickly strewn among the dark gardens on the Scutari shore; clustered, like swarms of bees from the top to the bottom on the hill of Galata; emerald and ruby, and large, upon the

94

masts in the Golden Horn, and upon the buoys, and upon the guard-boats, reflected full-length in the mirror-like water; rare and somnolent in Stamboul, which is sleeping with open, glittering eyes on its knolls against the moon. I distinguished the stone and wooden houses of its suburbs, the ethereal, infinitely high minarets around the chalice-like cupolas of the white Ahmedieh, the ancient cupola, so dear to me, of Sophia, the gardens of the Serail, and the grey wall of the Palace of Constantine. Once more I was inhaling that peculiar aroma, sweet and dry, of the shores of Turkey.

Suddenly, somewhere from afar, there floated through the silence someone's faint, sobbing call:

"Yu—ussouf!"

Ever nearer and nearer swarmed the fiery bees on the hill of Galata. We were moving along, and the little red lanterns on the guard-boats were being borne back past us. I reflected: "This may have been someone on a guard-boat calling out; perhaps there is murder being done, and the victim has screamed for mercy; perhaps they've caught a Greek smuggler; but what have I to do with it?"

Again there comes a low-voiced command and then the alto of the helmsman. The moon shifts its position; the Scutari shore moves forward from starboard—far upon the mirror-like water has its shadow fallen. The hill of Pera and Galata has already passed, all covered, as if with a cascade, by the stone buildings of the city and swathed in a transparently white pall. The two somnolent, translucent emeralds hanging low over the water, one above the other— there, where the small white tower of Leander sticks out of the water—have been left far behind. The nose of the steamer slowly turns; the Sea of Marmora, glittering like a glassy-golden field near the Serail cape, closes behind us. This field fades away; the short, crystal-clear ring of the telegraph breaks the silence. We are turning ever more sharply to starboard. Now there is no more glitter any-where: the Bosporus has narrowed. The white, marble palaces of the Sultan stretch out along the left littoral, bath-ing the broad steps of their landings in the water. The shadow reaches them as well; in this shadow the marble takes on a greenish pallor. . . .

"Yussouf!"—again the cry comes floating from some-where afar off.

I raise my eyebrows, and listen closely. . . . And again I forget about this scream.

Because of the shadow the chilly spring night seems brighter and greener, the moon more mirror-like. Clearer, bluer had the starry sky become. At times the summits of the Asia Minor shore, with its lowlands covered with villas, gardens, and groves, are receding. Ahead I see a high, rounded knoll—how softly and distinctly it stands out against the light sky! How unruffled and ethereal are the outlines of several Italian *pini* wreathing its crown, with their short trunks and dark, spreading tops! And here is a great saddle-shaped hollow between the mountains—and now the moon, which had been standing behind this hol-low, grows a trifle paler; the vernal groves, still denuded, let its light filter through; the transparent mist among the trees shows silvery under the moon. But this hollow disappears from view as well; we are now sailing under a dark slope, closely covered with gardens, where black cypresses rear over tile roofs. The first timid nightingale

sends his sonorous and sweet call through the gardens, and
falls silent. . . . The vernal chill of the earth and the
odour of last year's leafage are wafted from the shore. . . .

"Yussouf!" a voice calls from the stern—passionately,
strangling from tears. "Youssou—ouf!"

Descending from the pilot-house, I quickly went toward
the stern. I ran down a trap from the boat-deck, passed near
the engine, sighing evenly and deeply, which breathed upon
me with its warmth and odour of heated oil.—The moon
has again shifted its place. It is far behind our stern, over
that enormous lake of gold into which the Bosporus, between its closed-in banks, has now been transformed. . . .
And, running down another ladder, I caught sight of a
small, dark, kneeling figure on a hatch, with its back toward
me. At times it would sit back, squatting on its heels, as the
Orientals do at prayer, raise itself impulsively, then seek
something in the matting doing duty as a prayer-rug, and
again throw itself backward, and, raising up its arms,
would cry out passionately, briefly, with unutterable pain
and supplication:

"Yussou—ouf! . . ."

And I comprehended everything.

He, this short little Turk, had fallen asleep after muttering to his heart's content and after having, in his
tipsiness, sung his fill of Greek songs. He had slept throughout the crossing of the Sea of Marmora. And suddenly he
had awakened near Stamboul itself—Stamboul, which had
taken his son from him. . . . Submissively, like a true
Moslem, he had accepted his sorrow and hidden it away in
his heart. None had remarked the traces of grief amid his

97

apathetic wrinkles, in his dispassionately arched eyebrows, and about his drooping moustache. And, besides, the nagging pain of this grief in his heart was far too dulled. But lo, something out of the ordinary had befallen him: he was on a journey to the Kovaki, on a strange deck, and amid strange men, who had begun by treating him to fiery vodka. Driven out of his mind by the drink, feeling that he was travelling to the Padishah's own city, he had begun to recall with painful rapture how his son had been carried off thither, to picture to himself with incomprehensible ecstasy how his son had been killed in Arabia. And the drink had felled him at last; he had lost consciousness and had slept for a long, long time. . . . And suddenly he had awakened. Something had been oppressively preying upon his mind in his drunken, heavy sleep. But when his eyes had opened, he had sensed that it was very late at night by that silence which was all around him, had beheld the grandiose and fantastic spectre of Stamboul in the moonlight—and had suddenly, with all his being, and perhaps for the first time, fathomed all the depth of that which Stamboul had done with his own life, pitiful and of no need to anyone, and with the splendidly beautiful youth of Yussouf. Why, it had been about him, about his son, that he had been telling these yapping, grinning Russian dogs! . . .

I walked up to him. He turned to me his face, pale in the moonlight, all moist from tears, with a moist, drooping moustache, and fixed me with his ram's eyes, goggling, grown glazed from the poison of alcohol, from his sobbing and the strain he had undergone.—Why did he have that bit of tangled matting under him? He may, perhaps, have also recalled that he had slept through the time of the evening prayer, and had made haste to spread this bit of matting, bowing and rising as he did so. . . . But was his a mood for prayer? Everything is becoming confused in his brain; he feels only horror and sad yearning. And suddenly he falls to screaming at Stamboul, at the moonlit night, that he is alone and is perishing. No, such a thing cannot be! His son is alive—he *must* be alive, he must return! His son must return, too, because his father, a beggared, lonely old man, had been put to shame, had been drugged. . . . And sobbing, growing frenzied from horror and grief, he had begun to scream wildly, strangling from his tears.

I took his ice-cold hand. He recoiled and snatched it away, heavily slumping back on his heels. His tears, unrestrainably rolling down, obscured his bewildered eyes; an alcoholic catarrh obstructed his breath; his moist moustaches straggled into his mouth.

"Yussouf!" he screamed dully and abruptly, like a man bobbing up out of the water.

And he began ululating, shaking from his sobs, chokingly, stretching his hands out toward Stamboul:

"Yussouf! Yussou—ouf! . . ."

The water was rushing past the ship's side. The lake of gold in its wake was fading.

THE STAR OF LOVE

⌒ ⌒

IT IS MAY; the hut stands in a thick forest; a glade spreads
out before the hut; in the centre of the glade grows a
spreading wild-apple-tree, all white and curly with blossoms. The sun has already gone down behind the forest,
but it will be light for a long time yet. Everything is fresh,
young; there is a superabundance of everything—of verdure, of flowers, of grasses, of nightingales, turtle-doves,
cuckoos. And the slight chill of evenglow smells sweetly of
the forest, the flowers, the grasses. Beyond those thickets,
over which is the radiant void of the vernal sunset and
which go down into the forest gullies, a pond shows like a
rosy mirror, and a frog croaks therein from time to time,
languidly, swooning with delight. The nightingales swoop
low across the glade, pursuing one another, chuckling and
chirruping as they fly.

A saddle-horse, seeming still lighter and more beautiful
because it is saddled, stands under the apple-tree. It
stretches its muzzle toward the small leaves among the
white blossoms, plucks them off, and is constantly and
noisily champing them. As for myself, I am sitting on a
tree-stump near the hut, and my heart rejoices at the sight
of my horse.

I still have the sensation I had when I was mounted on it. I feel pleased because I have well-made riding-boots on; because I am strong, young; because I am a good rider and because the horse appreciates this, and loves me; because there is so much of the woman in her, and she is such a thoroughbred; because she so ardently and with such enjoyment rushes along with me on her back, wherever I may want to go; because, equally pleased, she submits to me in everything: accepts the saddle on her back, feels the surcingles which gird her firmly, goes at a round, free pace or at a lively, swinging trot, or gallops full speed ahead, or stands near the front steps or on a boundary between two fields or under a tree in a forest. . . .

I slap the tops of my riding-boots with my short, wicked whip, which I take along only for diversion; I am sitting and smoking. In the hut, on a bench near the small window, lies a little girl of three years or so, in a baby-cap. She is absorbed in drumming upon her lips; *bam, bam, bam!* The interior of the hut behind her is dark and hot. There is a smell of warm loaves of bread, lying on the table and covered with a long peasant coat of denim.

The breadth and depth of the radiant sunset have contracted and dimmed. It is growing dark; dusk is coming on. In the bottomless height, greying over the glade, the woodcock come whirring in pairs, halt for an instant, and fly on. The frog has fallen silent; there is a sensitive quiet throughout the forest, save that two tiny birds are chirping somewhere near, but even they are doing it somehow lifelessly, on the verge of dozing off. And the hunch-backed girl who has been sitting quietly all evening on the grass not far from the apple-tree is gazing ever more frequently, ever more strangely, upward, at the greying azure, where the first seeds of the stars are already springing up thickly.

Above is the sky; to the right is the faded evenglow; ahead, beyond the apple-tree, are the far-off reddish gaps amid the bottomlands of the forest. And I, too, am gazing —now up at the high heavens, now at the gaps, now at the horse, now at the hunch-backed girl. And at such times she at once senses my gaze, without looking, and modestly tucks her feet under her and pulls down the hem of her skirt. She is neatly and pleasingly dressed. Her face is somewhat broad of cheek, but is finely featured, made spirituelle by a transparent and lovely pallor. There is something touching about the necklace upon her gaunt clavicle, about her virginal linen shift, her small bare feet —and strange, even a little frightening, is her frequent and timorous glance heavenward.

Her mother approaches; she has come back from the settlement, bringing a small bag of millet and a bundle of cracknels.

Having greeted me, she sits down on the threshold of the hut and sighs.

"I was over to the settlement, an' bought a thing or two. . . . But you been here long? Was Aniutka cryin'? There ain't no trustin' her," she says meaning the hunch-back, who listens as if it were somebody else being discussed, and not herself. "You yourself ought to know how this girl of ours is. . . ."

I do know, but say nothing, and the peasant woman tells me in detail and leisurely (or, rather, ruminates aloud) all that which I have already heard many times:

"Why, things once come to such a pass that we had to

drag her out of the deep pool. . . . It so happens that I'm comin' from the croft one mornin', when she'd got into the pond, into the deepest place itself, wantin' for to drown herself. . . . An' just the other day I took her down off a small aspen; I was pickin' up faggots in the forest, when I looks up, and there she was, hangin' on a bough, her feet barely touchin' the grass, and her face already turnin' all colours. . . . She's forever sayin': '*He* is comin' to me all the time, stranglin' me, catchin' up with me. . . .' I wake up in the night, an' she's stiflin', cryin' out: 'What you doin'? What you doin'? Le' me go! I don't want to!' But I can tell by her voice that she's really feelin' flattered and finds it sweet. . . . She'll never go to sleep without she prays an' says over an' over: 'Don't count on it—don't count on it! I ain't goin' to let you in bed with me! I'm goin' to put the sign of the cross all over the bed!' She's wastin' away downright to nothin'; all that's left is to dress her for the last time an' to put her in her coffin. . . . I don't even open my mouth to her about her workin'—'twould be a downright sin even to ask her. . . . Where's all her spirit gone to? And yet afore this she was all fire, all tender, easy to take offence. . . . The main thing is, this evil spell has drove her out of her mind; she ain't sayin' nothin', but, never fear, she's bearin' some torment, some shame within her. She's a young thing an' keeps her own secrets; an' what thoughts don't she have in her head! Now an' then she'll let somethin' out by chance; she'll drop her eyes, turn all red, an' whisper to herself: 'Well, what of it? What if I be hunch-backed—what if I be mis-shapen? Still, as far as my face goes, I ain't worse nor the others. . . . Well, even sup-posin' no one takes me, bein' ashamed to stand up before the altar with the likes of me. . . . I'll find me a better deary-dear—a secret deary, one that comes in the dead of night. . . .' Oh, well, it's all true enough: she has no father, no dowry. . . . What frightfully sinful things she says! An' yet a body can't help always thinkin': When she dies, the good Lord will forgive her everythin'. . . ."

The girl is sitting erect, without moving; she is not listening, or else does not hear anything; intently and oddly, almost wildly, she is peering into the darkness of the forest.

I ride home across fields. The earth is inundated with darkness; the darkness rises from below; it floods the distant evenglow, floods its last trace. The air is fresh; there is a smell not only of the green sprouts in the fields of rye, but also of the dewy grass on the boundaries between and of all those things of the field and of the night amidst which I was born and had grown up and which form the sweet substance of my life.

The peasant woman had said: "I sleep on a cot, with Aniutka, but she sleeps on a chest, underneath the images of the saints. . . . For all the world like a dead woman— it even makes you feel creepy in the night. . . . I may wake up in the night, and there she'll be, sittin' and lookin' out of the little window at the stars, at the night, at the forest. . . . 'I have,' says she, 'one star I love the best, faithful and unchanging—the Midnight Glow. . . .' "

The Midnight Glow, or Midnight Star: the star of love, the star that heralds the dawn.

The horse picks her way, just as though she were sentient of my meditations— I can see her small ears, pricked up,

against the faint light of the afterglow. . . . Oh, my
beauty, my clever girl, my beloved! How can one transmit
in words this our intimacy, our love—there is naught finer,
more mystical, and purer than this love, forever unvoiced,
forever faithful, never deceiving: the love between man
and brute! And how may one comprehend all that is un-
uttered, all that apparently has no existence, having no
image nor name, resembling naught else in this world, and
yet so real, perceptible with such keenness as that which
exists between this four-footed creature and myself? A
creature in reality so incomprehensible to me, and even
frightful, and with which I am almost one. . . .

And what of this forest, already so dark and so sinister;
and what of her, this fearful and lovely hunch-back? Her
mother must surely be sleeping now, but she, the living
dead woman, is sitting on the coffer underneath the images
of the saints and is gazing, is hearkening—alone in this
whole world. And everything—save man—everything is
with her and within her: the night, and the forest, and all
creation, and all of this creation's abyss and all its mystery.
And everything with her and within her is of such nature
as is given to none of us, inasmuch as she is already altogether out of this world, altogether not of us, already almost under the full sway of this Hidden, Midnight Entity,
whose wondrous and awesome Star flames before dawn over
the forest. . . .

And I clasp and kiss the strong and satiny neck of my
speechless beloved, so that I may scent her gross odour,
may feel the flesh of this earth, inasmuch as without it,
without this flesh, I find the world too uncanny. And I

tauten the reins, grip the saddle between my knees, and the horse immediately responds to me with all her being, and lightly, spiritedly rushes over the dark road, homeward.

TRANSFIGURATION

～ ～

THE HOMESTEAD WAS WELL-TO-DO; the family was a large one.

The old man, having brought forth many children and grandchildren, had died when his time came; but the old woman proved long-lived, and lived so long that it seemed as if there would never be an end to her sorry and dragging existence.

It was they, she and the old man, who had been the builders and sovereigns of this nest, straggling, sturdily made, by now long lived in, firmly rooted in its place, dirty and snug, with its threshing-floor, its hollow-trunked willows, its storehouses, its *Pi*-shaped hut for the workers, its cattle-yard, crude to the verge of savagery, sunk in manure and overcrowded with well-fed cattle. It was they who, once upon a time, had been young, good-looking, shrewd, and stern; but later on they had begun, little by little, to yield and yield, becoming nonplussed before the young folk, who were growing ever more numerous and stronger, letting their old will give way to them now in one thing, now in another, and finally they were reduced to nothing, had begun to pine, to shrivel, to hunch over, to huddle in

107

their suspended bunks or in the warm nook atop the oven; they became estranged, at first from their family and later from each other as well, only to go apart forever, to their graves.

After the old man's death the old woman came to feel herself especially ill at ease and became abbreviated to the last degree. It was, altogether, as if she had forgotten that it was she, she herself, who had raised all this young, strong kingdom, in which she had become so unnecessary. Things so fell out, somehow, that she turned out to be the most insignificant creature about the whole place, living there as though out of charity, fit only for a snug berth atop the oven in winter, and, in the summer, for keeping an eye on the chicks or watching the hut when the others were out working. . . . Who would ever even think of being afraid of her—pitiful, watery-eyed, bowed down both from old age and from constant fawning timidity! Come dinner-time or supper, just you take your wooden bowl of thin soup take your crust of bread, and take yourself off somewheres, as far as you can from the crowded table, into some corner (under the hanging bunks, say)—and that's all there is to it. . . .

But the time came when she was taken sick right proper —she crept into a corner atop the oven, without any shamming now; she closed her eyes, breathing feverishly and helplessly, with such great weariness that even the hearts of her broad-shouldered daughters-in-law were turned by pity: "Mother dear, mebbe we'd better make a sup of chicken-broth for ye, or some noodles and milk? Mebbe there's somethin' ye'd like to have? Would ye like to have us put up a samovar?" But all she could do was to breathe hard, almost unconscious, merely moving her hand a little, faintly and gratefully.

Finally she freed them all of their bonds—she passed out.

It is the height of winter, and night—for her the last night among the living. Out of doors a blizzard is raging and the darkness is profound. The whole village is asleep; asleep, too, is the whole farm; both wings of the hut, where the living-quarters are, are filled with sleepers. And, over all this winter night and this blizzard, over all this slumber and the deserted stillness of farm and village, there reigns the One Who Has Died—yesterday's pitiful and downtrodden little crone has been transformed into something awesome, mysterious, the greatest and most significant thing in the whole world, into some inconceivable and fearful deity, into one who had gone to her rest.

She is lying in the cold part of the hut, already in her coffin and as cold and white as the snow, deeply withdrawn into her coffined world, with her head, raised by a pillow of straw, thrust against her chest, and her eyelashes casting a shadow which shows dark and sharp upon her white face. The coffin, covered with a cloth-of-gold pall which is flimsy from age, stands behind a table which is brightly lit up by a whole cluster of wax candles stuck to it and blazing hotly and restlessly. The coffin is placed underneath the images of the saints, resting on a bench near a small window, outside of which the frost and blizzard are raging and whose black panes gleam and sparkle from the snow which freezes to their outer surface.

The Psalter is being read by Gavril, the dead woman's

youngest son, who had recently married. He had always stood out in the family because of his good looks and neatness, his even temper, and his love of reading, of church services; who, then, was to read the Psalter over his mother if not he? And so he had gone into this icy and isolated part of the hut—had gone without any ado, not at all afraid of the long night before him all alone with the dead woman, without thinking of this night, without having pictured to himself that which awaited him. . . . And now he has been feeling for a long time already that something fatal and irreparable has come into his life.—He stands and reads, bending toward the hot and trembling candles; he reads, and his voice is never still, and always at the same pitch; just as he had first raised his voice, in churchly fashion, so has he kept it up on a high note. He reads without understanding anything, and it is beyond his power to cease reading, because of the strange terror ever growing within him. He feels that there is no longer any escape for him; that he is utterly alone, not only in this icy hut, eye to eye with this frightful being (all the more fearful because it is the mother that bore him), but in the whole world; and he feels, as well, that the night is so far gone, the hour so late, that he can no longer expect defence or help from anyone.

What has befallen him? That he had miscalculated his strength, having resolved to read the Psalter over the dead woman in the night, at an hour when all are asleep? That he had suddenly become possessed by fear, and that he cannot stir because of this fear, cannot flee from this hut? No, something more wondrous had befallen. A miracle had befallen, and it is by no common fear that he is stricken, but precisely by this miracle, by a wondrous amazement over the mystery which has taken place before his very eyes. Where is she now, whither has she gone, that pitiful little crone, made lowly by old age, timidity, and helplessness, who for so many years had been almost unnoticed by anybody in their big family, so rough because of its strength and youth? She no longer is, she has vanished. For was that she—this Something, icy, motionless, without the breath of life, without a voice, and yet altogether different from the table, the wall, the panes, the snow? Something altogether no mere thing, but an entity, whose secret being was just as incomprehensible as God? Why, was that which was lying motionless and silent in this new, handsome coffin, lined with dark-lilac velveteen and adorned with white crosses and winged cherub heads—why, was that she who, no longer ago than the day before yesterday, had been seeking a snug nook atop the oven? No, a certain transfiguration had occurred in her—and everything in the universe, the entire universe itself, had become transfigured for her sake. And he is alone, alone in this transfigured universe.

He is ensorcelled, enclosed therein, and he must stand therein until dawn and read without ever falling silent in that extraordinary, eerie, and majestic tongue which, too, is a part of this transfigured universe, its perilous logos, of ill omen for the living. And he gathers all his forces to see, to read, to hear his own voice, and to stay on his feet, with all his being, and is ever more deeply receptive of that inexpressibly eerie and inexpressibly sorcerous something which, like some liturgy, is being consummated within his own self and before his eyes.

And suddenly the cloth-of-gold pall upon the dead woman's breast slowly rises and, still more slowly, sinks—

it is as though she were slowly breathing! And still higher and more vivid grows, trembles, dazzles the glitter of the candles—and by now everything around him turns into a single frenzy of rapture and horror, from which his head and shoulders and legs turn to wood. He knows, he is still able to comprehend, that there is a frosty wind blowing through the window, a wind bringing a January snow-storm at its heels, that it is this wind that is puffing up the pall and blowing up the candles. But that makes no difference: this wind, too, is she, the one who has gone to her eternal sleep; it is from her that there is wafted this breath, as pure as death and as icy as eternity; and it is she who will arise right away to judge the whole universe—the whole universe of the living, thoroughly despicable in its animality and corruptibility!

Gavril is now a youngish-looking mujik, with grey, neatly combed hair. He does not concern himself with the management of the farm—he has left all that to his brothers, to his wife. He is childless. He has chosen his work —something he does not have to do, being a man of means, but the only work he loves: he drives a stage.

He is forever on the road. And the road, the distant vista, the pictures, changing according to the time of the year, of sky and field and forest, the driver's seat of his cart or sleigh, the pace of his two horses, intelligent and faithful to him, the sound of his little bell, and a long conversation with an agreeable fare—all these form a happiness which never fails him.

He is simple, kindly, always cheerful in moderation. His face is clean-cut, rather gaunt; his grey eyes are truthful and clear. He is not talkative, but willingly tells to anyone he finds worthy that incident, difficult to relate, resembling a yuletide story, but truly wondrous, which he lived through by the coffin of his mother, on her last night among the living.

THE CRICKET

~ ~

This slight story was told by Sverchok (the Cricket), a harness-maker, who, with another harness-maker by the name of Vassilii, had worked all through November for Remer, the landowner.

November, murky and miry, persisted; winter was constantly failing to hit the right stride. Remer and his young wife, who were thriftily and capably managing the ancestral estate, felt bored, and so, of evenings, they took to leaving their two-storey, boarded-up building, where there was but one tolerable and habitable room on the first storey, under the colonnade, and dropping into the old wing of the house, with the plaster peeling off its walls, where the disused counting-house was: there, too, were the winter quarters for the poultry and the living-quarters of the harness-makers and the hired couple.

On the eve of the Presentation of the Holy Virgin a wet, impenetrable blizzard was raging. It was very warm and damp in the low-ceiled and spacious counting-house, which, on a time, had been whitewashed; there was a dense stench of atrocious tobacco, of the small tin lamp burning on the work-bench, of cobbler's wax, of varnish, and of the minty acidity of leather, pieces and scraps of which, together with the tools, new and old harness, hide for horse-collars, sad-dle-cloths, waxed thread, and brass harness-fittings, were strewn over both the work-bench and the floor, covered with rubbish and as worn and trampled as that of a kennel. There was also a stench of poultry from the dark kitchen, the door of which was open; but the Cricket and Vassilii, who slept amidst all these stenches and who sat therein day after day, with bent backs, for not less than ten or eleven hours at a stretch, were, as always, very much satisfied with their diggings—but especially by the fact that Remer was not sparing of fuel.

Moisture was dripping from the narrow little window-sills; the wet, viscid snow sparkled and showed dazzlingly white against the black window-panes. The harness-makers were working intently; the cook, a small woman in a sheep-skin jacket and mujik boots, who had become chilled through and through during the day, was resting on a chair the seat of which was torn through, near the hot oven. She was warming her back and hands and, with her shawl-wrapped head inclined to one side, without taking her star-ing eyes away from the fire, was hearkening to the bluster-ing of the wind, which from time to time shook the whole wing, to the tapping of Vassilii's hammer on the horse-collar he was making, and to the senilely childish breathing of the bald-headed Cricket, who was fussing with hip-strap and breeching, and who, during critical moments, thrust out the red, quivering tip of his tongue.

The small lamp, drenched with kerosene, stood on the very edge of the work-bench and just half-way between the two workers, so as to afford the best visibility to both, but Vassilii was forever moving it toward him with his strong,

sinewy, swarthy hand. His sleeves were rolled up to his
elbows; strength, and an assurance in that strength, could
be felt, as well, in the whole figure of this dark-haired man,
who looked like a Malay—in every convexity of his muscu-
lar body, clearly defined under a shirt so thin that it seemed
falling to pieces and which at one time had been red; and
it always seemed as if the Cricket, small and, despite all his
seeming sprightliness, altogether broken up, like all farm
workers, were afraid of Vassilii, who had grown up in the
city and had never feared anybody. This seemed so to Vassilii himself, who had even, as if in jest, for the amusement
of those around them, fallen into a way of shouting at the
Cricket, who also willingly abetted this jest, either in earnest or for the fun of the thing becoming scared at these
shouts.

Vassilii, holding a new horse-collar between his knees,
which were protected with a greasy apron, was drawing
thick, dark-lilac, odorous leather over it; with one hand he
would seize the leather firmly, and, pulling it tight over the
wooden frame with a pair of pliers, with his other hand
taking brass-headed tacks out of his pursed lips, would
thrust them into slits previously punched with an awl, and
then with a single stroke would drive each tack powerfully
and deftly home into the wood. He bent low his great head
with its black hair, curly from the moisture and bound with
a narrow strap, and worked with that smooth intentness,
satisfying both to himself and to those around him, which
is acquired only through well-developed strength, through
talent.

The Cricket, too, worked intently, but his intentness was
of a different nature. He was stitching together a hip-strap,

116

new, of a flesh-pink tint, holding it gripped, just as Vassilii
was doing with his work, between his knees, and it was hard
for him to punch the slits, mighty hard: he had to thrust
out the tip of his tongue, and tried to keep his head to the
light. He managed to get the bristles into the small holes,
pulled the ends with a will in opposite directions, and then
made the stitch hard and fast, also with deftness and
strength, even with a certain bravado—the bravado of an
old, mellowed master.

Vassilii's face, bent over the horse-collar, was broad, with
prominent bones under the oily, yellow-swarthy skin and
with coarse black hairs above the corners of the lips; it
wore a stern, frowning, and grave expression. But from the
Cricket's face, bent over his hip-strap, one could see only
that he found the light poor and his work hard. He was
exactly twice Vassilii's age and almost half his height. Nor
did it make any great difference in his height whether he
sat or stood, so short were his legs, clad in trodden-down
boots which had become soft from age. He walked (also
from his age and his rupture) awkwardly, all bent over, in
such a way that his apron fell away and one could see his
belly, deeply sunken in, as loosely belted as a child's. As
dark as a child's, too, were his little eyes, resembling small,
black, cured olives, while his face had a slightly crafty,
mocking air: the Cricket's lower jaw projected, while his
upper jaw, upon which two slender rat-tails, always moist,
showed darkly, was sunk in. He dropped his *r*'s and substi-
tuted *v* for *l* and frequently gulped the air, wiping his tiny
drooping nose, on the tip of which a transparent little drop
was always hanging, with his right hand, big and cold. He
gave off an odour of shag, of leather, and of something else,

that pungent something which is common to all gaffers who bathe only two or three times a year.

Through the blustering of the blizzard came the stamping of feet knocking off the snow, the slamming of a door, and then the master and mistress entered, bringing in with them a pleasant odour of freshness, plastered with white flakes, their faces wet, and with moisture sparkling on their hair and garments. Remer's russet beard and his bushy eyebrows, beetling over his serious and animated eyes, the glossy Persian lamb collar of his shaggy overcoat, and his Persian lamb cap seemed, because of the sparkling moisture, still more magnificent, while the tender, charming face of his wife, her soft, long eyelashes, her blue-grey eyes, and her downy, grey head-shawl seemed to have an added tenderness and charm. The cook was about to offer her the seatless chair, but she thanked her kindlily, made her stay where she was, and sat down on a bench in another corner, carefully removing a bridle with broken bits to make room; then, with a faint yawn, and moving her shoulders a little, she smiled and in her turn became lost in wide-eyed contemplation of the fire. Remer began smoking and took to pacing the room, without taking off his overcoat or cap. His wife, likewise, did not take her things off, but sat lost in pleasant thoughts: now about her pregnancy; then of that new, agreeably unaccustomed life which she had been living in the country for half a year by now; then, again, of far-off Moscow, of its streets, its lights, its trams. As always, the master and mistress had dropped in for just a minute—for the air at the harness-makers' was altogether too heavy and warm; but then, as always, they forgot themselves, lost their sense of smell, and became absorbed in talk.—And it was just then that the Cricket, unexpectedly for all, told how his son had been frozen to death.

"You're pretty slick, though, brother, I must say," he lisped out when Vassilii, after having greeted the master and mistress with a nod of his head, had once more moved the little lamp toward himself. "You are that, I must say, brother. I'm summat older nor you be, never fear," said he, gulping the air and wiping his nose.

"What!" Vassilii yelled at him in simulated wrath, contracting his eyebrows. "Mebbe you'd like me to light a gasjet for ye? If you've gone blind, then get into a home."

Everybody smiled—even the mistress, who found these jests unpleasant: one always felt sorry for the Cricket—and thought that the Cricket would, as always, perpetrate something funny. But this time he merely tossed his head and, after a sigh, straightened up and fixed his gaze on the black window-panes, plastered over with wet, white flakes. Then, picking up the awl in his great hand, gnarled with big veins, and with the joints on his thumb and index-finger far apart, he plunged the tool awkwardly and with difficulty into the rosy rawhide. The cook, having noticed his look at the window-panes, began to voice her fears that her man, who had gone to Chicherino to fetch a horse-doctor, would freeze to death or lose his way in such a ragin' snow-storm—the snow now seemed as thick as smoke—when the Cricket, making believe he was very busy with the hip-strap as he leaned back and inspected it, suddenly spoke with pensive good-nature:

"Yes, brother, I *have* become blind. . . . A fellow's bound to go blind, whether or no! You just live to be as old as me and go through and feel all that I have! But you never could. . . . I've been the way you see me now for ages an' ages; nobody knows how I keep body and soul together; yet I've always pulled my load, have lived, and would like for to live as long again, if only there was somethin' to live for. I wanted to live, brother—even very much so, so long as things was interestin'; an' live I did, nor would I give in to death. But as for *your* endurance—why, we don't know nothin' about it yet. You're kind o' young— you ain't been through much, so far. . . ."

Vassilii looked at him intently, just as the master and mistress and the cook did, struck by his unusual tone; for a moment, in the stillness, the blustering of the wind around the wing of the house became clearly audible. And then Vassilii asked, gravely:

"What are you belly-achin' like that for, now?"

"Who, me?" asked the Cricket, raising his head. "No, brother, I ain't belly-achin'. I was reminded of my son, now. You've heard, never fear, of what a fine lad he were? He'd have turned out better nor you, like as not, nor would he have yielded to you in strength; and yet he weren't able to go through what I did."

"Why, he froze to death, I believe?" Remer asked.

"He did that; I knew him," answered Vassilii, and, without feeling any constraint, as people speak of a child in its presence, he added: "Why, they do be sayin' he weren't even a son of his—of the Cricket's, that is. He looked neither like his mother nor his father, but a chance-come stranger, rather."

"That's something else again," said the Cricket, just as straightforwardly as Vassilii. "All that may be as you say, but he respected me just as much as if I'd been his father—

God grant your own sons may respect you as much. And besides, I didn't go probin' for to dig out if he were my son or no, my own flesh an' blood or some other man's. . . . I guess we all have the same flesh an' blood! The main thing is that mebbe he were dearer to me nor half a score of my own sons might have been. You, now, master, and you, missus," said the Cricket, turning his head toward Remer and his wife and pronouncing "missus" with particular kindliness, "you just listen to how all this come about— how he come to freeze to death, now. Why, I lugged him pig-a-back all night long!"

"Was there much of a snow-storm at the time?" asked the cook.

"By no means," answered the Cricket. "There was a fog on."

"What? A fog?" asked the mistress. "Come, can one freeze to death in a fog? And what ever did you have to— 'lug'—him for?"

The Cricket smiled meekly.

"Hm!" said he. "Why, now, missus, you can't even imagine how a fog like that can torture a man to death! And the reason I lugged him along was 'cause I felt no end of pity for him, thinkin' all the time I might be able to fend this fate off him—fend off this death, now. This is how it all come about," he began lispingly, addressing neither Vassilii nor the master, but the mistress alone. "It all come about on the eve of St. Nikola's day—"

"But was this a long time ago?" asked Remer.

"Why, some five or six years back," Vassilii, who was listening gravely and rolling a coffin-nail, answered for the Cricket.

The Cricket, with senile sternness, threw a passing look at him.

"Leave enough for me to have a good lungful," said he, and went on: "We was workin,' missus, at Squire Savvich's, in Ognevka. He—my son, that is—always went with me; he never strayed from me, knowin' I wouldn't teach him nothin' bad. Well, then, we worked an' we worked, and we had lodgin's hired in the settlement near by,—after his mother died we lived together, like two close chums, you might say. Then, at last, Nikola's Day is comin' along. It's time, us thinks, we was leavin' for home, time we was puttin' ourselves to rights a little, for, in all conscience, I must say there was entirely too much dirt on us. Toward evenin' we're gettin' ready to go, but we don't even notice that there's an awful cold spell gatherin' toward nightfall, and with such a fog, at that, that you couldn't see the village beyant a certain little meadow, to say nothin' of the region all around bein' very lonely. There we were, putterin' aroun' an' puttin' away our tools in this here bath-house—the same where we'd been seekin' salvation from our dirt, I mean; we couldn't find nothin' in the darkness, nohow—our master was that stingy, now, you couldn't get as much as a candle-end out of him. And we feel that we've overtarried a bit, and, would you believe it, such a fit of blues took aholt on me, sudden-like, that I ups an' says: 'Maxim Iliich, my dear mate, mebbe we'd better stay on here an' wait for mornin'?' "

"Why, is your name Ilya?" asked the mistress, suddenly recalling that even up to now she did not know the Cricket's first name.

"Ilya it is, ma'am," said the Cricket kindly, and, after

sniffling, made a dab at his nose. "Ilya Kapitonov is my right name. Only my son, too, used to call me Cricket, an' that's all there was to it, every whit like this Jack the Giant here, I mean Vassil' Stepannich, does; he used to make fun of me an' was pretty pert. Well, of course, he'd have his joke, an' started yellin' at me this time as well—for does a young lad ever think of death? . . . 'What's all this, now? I'll teach you to talk!' He shoved my cap down over my ears, put on his own, pulled in on his strap (a handsome lad he were, an' it's the holy truth I'm tellin' you, missus!), picked up his bit of a stick, an', without any more talk, marches out onto the front steps. I follows him. . . .

"I see that the fog is somethin' dreadful, an' that it's grown altogether dark by now; the trees in the squire's garden was all wearin' dove-coloured caps, like, an' was grown over with hoar-frost—the whole garden was loomin' like a cloud or somethin' through this murk, through this fog. But there was no help for it now; I don't want to hurt the young fellow's feelin's, so I says nothin'.

"We crossed the little meadows, went up a small hill, an' looked behind us; but by now we couldn't see the squire's windows—everythin' had turned grey, murky; everythin' was motionless, an' right on top of us; you felt uncanny just lookin' at it. I turned my head away from the wind— it had took the breath right out of me all inside a minute; there was a downright chill comin' together with this murk an' fog, like it was a breath of somethin', sort of. I hadn't took more'n two steps when I feel that I'm soaked through to the very bone, whilst our boots, mind you, was put right on our bare feet, and, besides that, our jackets wasn't any too well made. And again I says: 'Aw, Maxim, let's turn back; don't be showin' off!' At that he did stop awhile, to think things over. But then, everybody knows young folks ain't like old folks—I guess you know that from your own experience, missus: how can one lose a chance of showin' one's pride? He scowled quickly an' started off again. We enter the village, an' of course things eased up a bit; there was lights in all the huts, an', even though they was blurred, they still meant there was folks livin' there. And so he rumbles out: 'There, you see? What was you shiverin' over? See—it's ever so much warmer when you're walkin', now; it was only at first that it seemed so chilly, but now it's altogether warm. . . . Don't you fall back, now, or else I'll start drivin' you along. . . .' But what warmth could there be, ma'am? All the water-carts was froze one hand high with hoar-frost, and not an osier but was bent close to the ground, and there weren't a roof to be seen for the fog and the frost. . . . Of course there was folks livin' there, but on account of their lights the fog was more treacherous than ever. . . . And all my eyelashes was covered with rime and had grown heavy, like you may have seen on a good horse. And as for the squire's windows on that side of his house—why, it was as if they had never been. . . . In a word, the night was a cruel one, nothin' less—just the very night for wolves to howl an' run abroad. . . ."

Vassilii frowned, let the smoke out through both his nostrils, and, giving what was left of the coffin-nail to the Cricket, interrupted him, mimicking his failings of speech:

"Oh, you and you' wo'ves! You won't get through by the Second Advent, at the rate you're goin'. Speed 'er up a little!" And he turned the horse-collar on his knees in a business-like manner, intending to go on with his work.

The Cricket took the cigarette-butt from him with the very tips of his sooty, nicotine-stained fingers, drew in a deep lungful of smoke, and for a moment became lost in sad thoughts, as if he were listening to his own childlike breathing and the blustering of the wind beyond the walls. Then he said, timorously:

"Well, God be with you! I won't spin it out so much. All I wanted to say was that we simply lost our way after we'd taken a couple of steps. And so, missus," he went on with greater assurance, after a glance at her and having caught the commiseration in her eyes, suddenly coming to feel more poignantly his grief, which he had long become accustomed to, "we lost our way, y'understand. No sooner had we passed out of the village and had gotten into this darkness, this murk, this cold, and had gone on for a mile or so, than we went astray. We come to a great upland, an ee-normous meadow, with ravines reachin' to the very settlement; well, above these there always used to be a road in the winter-time, and so we hit upon it, thinkin' all the time we was keepin' a true course. But, instead of that, we went too far to the left, followin' somebody's tracks, toward the Bibikov ditches; an' then, as bad luck would have it, we lost them tracks as well. An' after that we just started in ploughin' through the snow, whichever way the wind carried us.

"But all this is an old, old story, missus—for who hasn't lost his way, at some time? Everybody has. What I was wantin' to tell, however, was all the torments I went through that night! I, truth to tell, grew so scary, so frightened after we'd been circlin' for two hours, or mebbe three, y'know, an' had become all petered out, all out of breath, all froze, and then come to a dead stop and seen that we was done for, for good an' all—I got so frightened, I say, that I felt real needles of fire goin' through my arms an' legs. . . . For every man, y'understand, finds his own life sweet. . . . Only it never entered my mind what was ahead of me, how the Lord would chastise me! I didn't have any other idea, y'understand, but that my end would come first—you can see for yourselves whether there's a great deal of vitality in me. But when I seen that I, now, was still alive, still keepin' on my feet, whereas he'd already squatted down on the snow —when I seen that—"

The Cricket emitted a slight cry at these last words, glanced at the cook, who was already in tears, and suddenly began blinking his eyes, as, with distorted eyebrows and lips, and quivering lower jaw, he commenced a hasty search for his tobacco-pouch. Vassilii grumpily thrust his own upon him, and the Cricket, rolling a coffin-nail with his twitching hands, while his tears dropped into the tobacco, again began to talk, but this time in a new tone, measured, firm, and somewhat higher:

"My dear missus, we once had a master by the name of Iliin; there weren't a meaner man in the whole province when it came to our sort—us workin' men, that is. Well, now, he happened to freeze to death. They found him near town, lyin' in his cart, all drifted over with snow an' turned stiff, he were, for a long time—why, there was ice inside his mouth. But right near him was a hound, still alive, squattin' an' shiverin'—a setter, it were, an' his favourite— an' it were covered over with a raccoon coat, now. . . . That means, though he were such a villain, that he must have taken his own fur coat off him, now, an' covered the hound with it, whilst he himself froze to death, an' his driver froze to death as well, an' so did his three horses, leanin' 'gainst the shafts as they froze, an' then passin' out. . . .

"But here it weren't no hound, but my own son, my dear maty! Yes, ma'am! What did *I* have to take off me, now? That there jacket of mine, mebbe? Why, that jacket was as old as I was; the one he had on was twice as warm. Why, here I couldn't have helped matters even with a fur coat! Here, though you was to take your very shirt off, there wouldn't have been any salvation—though you was to shout for all the wide world to hear, you couldn't have roused a livin' soul for all your shoutin'! In a short while he grew even more frightened nor I were, an' it were for that very reason that we was done for. Just as soon as we had lost them tracks he begun to dash about. At first he kept on callin' out all the while, his teeth clickin' an' him puffin' to catch his breath all the while—that's how the wind an' the frost had gone through us, to our very bones. Then he sort of got locoed.

"'Hold on!' I calls out to him. 'Hold on, for Christ's sake! Let's sit down an' get our wits together!'

"He don't say nothin'. I grabs him by the sleeve an' yells at him again. . . . He don't say nothin', an' that's all there is to it. Either he don't understand a thing or else he don't hear me. It's so dark you might as well be blind. We no longer feel our hands or our feet. Our faces is all covered with rime by the wind, an' like as if they was made of wrought iron; it was just as if we had no lips at all—like as if we had only our bare jaws. An' you couldn't understand nothin', couldn't see nothin'! The wind is bellowin' in our ears, dashin' all this murk along with it; but he—my son, that is—he keeps on circlin', dashin' about, an' won't listen to a word I say. I'm runnin', gulpin' down the fog, sinkin' in the snow up to my waist. . . . 'First thing you know,' I'm thinkin', 'I'll be losin' sight of him—' When all of a sudden, bingo! we step off into space and then start rollin' down, chokin' in the snow. . . . Then I have a feelin' we've struck the bottom of a deep ditch. We said nary a word for quite a while; by an' by we had our breath back, an' he ups an' says: 'What's all this, now, father? The Bibikov ditches? Well, set still, set still—let's take a rest. Then we'll climb out of here an' go back all the way to where we started from. Now I've got it all clear in my mind. Don't you be afraid, now—don't you be afraid—I'll bring you there all safe!' But his voice, now, is already crazed, sort of, an' not like that of a livin' man. It don't sound so much like a man talkin', but more like wood bein' chopped. . . . An' it was right then an' there that I understood we was all done for. We clambered out; we started walkin' again—an' again we got in a daze. . . . We churned that snow, and we kept on churnin' it, for two hours more or thereabouts; we got into some oak undergrowth. An' when we run into it an' understood that we was already some fifteen miles away from Ognevka, out in the open steppe— why, it were then that he slumped down all of a sudden: 'Good-bye, Cricket!'—'Hold on, there—what d'you mean, good-bye? Pull yourself together, Maxim!' But no such thing; he sat down an' became still. . . .

"No use drawin' the story out, ma'am," said the Cricket suddenly, his voice ringing again and his eyebrows distorted. "Right then an' there all my fear vanished. Soon as he slumped down, somethin' seemed to hit me over the head. 'So—o,' thinks I, 'so that's it! Well, it's plain enough this ain't no time for *me* to be dyin'!' I fell to kissin' his hands, to implorin' him, now: 'Keep on goin', if but for a little while longer; don't sit down; don't give in to this deathly sleep; let's get goin' as fast as ever we can; lean on me!' No; he's fallin' off his feet all the while, an' that's all there is to it! As for me, I'd have been willin' to die from the dreadful fix we was in, but I just couldn't. . . . I weren't in no mood for it! . . . An' when he had breathed his last an' was all quiet, had grown heavy an' turned to ice, I took him, though he were a man amongst men, an' threw him onto my shoulders, got a holt of him round his legs, an' started travellin' for all I were worth. 'No you don't!' thinks I. 'Hold on, there; no, you got another guess comin' —I ain't a-goin' to give him up! I'll drag him around, dead as he is, for a hundred nights if I have to!'

"I run along, sinkin' in the snow, while my own breath comes thick an' fast, because of the weight of him, an' my hair stands up on end from terror, the way the icy head of him slithers over my shoulders an' touches my ear now an' then—his cap had fallen off long ago. But I keeps on runnin' an' screamin' all the while: 'No, hold on there! I ain't a-goin' to give him up! It ain't no time for me to be dyin', now!'—You see, ma'am, I was figgerin' all the while," said the Cricket, in a voice that suddenly sank, bursting into tears and wiping his eyes with his sleeve, picking out the least soiled spot, near the shoulder, for the purpose, "I was figgerin' I'd bring him to the settlement—mebbe he'd thaw out. . . . Mebbe I'd bring him back by massagin'. . . ."

After a long interval, when the Cricket had already

calmed down and, having lit a new coffin-nail, was staring at a point ahead of him with his fixed red eyes, when both the mistress and the cook had dried their eyes and heaved sighs of relief, Vassilii spoke gravely:

"Well, now, it's a pity I cut you short. You tell a story well. I didn't even expec' such spirit from you."

"Well, that's just it," answered the Cricket, also gravely and simply. "A fellow could go on tellin' a story like that all night long, brother, an' never tell it all, even then."

"And how old was he?" asked Remer, with an occasional look out of the corners of his eyes at his wife, who was gently smiling after her tears and uneasily wondering whether the story might not prove harmful to one in her condition.

"He were goin' on twenty-five, sir," answered the Cricket.

"And you had no other children?" his mistress asked timidly.

"No, ma'am, I didn't."

"But you take me, now—I've got all of seven," said Vassilii, frowning. "My hut is but two paces long an' two paces wide, but there's a whole heap of 'em. Children, now—it ain't all honey havin' 'em, neither. The sooner we die, 'tis plain to see, the better off we be."

The Cricket cogitated awhile.

"Well, that's a matter that ain't for our heads to decide," he answered, still more simply, gravely and pensively, and picked up his awl once more. "If he hadn't froze to death, brother, there ain't any death that would get me afore I'd be a hundred years old."

The master and mistress exchanged glances and, buttoning their outer garments, got ready to go. But for a long while yet they remained standing and listening to the Cricket as he answered the cook's questions as to whether he had succeeded in carrying his son to the settlement and how the matter had ended. The Cricket answered that he had carried his son to the bitter end—not to the settlement, however, but as far as the railroad, and that he had fallen, having stumbled against the rails. His hands and feet were already frozen, and he was just about to lose consciousness altogether. Daylight came. There was a blizzard raging. Everything around him was white, but he sat on in the open steppe and watched the snow burying his dead son, watched the snow powdering his son's sprouting moustache and filling his frost-white ears.

They had been picked up by the crew of a freight train coming from Balashov.

" 'Tis a miraculous thing," said the cook when the Cricket had finished. "But there's one thing I can't understand—how is it you yourself wasn't froze to death in such fierce weather, now? . . ."

"I had no time for that, mother," the Cricket answered absent-mindedly, searching for something on the workbench, among the scraps of leather.

LONG, LONG AGO

∽ ∽

LONG, LONG AGO, a thousand years back, there lived and had his being, at the same time as I, on Arbat Street, in the Hotel North Pole, a certain inaudible, imperceptible Ivan Ivannich, the most modest of the tribe in all the world, a fellow already somewhat old and rather shop-worn by life. From year to year Moscow lived on and did her enormous work. He, too, did something or other, and, for some reason or other, lived on in this world. He would go away about nine in the morning; about five he would come back. Cogitating upon something subduedly, but not the least whit sadly, he would take his own key down from its nail in the conciergerie, would mount to the second floor, and pass through a corridor of many turns. This corridor had an exceedingly complicated and exceedingly vile smell, and it smelt particularly of that special something, stifling and acrid, which is used for waxing the floors of execrable hotels. Dark and sinister was this corridor (the rooms themselves had windows looking out on an inner court, while the transoms gave but little light), and all day long, at the end of each *cul-de-sac*, there burned a small bulb with a dazzling reflector. But Ivan Ivannich, it seemed, did not experience the least moiety of those oppressive emotions which this corridor aroused in people unused to the North Pole.

He walked along this corridor calmly, unassumingly—in general in such a way that people hardly noticed him. He usually encountered some of his fellow-guests: a student alertly hastening along, with youthful beard and bright gaze, who was putting on the sleeves of his uniform overcoat as he went; a lady stenographer with an independent air, well grown and enticing, despite her resemblance to a white Negro; a little old lady, always tricked out, rouged, brown of hair, with phlegm eternally gurgling in her chest,—which lady's advent was always heralded by the babbling of jingle-bells, quickly flying through the corridor upon her pug-dog, which had a prognathous lower jaw and ferociously and senselessly goggling eyes. . . . Ivan Ivannich would make polite and elaborate bows to all those he encountered, and did not object in the least to the fact that the others barely nodded to him in answer. He passed one *cul-de-sac*, turned into another one, still longer and blacker, where the wall-light shone and showed redly still farther off, thrust the key into his door, and closeted himself behind it until the following morning.

What did he occupy himself with in his sanctum, with what means did he shorten his leisure? Why, God alone knows. His domestic life, evinced by no outward signs, utterly unnecessary to anyone, was also unknown to anybody—even to the chambermaid or the hall-boy, who disturbed his monastic seclusion only by bringing a samovar, making his bed, and cleaning his vile wash-stand, whose jet of water always came as a surprise, and never either on the face or on the hands, but always squirted very high, to one side, and obliquely. With (I repeat) rare unobtrusiveness, with rare monotony, did this Ivan Ivannich exist. Winter would pass; spring would advance. The horse-trams sped, rumbled, jangled on Arbat Street; people cease-lessly hurried along somewhere, passing one another; light carriages rattled by; hucksters, bearing trays on their heads, cried their wares; of evenings, in the far-off hiatus of the street, glowed the lightly aureate sunset sky; musically, above all the noises and sounds, floated the bassy ringing of a tabernacle-like ancient belfry. But Ivan Ivannich ap-parently did not see, did not hear anything of all this. Nor winter, nor spring, nor summer, nor autumn had any per-ceptible influence either upon him or upon his mode of life.

But lo, once, in the spring, there arrived from somewhere, and took a room, and became the nearest fellow-guest of Ivan Ivannich, a certain prince. And there took place in Ivan Ivannich something utterly unexpected, something one could never have guessed.

Wherewith could the prince have overwhelmed him? Not with his title, surely; for the oldest fellow-guest of Ivan Ivannich's, the little old lady of the pug-dog, was likewise a titled personage, and yet he was utterly unimpressed by her.—Wherewith could the prince have captivated him? Not with his riches, surely, and not by his appearance: the prince was a man who had most decidedly gone through all his means, and, to look at, was most decidedly negligent, unwieldily enormous, with pouches under his eyes and with a heavy, stentorian asthma. And yet, notwithstanding, Ivan Ivannich was both overwhelmed and captivated. Most im-portant of all, however, he was absolutely knocked galley-west out of his rut of many years. He transformed his existence into some sort of incessant excitement. He plunged into uneasy, petty, and ignominious aping.

The prince arrived, settled down, began to come and go, to see certain people, to concern himself with certain affairs—in the very same way, of course, as all those who put up at the North Pole did, and of whom a very great number had come and gone within the memory of Ivan Ivannich and with whom it had never even occurred to Ivan Ivannich to force an acquaintance. But, for some reason, he had singled the prince out from all the others. For some reason, upon meeting him in the corridor for the second or third time, he scraped and bowed and introduced himself and, with all sorts of exceedingly amiable apologies, requested the prince to tell him, as exactly as possible, what time it was. And, having struck up an acquaintanceship in this adroit manner, he simply fell in love with the prince, brought into utter disarray his customary life-pattern, and began to imitate the prince slavishly at almost every step.

The prince, for instance, went to bed late. He returned home about two in the morning—and always by cab. And so Ivan Ivannich's lamp, too, began to burn until two in the morning as well. For some reason or other he waited for the prince's return, for his ponderous steps through the corridor, for his wheezing asthma. He waited with joy, well-nigh with trepidation, and at times would even thrust his head out of his cubby-hole in order to catch a peep of the approaching prince, in order to exchange a word with him. The prince walked along leisurely, as though he did not see Ivan Ivannich, and always asked him the one and the same thing, in a profoundly indifferent tone:

"Ah, but aren't you asleep yet?"

And Ivan Ivannich, swooning from delight—although, on the whole, without any timidity and without any fawning—would answer:

"No, prince, I'm not asleep yet. The day is still young— it's only ten after two. . . . Have you been diverting yourself? Having a good time?"

"Yes," the prince would say, breathing stentoriously and unable to get his key into the keyhole. "I met an old acquaintance; we dropped into a bar and sat there awhile. . . . Good night!"

And thus the whole business usually terminated—so coldly, even though politely, did the prince cut short his night conversations with Ivan Ivannich. But, for Ivan Ivannich, even that sufficed. He would go back on tippity-toe into his own room; would do, by routine, all those things which are supposed to be done before going to sleep; crossing himself sketchily and with a nod toward the corner where the icons were supposed to hang, he would inaudibly get into his bed, which stood behind a partition, and immediately fall asleep, perfectly happy and perfectly disinterested in his further intentions concerning the prince, that is, if we do not count a most innocent braggadocio before the hall-boy in the morning:

"My, but I sat up late again last night! . . . The prince and I kept on talking until the third cock-crow again. . . ."

The prince used to put his big, trodden-down shoes outside his door in the evening and to hang out his pantaloons —of the widest, and silvery-grey. Ivan Ivannich, too, took to putting out his wrinkled little boots, which had hitherto been shined only once in a blue moon, and to hanging out

his diminutive trousers—shiny, with buttons missing—
which had never been hung out hitherto—no, not even before Christmas or Easter.

The prince would awake early, then cough terribly,
avidly light a thick cigarette, and after that, opening the
door into the corridor, would start shouting so that he could
be heard all over the house: "Hall-boy! Let's have tea!"—
and, with his slippers flapping, in his bath-robe, would go
off for a long session. . . . And Ivan Ivannich took to
doing the same (things, mind you, which he had never
done before in all his born days): he shouted into the corridor for *his* samovar, and, with galoshes on his bare feet,
in a wretched little spring overcoat atop his much-worn,
soiled underwear, went off for *his* session, although hitherto
he had always done so in the evening.

The prince, just like Ivan Ivannich, rolled his own cigarettes; every other day he purchased three ounces of tobacco and spread it out on a newspaper to dry on the window-sill. Having spied this out, Ivan Ivannich began to do
this with his tobacco as well.

The prince had once happened to say that he was very
fond of the circus, and that he frequently went there. Ivan
Ivannich, who did not like the circus, who had last gone to
one not less than forty years ago, also decided to go to the
circus, and once actually went there, and, that night, told
the prince with rapture what enormous enjoyment he had
derived from it. . . .

Ah, spring—spring! The nub of the whole matter was
that all this nonsense took place in the spring.

Every spring is, as it were, the end of something lived
through and done with, and the beginning of something

new. In that Moscow spring of long ago this deceptive feeling was especially sweet and strong: for me because of my youth and because my student years were coming to an end; and for many others simply because it was spring—a rarely wondrous spring. Every spring is a festival, but that spring was especially festive.

Moscow had lived through its involved and tiresome winter. And after that she had lived through Lent, through Easter, and again had sensed that apparently she had done with something, had dropped something off her shoulders, had, after long waiting, attained something real. And there was a great number of Muscovites who were already changing their lives, or preparing to change them, to begin them all over again, as it were, and this time live after a different fashion than hitherto; they intended to lead more sensible, more regular, more youthful lives. And they were hastening to spruce up their quarters, to order summer clothes, to make purchases—and making purchases (even if it be but of naphthalene) is a jolly thing! They were preparing, in a word, for departure from Moscow, for rest in country-houses, in the Caucasus, in Crimea, or abroad; preparing, in general, for summer, which, as it always seems, was bound to be happy and long—oh, ever so long!

How many resplendent suit-cases, gladdening to the soul, and how many brand-new, creaking hampers were bought at that time in Leontievski Lane and at Miur-Meriliz's! What a multitude were taking hair-cuts and shaves at Basile's and Theodore's! And, one after the other, there followed sunny, stirring days, days with new odours, with a new cleanliness about the streets, with a new glitter on church-domes against the vivid sky, with a new Strastnoi

Nunnery and a new Petrovka, with new, radiant raiments upon beautiful women and feminine fashion-plates, flying by in fine light carriages over the Kuznetzki Bridge, and with a new light-grey fedora on a famous actor, who is also speeding somewhere on pneumatic tires over Gazette Row. . . .

Everyone was nearing the end of a certain zone of his or her former life, which zone had not been all it should, and for well-nigh all of Moscow it was the eve of a new life, and that, inevitably, a happy one. And I, too, was on the eve of such a life; especially I, and far more so than the others, as it seemed to me then. And the time of my parting with the North Pole was ever nearing, nearing—the time of my parting with all that which had made up my life there, in a student's way, in a youth's way. And from morn till night I was taken up with my affairs, with riding about Moscow, absorbed in all sorts of joyous cares.

But what was the occupant of the room next to mine doing—the most unassuming of all those staying in the North Pole at the same time as the rest of us? Why, approximately the same things as we. The same thing had befallen him, in the upshot, that had befallen all of us.

There was a succession of April and May days; the horse-trams rolled along, jangling; men and women were ceaselessly hurrying by; cabs rattled past; tenderly and pensively (although the matter at hand may have had to do only with asparagus) came the cries of hucksters with trays on their heads; there was a sweet and warm smell emanating from Skachcov's pastry-shop; tubs of laurel were standing near the entrance of an expensive restaurant, where the better sort were already partaking of young po-

tatoes in sour cream. The day would imperceptibly near
evening, and, lo, the aureately radiant pre-sunset sky was
glowing in the west, and over the happy, thronged street
floated the musical, bass pealing of a tabernacled belfry.
. . . Day after day the city, in its vernal mood, lived its
tremendous, variegated life, and I was one of the happiest
participants in that life. I lived with all its odours, all its
sounds, all its bustle, encounters, affairs, purchases. I hired
cabs; with friends of mine I would drop into the Café
Tramblais; I would order at the Hermitage an iced soup of
beet-leaves and pot-herbs and, after a pony of cold vodka,
would sink my teeth in a fresh gherkin. . . .

But what of Ivan Ivannich? Why, Ivan Ivannich, too,
would go off somewhere; he, too, went to this place or that,
attended to certain affairs of his own—certain small affairs,
certain exceedingly small affairs—acquiring thereby a right
to further existence in our midst: that is, to a thirty-kopeck
table-d'hôte in a cook-shop across the way from the North
Pole, and to a room in the North Pole itself. He earned only
this modest right somewhere and in some way, and, it
seemed, was altogether a stranger to all our hopes for some
new life, for a new suit, for a new hat, for a fresh hair-cut,
for catching up with somebody in something, for forming
an acquaintance, a friendship. . . . But lo, the prince had
come. . . .

Wherewith could he have enchanted, overwhelmed Ivan
Ivannich? However, it is not the object of enchantment
which matters so much; what matters is the thirst for being
enchanted. And who is there in whom this thirst does not
abide to the very grave? Besides that, the prince was a guest
who did not resemble any of the usual run of guests in the

North Pole; he was a man with remnants of seigniorial
ways, of a seigniorial independence; a man who had lived
through a great deal of his money, but, for that very reason,
also one who, in his time, had lived as one should. Well, and
so poor Ivan Ivannich as well had got the dream into his
head, together with all of us, of starting to live in a new
way, in a vernal way, with certain seigniorial whims and
even diversions. Oh, well, is that such a bad thing—to brace
up a little, not to hit the pillows as soon as the clock struck
ten, for instance, to hang out one's suit to be cleaned, to go
into session before washing, before dressing? Why, doesn't
it refresh one to go to a summer garden, to a circus, to take
a ride in a cab through Moscow, clean and vernal under
the starry sky? Doesn't it rejuvenate one to drop in for a
hair-cut, to have one's beard shortened, trimmed, to buy
a greyish hat that takes years off one's age, and to return
home with some modest purchase or other, even though it
be but a quarter of a pound of something trifling, prettily
tied by the rosy hands of a rather good-looking, amiable
salesgirl?

And Ivan Ivannich, gradually and ever more and more
yielding to temptation, went through all these things in his
own way; that is, he fulfilled, as far as he was able and as
far as his means permitted, almost all that the others did.
Not only did he form an acquaintanceship, but also he
took to aping (true, no more so than the others!) and
gathered spring raiment unto himself, and brought a certain moiety of the dissoluteness of spring into his life, and
acquired certain seigniorial airs, and clipped his beard, and
took to carrying some little parcels or other whenever he
came home to the North Pole, just before evening, and,

what is even more, bought a little greyish hat for himself,
and a bit of luggage (a small suit-case, costing a rouble and
seventy-five kopecks and studded all over with glistening
tin tacks), since he cherished a dream of going this summer,
without fail, to the Trinity Abbey, or the New Jerusalem
Monastery. . . .

Whether this dream was ever realized, and how, in general, Ivan Ivannich's impulse toward a better life ended, I
really do not know. I think that it ended in the same way
as the majority of our impulses: none too grandly. But, I
repeat, I cannot say anything definite. And the reason I
cannot is that all of us (that is, the prince, Ivan Ivannich,
and myself) shortly, one fine day, parted, and parted not
for the summer, nor for a year, nor for two, but for all
time. Yes, for all time, no more, no less—that is, never to
meet again, at any time, till the end of the world, which
thought, despite all its seeming oddity, is simply horrible.
Just think of it—never! In reality, all of us who live during
a certain period on earth together and who together experience all the earthly joys and sorrows, seeing the one and
the same sky, loving and hating, in the final analysis, the
same things, and all, without a single exception, doomed to
one and the same execution, to one and the same evanish-
ment from the face of the earth—we all, I say, should culti-
vate toward one another the greatest tenderness, a feeling
of nearness that should move us to joyous tears, almost to
ecstasy. And we ought to be simply screaming from fear
and pain whenever fate separates us without our ever knowing for how long a space, every time with the perfect possibility of turning our every parting, even though it be for
but ten minutes, into an eternal one. But, as everyone

knows, we are generally far removed from such emotions, and frequently part even with those most near to us in a way that could not possibly be more frivolous. And thus, of course, we too parted—the prince, Ivan Ivannich, and myself. One day, toward evening, a cab was called for the prince to take him to the Smolenski station—a wretched little cab, whose hire would not be more than sixty kopecks; whereas the cab they called for me, whose tariff to the Kurski station would run to a rouble and a half, had a lively dun—and we parted without so much as a good-bye to one another.

And Ivan Ivannich was left in his gloomy corridor, in his cage, the transom of which had a dull pane, and the prince and I, after having thrust tips right and left and having got into our light carriages, drove off in different directions— the prince, apparently, rather indifferent, and I radiant, alert, all in brand-new clothes, vaguely anticipating some wondrous encounter on the train, during my journey. . . . And I remember, as if it were now: I was riding toward the Kremlin, while the Kremlin was peacefully and joyously lit up by the direct rays of the evening sun; I drove through the Kremlin, past the cathedrals—and, my God, how beautiful they looked!—then through the Iliinka, odorous with all sorts of chandlery wares, where the evening shadows were already lying; then through the Pokrovka, still thronged with fashionable people and noisy, but already under the benediction of the pealing and rumbling of church-bells, blessing the happily ended bustling day. . . .

I rode along and not merely rejoiced over myself and the whole world, but was veritably sinking in the joy of being, having forgotten, somehow instantaneously, even while I had been on Arbat Square, not only the North Pole, but the prince and Ivan Ivannich, and I would probably have been very much astonished had I been told that they, too, would be preserved forever in that sweet and bitter dream of the past, whereby my soul will live till I am in the grave itself, and had I been told that there would come a certain day when I would be calling out to them also, and in vain:

"Dear prince, dear Ivan Ivannich, where are your bones rotting now? And where are our common, silly hopes and joys, our long-gone Moscow spring?"

CICADAS

~ ~

THE VILLA IS DARK, the hour being late, and all around is a streaming, ceaseless, liquid murmur. I have come back from a long ramble on the cliffs overhanging the sea, and have lain down on a reed-work easy-chair on the balcony. I am smoking, thinking, and listening . . . listening. There is some sort of witching spell about this crystal-clear murmur.

The nocturnal, dark-blue abyss of the sky is overflowing with the vari-coloured stars suspended therein, and in their midst the Milky Way, transparent and in its turn star-filled, shows ethereally grey, sloping in two uneven masses of haze toward the southern horizon, which is starless and, because of that, almost black. The balcony overlooks the garden, the trees of which are few and low; its paths are strewn with shingle. A vista of the night sea is revealed from the balcony. Wan, milky-mirrorous, it is profoundly silent. And because it is silent I have a feeling as if the stars, too, are silent. And the crystal-clear ringing, monotonous, never ceasing for even a second, regnant throughout this silent, nocturnal world, resembles some tinkling dream. En-sorcelled by its own self, it seems to grow, to spread, and yet does not increase, does not attain to any ultimate growth

—and finds no culmination. And I recline, listen, and think . . . think.

Of what do I think?

"And I gave my heart to seek and search out by wisdom concerning all things that are done under heaven: this sore travail hath God given to the sons of man to be exercised therewith. . . . Lo, this only have I found, that God hath made man upright; but they have sought out many inventions." And the Preacher gives one fatherly advice: "Be not righteous overmuch; neither make thyself over-wise. . . ." Yet I am forever tormenting myself, forever being over-wise. I am "righteous overmuch."

Of what do I think? When I had suddenly put this question to myself, I had wanted to recall what, precisely, I had been thinking of—and immediately had thought of my thinking, and that this thinking is, apparently, the most amazing, the most incomprehensible, and, indubitably, the most fatal thing in my life. What had I been thinking of, what had been going on within me? As always, there had been fragments of some recollections or other, some thoughts or other about my surroundings, and a desire, for some reason, to realize and impress upon my memory (that is, to preserve, to retain within myself) these surroundings. What else had there been? Why, there had also been a feeling of great happiness, because of this great peace and great harmony of the night, and because of my beholding, my sensing this splendour; and, side by side with all this, there was the feeling of a certain yearning and of a certain covetousness which forever haunts me: an avidity to avail myself, somehow, of this happiness, and even of this very yearning and avidity. My eternal cross, this!

Whence comes this yearning? From a hidden feeling that it is only within me, alone, that there is no calm, no harmony, no submissiveness, and no absence of thought. Whence this covetousness? It is a consequence of my trade. And just what is my trade? An impulse to creativeness is the basis of man's nature. Life is a certain form, a certain incarnation of something unknown to us. And we eternally feel the brief tenure and instability of this form and are afraid of leaving no vestiges of ourselves. "There is no remembrance of former things; neither shall there be any remembrance of things that are to come with those that shall come after. . . . The dead know not anything, neither have they any more a reward; for the memory of them is forgotten. Also their love, and their hatred, and their envy, is now perished; neither have they any more a portion for ever in any thing that is done under the sun."—And also: "I made me great works; I builded me houses; I planted me vineyards: I made me gardens and orchards. . . . I got me servants and maidens. . . . I gathered me also silver and gold, and the peculiar treasure of kings and of the provinces. . . ."

Wherefore? For this: that labouring, and through his labours attaining power, glory, man rejoices over that power, over that glory, even as he rejoices over fertility in his struggle against death, the ravager of forms. And he to whom it is given to feel peculiarly the instability and insecurity of these forms, that one is peculiarly possessed by an avidity for such a struggle. And I am of the number of precisely these peculiar ones. Why, then, am I being over-wise and seeking out "many inventions," which lead to barrenness and to a wisdom as old as the world: "What profit hath a man of all his labour which he taketh under the sun?" For has there not been allotted more power to me for this struggle than has been allotted to many others? Yes, but not at all in proportion to my ever-growing sensation of the fatal insecurity, instability, of my life-form. Here one always comes upon a certain enchanted circle. "For unto whomsoever much is given, of him shall be much required: and to whom men have committed much, of him they will ask the more." The more passionate the singer of *The Song of Songs*, the more surely he winds up with *Ecclesiastes*.

Of what had I been thinking? But it does not matter a great deal what I had been thinking of; what matters is the fact of my thinking, a process perfectly incomprehensible to me; but of still greater importance and incomprehensibility is the fact of my thinking about this thinking and about the fact that I do not understand anything either in myself or in the universe, and, at the same time, understand my lack of understanding, understand my bewilderment in the midst of this night, and of this sorcerous murmur, now living, now dead, now devoid of all meaning, now imparting to me something most esoteric and most needful.

I am consoling myself:

"This thought about one's own thought, this understanding of one's own lack of understanding, constitute the most irrefutable proof of my participation in something that is a hundredfold greater than I, and, therefore, a proof of my immortality: there is within me a certain something, a certain *additum*, evidently unanalysable, cardinal—of a verity a particle of God Himself."

But I myself answer this consolation:

148

"That is, I am a particle of that which has nor form, nor time, nor space; that which as far as it concerns the earth and my existence upon the earth, constitutes my very perdition! This something within us gives us wisdom—in other words, death. 'Taste thereof . . . and ye shall be as God.' But 'God is in heaven, and we upon earth.' Tasting thereof, we increase cognition, consciousness—that is, sorrow. Tasting thereof, we die for the earth, for earthly forms and laws. God is infinite, illimitable, omnipresent, innominate. But it is these very attributes of God that are terrible to me. And if they are ever increasing within me, I am perishing, as far as my human life and this my earthly 'being' are concerned."

The stunted trees in the garden show motionless, dark.

The shingle shows grey between them, the white flowers glimmer on their bed, and farther off are the cliffs, and the sea, like a milk-white cerement, rises upward to the sky.

There is a mirrorous quality about this milky whiteness of the sea, but the horizon is dark, crepuscular, sinister; this is because of Jupiter, and because there are almost no stars on the southern rim of the sky.

Jupiter—golden, enormous—blazes at one end of the Milky Way, so regally and vividly that the table and the chairs cast barely perceptible shadows on the balcony. This star seems to be the small moon of some other world, on the other side of this, and its glow falls as a mistily aureate pillar upon the mirror-like milky whiteness of the sea from the great height of the skyey rim, while something that seems like a dark knoll is, by forceful contrast with the light, sombrely outlined against the horizon.

And the ringing—ceaseless, never silenced for even a

second—which fills the silence of the earth, the sky, and the sea with its apparently transparent murmur, now has a sound like that of millions of rills flowing and converging, now the semblance of some wondrous blossoms, which somehow seem to be forever growing in crystal spirals.

And I listen . . . listen to this ringing, and think.

I think of how happy I am made by these nights, by this summer, by the south, by the fact that the foot-hills of the south are all around me, while under those cliffs, two paces away from me, there rests, in a starry lethargy, that miracle which men call the sea. And I also think of how infinitely unhappy I am, oppressed by my happiness, which is forever lacking something and which is so fleeting, so traceless, and so envenomed by a madness ever growing within me: the madness of my detachment from the universe, and even from my own self; the madness of my great wonder before the universe and before my own existence; the madness of my incomprehension either of the universe or of myself. Thus, in my childhood, I would look at myself in a mirror: What is it—who is that whom I am seeing, who is *I*, and of whom *I myself* am thinking? And who is looking at whom?

Only man finds his own existence a matter of wonder. And therein lies his chief distinction from other creatures, which are yet in paradise, without any thought of themselves. But even human beings differ from one another in the degree, the measure, of this wonder. For what reason, then, has God so doubly marked me out with the fatal mark of great wonder, of being "over-wise"? Wherefore does this over-wisdom keep forever increasing within me? Are the myriads of cicadas, which seem to fill all creation around me with their nocturnal love-chant—are the cicadas being "over-wise"? No; they are in paradise, in the beatific sleep of life, whereas I have already come out of my sleep and am wide awake. The universe is within them, and they are within it, whereas I am already looking at it from the side, as it were. And what does that lead to? "The fool foldeth his hands together, and eateth his own flesh. . . . He that observeth the wind shall not sow; and he that regardeth the clouds shall not reap."

I listen and meditate. And it is because of that that I am infinitely lonely in the midst of this midnight silence, sorcerously ringing with myriads of crystal well-springs, inexhaustibly, in great submissiveness, and without reasoning flowing into some abysmal Bosom. The celestial light of Jupiter weirdly lights up the vast expanse between sky and sea: an expanse forming part of the grand temple of the night, over the Holy Gates of which this star is elevated as a sign of the Holy Ghost. And I am alone within this temple: I blasphemously keep vigil therein.

The day is the hour of action, the hour of bondage. The day belongs to time, to space. The day is a fulfilment of earthly duty, of service to earthly life. And the law of the day decrees: Be thou at work, and interrupt it not for a realization of thine own self, thy place, and thy goal, inasmuch as thou art but a slave of life, and a known assignment, calling, name, have been given to thee in life. . . .

But what is night? And is it seemly for any man to be keeping vigil before its face, to be in that incomprehensible state which constitutes our thought, our over-wisdom? It was commanded that we taste not of the forbidden fruit—hearken, therefore, do but hearken to the cicadas, these self-oblivious singers, indisseverable from their delectable love-songs: they have not tasted, nor do they now taste thereof! And what other than eulogy for these singers have the Ecclesiasts derived out of all their wisdom? It was they who said: "Vanity of vanities; all is vanity. What profit hath a man of all his labour which he taketh under the sun?" But it was also they who added: "The sleep of a labouring man is sweet. . . . There is nothing better for a man than . . . that he should make his soul enjoy good in his labour. . . . Go thy way, eat thy bread with joy, and drink thy wine with a merry heart. . . ."

What is night? This: that a slave of time and space is, for a certain period, free, that he has been relieved of his earthly assignment, his earthly name, calling—and that there has been prepared for him, if he keep vigil, a great temptation: a sterile over-wisdom, a sterile aspiration toward comprehension—that is, a twofold incomprehension: an incomprehension both of the universe, and of one's own self, surrounded by that universe, as well as of one's beginning and one's end.

I have them not: nor beginning nor end.

I know that I number so many years. But then, I was told this—that is, that I was born in such and such a year, on such a day and at such an hour. Otherwise I would be ignorant not only of the day of my birth (and consequently of the account of my days as well), but even of my existing by reason of my birth.

And, in general, my birth is by no means my beginning. My beginning lies not only in that darkness (utterly incomprehensible to me) in which I had my being from inception to birth, but also in my father, in my mother, in my grandsires and my great-grandsires, inasmuch as they, too, are I, only in a somewhat different form, of which quite a great deal was almost identically repeated in me. "I remember that on a time, myriads of years ago, I was a yeanling." And I myself once (in the very land of Him who said this, in the tropics of India) experienced the horror of an unusually keen sensation: that I had already, at some time, been in the midst of this paradisaical warmth and these paradisaical riches.

Self-suggestion? Self-deception?

But then, it is very probable that my forefathers dwelt precisely in tropical India. How could they have failed, then—they who had so many times transmitted to their descendants (and had at last transmitted to me as well), in almost exact form, the family ear, chin, arches of the eyebrows—how could they have failed to transmit, as well, the finer, more imponderable corporeity bound up with India? There are persons who are afraid of snakes, of spiders, who are afraid of them "insanely" (that is, contrary to all reason), and yet this is that precise feeling of some former existence of long ago, a dark memory, for example, that on a time an ancient forebear, who was afraid, was constantly threatened by death from cobra or scorpion or tarantula. My forebear dwelt in India. Why would it be impossible, then, at the sight of coco-nut palms leaning forward on an ocean littoral, at the sight of dark-brown natives in warm tropical waters—why would it be impossible for me to recall that which I had on a time felt when I had been my own dark-brown ancestor?

Neither have I an end.

Not understanding, not feeling my birth, I do not understand, I do not feel, my death, of which I would likewise have had not even the least conception, awareness, and, perhaps, sensation as well, had I been born and were I living on some island utterly uninhabited and without a single living being save for myself. All my life I am living under the fearful sign of death—and still, all my life, I have a certain feeling as if I shall never die.—Death!—Yes, but man is reborn every seven years; that is, he is imperceptibly dying as he is being imperceptibly reborn. Therefore I, too, must have been reborn more than once, that is, I had been dying as I had been reborn. I was dying, and yet had lived; had died many times already, and yet, basically, I am still the same as I had formerly been, and, to boot, am still filled with my own past.

The beginning, the end! But my conceptions of time, of space, are frightfully unstable. And, with the years, I not only feel but realize this, more and more.

I have been set apart from many others. My imagination, my memory, my susceptibility to impressions, my ability of expression, have all been set apart. And although almost the whole of my life is an almost continuous and excruciating consciousness of the weakness and insignificance of all those qualities of mine which I have just enumerated, I, by comparison with certain others, am really not altogether an ordinary man. But it is precisely because of this (that is, on the strength of a certain extraordinariness of mine, on the strength of my appertainance to a certain special category of men) that my conceptions, my sensations of time, of space, and of my own self, are especially unstable.

What sort of category is this, what sort of men are these?

They are those who are styled poets, artists. What qualifications must they be possessed of? They must possess, with especial force, the ability of sentience, not only of their own times, but of the times of others, of the past; not only of their own land, of their own tribe, but of the lands and tribes of others, of those foreign to them; not only of their own selves, but of the selves of others—that is, they must be possessed, as the accepted phrase has it, of the ability of re-incarnation; and, in addition to that, of an especially lively and especially imagistic (sensuous) memory. And in order to be one of these men, one must be of a species which, through the chain of its ancestors, has covered a very long course of existences, and which has suddenly evinced in itself an especially complete image of its wild forebear, with all the freshness of that forebear's sensations, with all the imagery of his processes of thought, and with all his enormous subconsciousness. And, at the same time, this species has been immeasurably enriched during its long course and is already possessed of an enormous consciousness.

Is a man of such a species a great martyr or a great favourite of fortune? Both the one and the other, inevitably. The curse of such a man is particularly potent, and so is his good fortune. I am the thirst of his greater affirmation, and, at the same time, I am a greater (on the strength of an enormous experience during the time of being in the enormous chain of existences) feeling of the futility of this thirst, an intensified sensation of the All-Being. And hence you have Buddha, Solomon, Tolstoi. . . .

Gorillas in their youth, in their maturity, are fearful in their bodily strength, immeasurably sensuous in their sentience of the universe, merciless in every satiation of their lust, and distinguished for their extreme spontaneity. But, toward their old age, they become hesitant, pensive, sorrowful, pitying. . . . What a crushing resemblance to the Buddhas, the Solomons, the Tolstois! And, in general, how many one can count in the regal tribe of saints and geniuses who provoke a comparison of them with gorillas—even in outward aspect! Everyone knows the arch of Tolstoi's beetling eyebrows, the gigantic stature of Buddha and the protuberance on his skull, and the seizures of Mohammed, when the angels, amid lightnings, revealed to him mysteries and abysses not of this earth and, "in the twinkling of an eye" (that is, outside of all laws of time and space), carried him over from Medina to Jerusalem—carried him precisely on to the Stone of Moriah, ceaselessly oscillating between heaven and earth and mingling, as it were, earth and heaven, the transitory with the eternal.

All these Solomons and Buddhas at first, with great avidity, take the world unto themselves, but subsequently, with great passionateness, curse its deceptive seductions. All of them are at first great sinners, but subsequently great saints; at first great accumulators, but subsequently great dissipaters. All of them are insatiable slaves of Maya—lo, there she is, this resonant, this spell-casting Maya: hearken to her, hearken!—and, at the same time, they are sentients of Nirvana, with its eternal bliss; which bliss is, nevertheless, always full of sorrow to the mortal who could never, while on earth, to his very end, make an utter, absolute renunciation of Maya, of the delectation of "being." All of these sages are distinguished by a religiousness that ever grows with the years—that is, by a fearful feeling of their bond

with the All-Being, and of an ineluctable vanishment
therein.

A faint stirring of the air, of the fragrance of the flowers
in the flower-bed and of the odour of the sea's freshness
are unexpectedly wafted to the balcony. And a minute later
a slight rustling is heard: the soft sigh of a half-slumbrous
wave, slowly rolling up on the beach somewhere below; a
wave happy, drowsy, unreflecting, submissive, dying, and
knowing not that it dies! It has rolled up, has plashed,
casting a pale-blue glow over the sands (the glow of countless lives)—and, just as slowly, has receded, has returned
soundlessly into the sea, into its cradle and its grave. And
countless lives are chanting all around, seemingly still more
ecstatically; and Jupiter, pouring in a golden torrent into
the great mirror of the waters, shines in the heavens and
seems still more awesome and regal. God, how beatified my
soul is, and how it grieves, deprived of Thy Edæn!

Why, am I no longer without a beginning, without an
end, without omnipresence?

Lo, decades separate me from my infancy, from my
childhood. And usually I have a feeling that the days of
my childhood, which are considered my first days, had
been an infinitely long time ago. Yet all I have to do is to
make a slight effort of thought: and time begins to con-
tract, to melt away. And thus has it been always. More than
once have I experienced something veritably marvellous.
More than once it has befallen me to return from some
distant journey; I would return to those fields which I had
once known as an infant, as a youth—and suddenly, after
having looked about me, I come to feel that the many and
long years I have lived through since then are as though

they had never been. And this is absolutely, absolutely *not a recollection*. No, it is simply that I am once more my former self, perfectly my former self. I am once more in the very same relation to these fields, to this field air, to this sky of Russia, I am once more in that same receptivity of the whole universe, which had been mine precisely here, upon this very cross-road, in the days of my childhood, of my adolescence. And one is unable to transmit all the pain and all the joy of these moments, all the bitter happiness they hold! Where is he, this infant, this youth, so near and dear to me? He is still alive, but already not of the flesh; he is I, but likewise not I. Yes, already, and despite everything, he is not I!

At such moments I have thought more than once: Every instant of that whereby I lived here on a time had been leaving its trace, had been occultly impressing it, as though upon certain countless, infinitely minute, most inwardly cherished laminæ of my *I;* and lo, certain ones of them have suddenly come to life, have evinced themselves. A second—and they again grow dim in the darkness of my being. But let them; I know that they are there. Nothing perishes—it does but change its outward form. But perhaps there is a something which is not subject even to an outward change of form, which is not subject to such a change, not only during the course of my life, but even during the course of millennia? Having increased the number of such impressions, I am obliged to transmit them to some other who comes after me, even as a great host of such impressions have been transmitted to me by my ancestors. More than once have I felt myself not only my former self, but also my own sire, my grandsire, my great-grandsire;

in due time someone must, and shall, feel that he is I.

And I have thought at such moments: The wealth of aptitudes, of talent, of genius—what is it save a wealth of those impressions (both hereditary and self-acquired)? What else save one or another sort of sensitivity to such impressions, and a number of their manifestations within the ray of that Sun which at times falls upon them from somewhere, now brighter, now fainter?

And I have said to myself: Rest assured that not a single particle of thy existence—not the very least particle, even —has ever been lost or ever will be; each particle has been recorded and will be preserved. All of them—and that for always, for all eternity—will grow dim, will perish in that ultimate Darkness whither we all pass when our time comes? But has it not seemed to thee, even once, that myriads of these particles have already perished, even during thy life? That they have lost their ability to come to life, to evince themselves? And wert thou not mistaken? And where is the dividing line between the darkness of the grave and that darkness within thee, wherein there lurks thy former life— that is, your life as an infant, as a child, as a youth—which life becomes illumined and alive only at rare moments? . . .

Recently, having chanced to awake at dawn, I was struck, for some reason or other, by the thought of my age. Once upon a time it seemed to me that a man who had lived forty or fifty years was some sort of peculiar, frightful being. And now I, too, had at last become such a being. "What am I, then?" said I to myself. "What, precisely, have I now become?" And, after having made a very slight effort of the will, after having looked at myself as at a stranger (how miraculous it is that we are able to do this!), I, of course, with absolute vividness sensed that even now I am absolutely the same being that I had been both at ten and at twenty.

I put on the light and looked in a mirror: Oh, yes, there is a certain gauntness and regularity of features; there is a silvery patina at the temples; the hue of the eyes is somewhat faded; but inwardly, psychically, only a great fund of worldly experience distinguishes my present self from my former one. I feel this with all my being!

And with especial buoyancy I got out of bed, put my feet right into the slippers, and went into the other rooms, still barely glimmering, still nocturnally peaceful, but already accepting the new day, now slowly coming to birth, which had faintly and mysteriously divided the semi-darkness of the rooms, at the level of my chest.

Quiet—a peculiar, pre-dawn quiet—still reigned, as well, in all that enormous human nest which is called a city. Taciturnly, and somehow differently from the daytime, the multi-windowed houses stood around with their multifarious dwellers, apparently all so different and yet so alike in their devotion to sleep, to unconsciousness, to helplessness. Taciturn, and as yet unpeopled, as yet clean, the streets lay below me; but the gas street-lamps, amid their pellucid murk, had already taken on a green glow. And suddenly, having comprehended that this pellucidity was none other than the birth of a new day, I again, again experienced that inexpressible emotion which I experience all through life whenever I chance to awake at early dawn; I experienced the emotion of a great happiness, of a childishly trusting, soul-touching sweetness of life; an emotion of something altogether new, good, beautiful, and of my nearness, my brotherhood, my oneness with all those living on this earth with me.

How well I always understand at such moments the tears of Peter the Apostle, who, precisely at daybreak, had felt so freshly, youthfully, tenderly, all the force of his love toward Jesus, and all the evil wrought by him, Peter, on the previous night, in his fear before the Roman soldiers!

And I recalled my journey (now, alas! distant) through Galilee, through Judæa; and once more, as though it were utterly a part of my own life, I lived through this far-off Biblical morning in the Grove of Olives, on the stony slope of the Mount of Olives; I lived through this denial of Peter's. Time vanished. With all my being I came to feel that two thousand years were, oh, such an insignificant period of time. Here I have lived for half a century; you have but to multiply my life fortyfold and you will have the times of Christ. of the Apostles, of "ancient" Judæa, of "ancient" mankind. The very same sun which on a time the tear-stained, pale Peter had beheld after his sleepless night will, at any moment now, rise over me as well. And almost the very same emotions which on a time crowded upon Peter in Gethsemane are crowding upon me right now, evoking from my eyes as well the very same sweet and painful tears which Peter broke into over the soldiers' fire.

Where, then, are my times, and where are his? Where am I, and where is Peter? Since we have blended so, if but for an instant, where is it, then, this *I* of mine, to establish and isolate which has been such a passionate desire of all my life, and is so even at this very moment? No, this signifies nothing—nothing whatsoever: the fact that I am fated to live on earth not in the days of Peter, Jesus, Tiberius, but in this so-called twentieth century. But come, *am* I living in it? During my life, which, after all, is a long one, with all its reflections, reading, wanderings, and dreams, I have become so habituated to thought and sensation that I seem to know and to picture to myself enormous expanses of place and time; in my imagination I have lived so many lives of others, strangers and remote, that it seems to me as if I had always been, forever and aye, and everywhere. And where is the dividing line between my actuality and my imagination—which, in its turn, is also actuality, something which indubitably exists?

Thus all my life, consciously and unconsciously, I am forever overcoming, forever destroying, space, time, forms. But does this bring me joy? Insatiable and inordinate is my thirst for life, and I live not only with my present, but with all my past; not only with my own life, but with the lives of thousands of others; with all that is contemporaneous with me, and with that which is far off, there, in the mist of the most distant ages. Wherefore do I do this? Is it for the purpose of destroying myself in this life-course, or is it, on the other hand, for the purpose of strengthening myself, through enrichment and intensification?

There are two categories of people. In the one (and it is enormous) are the people of their own, definite moment, people of worldly-wise constructiveness, of action, people of almost no past, no ancestors, as it were; true links, these, of that Chain of which Hindu wisdom saith: "What matters it to them that both the beginning and the end of this Chain are so frightfully slipping away into infinitude?" While in the other category (and it is very small by comparison) are those who not only are not men of action, of constructiveness, but are veritable destroyers, who have already learned the vanity and vexation of action and constructiveness; men of reverie, of contemplation, of great wonder before themselves and before the universe; the men who are "over-wise"; men who have already, in secret, responded to the ancient call: "Come thou forth out of the Chain!" —men who are already a-thirst to be dissolved, to vanish in the All-One, and, at the same time, still cruelly suffering, still yearning for all those aspects, those incarnations in which they had existed, but yearning especially over every instant of their present.

These are men gifted with a great wealth of apperceptions, which they had received from their countless predecessors; men sensitive of even those links of the Chain which are infinitely remote; beings who have wondrously (and is it not for the last time, perhaps?) resurrected within themselves the strength and freshness of their forefather in Edæn, of his corporeity. These are men who are paradisaically sensuous in their sensations of the universe, but who are, alas! already bereft of paradise. Hence, too, is their great divarication: the torment of their leaving the Chain, their parting with It, a realization of Its futility— and their intensified, fearful bewitchment with that same Chain. And every one of these men has fully earned the right to repeat the ancient wail: "Thou Eternal and All-Embracing! There was a time when Thou didst not know Desire, didst not know Thirst. Thou wert dwelling in great peace, but Thou Thyself didst disrupt it: Thou didst conceive and lead forth the immeasurable chain of incarnations, of which each one was ordained to be ever less carnal, ever nearer to the blissful Beginning. Now Thy call sounds ever more loudly in mine ears: 'Go thou forth out of the Chain! Go thou forth without leaving a trace, without any heritage, without any heir!' Thus do I hear Thee by now, O Lord. Yet still bitter to me is the parting with the deceptive and bitter sweetness of Being. Still am I frightened by Thy having no beginning and Thy having no end. . . ."

Ay, if one could but leave an impress of this deceptive, and yet, nevertheless, unutterably sweet Being, even though it be in the speech of men, if not in the flesh!

Even in my most ancient days, thousands of years ago, I spoke in measured words of the measured surging of the sea; I sang of being joyous and sorrowful—that the blue of the heavens and the whiteness of the clouds are far off and beautiful in splendour, that the forms of woman's body are excruciating in their inconceivable loveliness. But now? Who has obligated me, and why, to carry, without ever a rest, the burden, crushing and exhausting, yet unavertible, of ceaselessly expressing my emotions, thoughts, conceptions —and of expressing them not simply, but with such precision, beauty, force as must charm, enrapture, bestow sadness or happiness upon men? By whom, and wherefore, has there been put within me an unquenchable compulsion to infect men with that whereby I myself live, to communicate myself to them, and to seek a fellow-feeling in them, a oneness, a blending with them?

Since my infancy I have never felt, have never thought or seen or heard or smelt anything without a covetousness of, without a thirst for, enrichment, which is necessary to me in order that I might express myself as richly as possible. I am possessed by an eternal desire not only to accumulate, and then to dissipate, but also to make myself stand out from the millions who are similar to me, to become known to them and worthy of envy, rapture, great wonder, and eternal memory. The crown of every human life is the memory thereof; the highest thing which is promised to man over his coffin is memory eternal. And there is never a soul which does not yearn in secret over a dream of such a crown. And what of my soul? Oh, how pitiful it is, how exhausted by this dream (wherefore? why?)— this dream of leaving in the universe, till the end of time, one's entity, one's emotions, visions, desires, this dream of overcoming that which is called my death, that which will inevitably befall me in due time, and which, nevertheless, I do not believe in, and cannot believe! I am tirelessly crying out without words, with all my being: "Sun, stand thou still!" And I am crying out all the more passionately since in reality I am not the architect but the demolisher of my own self—and incapable of being any other, since it has already been given to me to overcome time, space, forms: these three; to feel my lack of beginning or end— that is, the Oneness, drawing me within Itself anew, as a spider doth its gossamer.

But the cicadas are singing . . . singing. And they, too, know this Oneness, but sweet is their song, and sorrowful to me alone; a song filled with a paradisaical unreflection, a babe-like submissiveness, a blissful self-oblivion!

Jupiter has attained its ultimate height. And the night has attained its ultimate silence, its ultimate immobility before the face of Jupiter, the ultimate hour of its beauty and grandeur. "Night unto night showeth knowledge." What knowledge? And would it show it at any other save this, its most secretly cherished, its highest hour?

Still more regal and awesome has become the unencompassable and unfathomable temple of the star-filled sky; by now many great pre-dawn stars have ascended to its heights. And from these great heights the nebulously aureate glowing pillar falls, by now altogether precipitately, into the milky, mirrorous surface of the sea, by now completely in the embraces of lethargy. And the stunted trees show darkly in a still greater immobility, having become still more stunted in this meagre southern garden strewn with pallid shingle. And the ceaseless ringing, falling silent for not even a second, filling the silence of earth, sky, and sea with its seemingly penetrant murmur, has taken on a still greater resemblance to some wondrous flowers which seem to be constantly growing in crystal spirals. . . . What, then, will this ringing silence finally attain?

But there it is again, this sigh, the sigh of life: the swish of a wave rolling up on the beach and spreading; and, following it, comes a slight stirring of the air, of the freshness of the sea and of the fragrance of flowers. And I awake, as it were. I look about me and get up from my place. I hasten down from the balcony and walk through the garden, the shingle crunching underfoot, and then run down, following the cliff. I walk over the sand and sit down near the very edge of the water, and, with intoxication, voluptuously plunge therein my arms, which instantaneously light up with myriads of glowing drops, of incomputable lives. . . . No, my time has not yet come! There is still a something which is stronger than all my over-wisdom, my philosophizings. Still as desirable as a woman is to me this watery, nocturnal bosom. . . . God, let me be!

And the cicadas sing on . . . and on.

THE NIGHT OF DENIAL

᠗ ᠗

The night is dismal, tempestuous, toward the end of the months of rain; darkness reigns, a hurricane is raging, and the clouds have burst.

On the shore of the sacred Isle of Lions the black jungle has advanced to the very ocean, which seems ready to inundate it.

There is a great roar from the foaming waves, which, in inwardly glowing mountains of water, incessantly charge against the island, and flood not only the near-shore shoals where sea-stars are lying in viscous rings, emitting a mysterious phosphorescence, and the crabs swish in their thousands as they crawl apart in every direction, not only the crags on the shore, but the very feet of those palms which are bending over the cliffs of the shore, twisting their slender trunks like serpents.

A raw and warm hurricane whirls by from time to time with redoubled impetuousness, with inexpressible force, so majestically and mightily that there comes rolling riotously out of the jungle toward the ocean a surge no less fearful and ponderous than the surge of the ocean itself. At such times the palms, which had been tossing from side to side like living creatures in the throes of a tormenting, uneasy slumber, suddenly bend low before the pressure of the storm as, in a rush, it reaches its goal, the shore; all sink low, as one, and myriads of dead fronds scatter noisily from their summits, while spicy fragrances are wafted through the air, borne from the heart of the isle, from the primeval depths of the jungle.

Clouds, sullen and heavily laden, as on the nights of the Deluge, are sinking ever lower over the ocean. But in the illimitable expanse between them and the abysmal trough of the waters there is a certain semblance of light: the ocean, to its most secret depths, is saturated with the most secret flame of incomputable lives.

The billows of the ocean, maned with seething fire, that run toward shore with roaring and rumbling, flare up, ere they break, with such vividness that they light up with their green reflection a man who is standing in the jungle, above the shore.

This man is barefooted, with closely shorn hair; his right shoulder is bared; he has on the tatters of an anchorite.

He is small, like a child, in the midst of the grandeur surrounding him—and is it not horror that has flitted over his exhausted face at the glitter and reverberation of a billow that has just shattered itself?

Firmly and sonorously, overcoming both this reverberation and the mingled din of the jungle and the hurricane, he lifts up his voice:

"Glory to the Exalted One, to the Holy One, to the All-Enlightened, to Him Who Hath Conquered Desire!"

Myriads of seemingly fiery eyes rush as a whirlwind through the jungle's black darkness together with the hurricane. And rapturously, passionately, sounds the voice of the man standing nigh the shore:

" 'Tis all in vain, Mara! 'Tis all in vain, Thou Thousand-Eyed, that Thou dost tempt me, sweeping by over the earth in life-creating hurricanes and cloud-bursts, as a fertile and by now fragrant corruption of graves, which give birth to new life out of their putridity and dust! Get Thee behind me, Mara! Even as a drop of rain rolls off the springy leaf of a lotos, so doth Desire roll off me!"

But victoriously, with squealing and laughter, in a downpour of leaves, rushes the whirlwind of incomputable fiery eyes, lighting up under the black canopy of the jungle a Something that seems like a colossal graven image: that of One Sitting upon the Earth, of One Whose Head Rears to the very summits of the palms.

His legs are crossed under Him.

From His neck to His loins He is entwined with the slate-coloured coils of a Serpent, which has puffed out Its rosy throat, which has spread Its flat, oblique-eyed head over His head.

Despite the immeasurable weight of the Serpent's coils, He Who Is Sitting is unhampered and stately, majestic and simple.

There is a divine node, a high and pointed protuberance, on the crown of His head. His blue-black, twining, but short hair is like the fan-tail of a peacock. His ruddy countenance is firm and calm. His eyes gleam, like to precious gems of the purest water.

And His awesome voice, a voice that sounds without any effort, yet is like to thunder, rolls majestically from the depth of the jungle to the man standing nigh the shore:

"Verily, verily, I say unto thee, My disciple: anew and anew shalt thou deny Me for the sake of Mara, for the sake of the sweet deception of mortal life, on this night of earthly spring!"

THE THIRD COCK-CROW

~ ~

At DAWN, in the mist and the dark, while yet all were asleep in the town, a sea-robbers' barque sailed up to Sinope.

The cocks were chanting all along the mountainous shore, all through the settlement, at this dark and delectable hour, and from the barque of the sea-robbers the ship's cock would crow back in answer, with friendly joy.

In Sinope the dogs and watchmen slept; slept, too, the women and children—all were asleep; but the robbers, talking to one another in subdued voices, lowered themselves over the ship's side into a skiff floating upon the water, redolent of freshness, rowed themselves to shore, and went toward the dwellings, stealthily.

They spared neither the old nor the young, the wolves!

And, having looted the place to their hearts' content, having sent five innocent souls to their last account—five of the blood-kindred of Phoca the Martyr, the patron saint of Sinope—they hastened back to their ship, hoisted sail, and put out to sea again.

And there, out on its free waste, they launched on a riotous spree.

They ate, and they drank, and they danced, and they

sang, until the very evening.

And toward evening they fell down all over the ship and in its cabins, wherever each one happened to be, without reefing sail, without lighting their lanterns, and without placing a helmsman or a look-out.

And then the dusk came down on the sea; low clouds gathered over it, and there fell a great silence.

Flapping its canvas, as if its sails were a cripple's empty sleeves, the ship drifted upon the sea, without any aim, without any direction.

And in the ship's cabins, in the vile-smelling darkness, the drink-sodden villains snored heavily.

And the Lord saith:

"Serve the evil-doers right!

"Be still, ye sea-birds white; swoop not down with your harsh, grating cries upon the sea-billow, awake not the silence and the sleeping robbers.

" 'Tis I that will arise in the wind out of the west, that will shower the Pontos with black sand, and speed over it as a whirlwind and as red lightning.

"Woe unto you, ye drink-sodden robbers!

"Keel upward, amid thunder and storm, shall I overturn your frail refuge!

"Into the bottomless trough of the sea shall I cast you down, who have trodden the decrees of man and of God underfoot!"

But who is that who glows like a slender, blue spectre at the prow of the robbers' ship?

Who has made the light to gleam warmly in the lantern and now descends into the dark cabins of the ship?

It is Phoca, the patron saint of the sea.

172

He nudges and awakes the robbers; he speaks to them in a rapid, creepy voice:

"Ah, up, up with you, quick, you robbers! Run up on deck—lower sail—place a helmsman—there's a great calamity about to befall ye!"

And the robbers, in affright, leap to their feet and run, each one his own way, all over the ship, all over the deck: seizing hold of ropes, of the spokes of the steering-wheel. But by now the wind is dashing this way and that over the sea, rending the canvas, blowing out the lights, knocking the robbers off their feet.

"Save yourselves, ye destroyers of souls, ye sons of Cain!"

And, while they are struggling and beating about, the Lord in His high wrath summons Phoca the Martyr to Him, to His dark heavens, under the red lightning-flashes.

"Tell Me, My saint, art thou not of the same town where those evil-doers have wrought their dark deeds?"

And the saint answers, all trembling in fear:

"I am from thereabouts, Lord."

"Was it known to thee that I had willed to destroy these robbers, who, because of their lust and self-willedness, had risen to such a pitch as to tread the decrees of God underfoot—who had slit the throats of five of your own blood-kindred?"

" 'Twas so, Lord."

"Wherefore, then, durst thou to oppose Me?"

And the saint sinks down on his knees before the Lord:

"For the sake of the third cock-crow, Lord, which on a time brought Peter the Apostle to tears of love and of repentance.

"When I thought that the robbers would never more hear

173

that joyous voice which comes just before the dawn, the soul within me came to sorrow with a bitter tenderness.

"Yea, verily, O Lord! Sweet is the earthly life that Thou hast bestowed!

"For the sake of this one voice alone, holding forth the promise of a new day, of a new path, to men dark and evil, may earthly birth be blessèd, for ever and aye!"

And the Lord forgives Phoca the Martyr.

OF EMELYA THE FOOL

AND OF HOW HE TURNED OUT TO BE
THE WISEST OF ALL

∽ ∽

EMELYA WAS A FOOL, 'tis true, but may God grant to you, an' you, to live on earth as sweet as he. He didn't sow, he didn't plough; an' work was somethin' he didn't know— for the most part he just lay there atop the warm oven, with the belly on him well-filled an' lined. Why, he rode on that there oven to the Tsar hisself when he had to plead his cause!

Well, now, this Emelya, he went out for to fetch some water (his brothers, they hired theirselves out to other folkses, but Emelya, he'd just be lyin' atop that there oven, an', just to pleasure his sisters-in-law, like, he'd mebbe go out, swingein' along, for to fetch some water, or he'd mebbe chop a little kindlin'-wood, now an' then, an' after that sleep sweet again). An' he comes to the river, an' there's a black pike a-swimmin' around in it. So he grabs a holt of it by its tail, quick as ever he could, an' begins haulin' it ashore, whilst that pike, sheddin' bitter tears, starts mercy to implore:

"Lemme go, Emelya! Some day I'll do you a good turn, I tell ya!"

Well, now, this Emelya, he weren't a fool for nothin', so he tosses it back inter the water, lettin' it go free—an' then it ups an' says:

"Ask for whatsomever you may wish—or may not wish!"

"Well," says Emelya, "I ain't wishful for to be luggin' no buckets around; let 'em git along of their own selves."

So the fish says, right quick:

"Obey the pike's command, an' by me own demand, get you goin' by your own selves, ye buckets!" An' they ups an' starts for Emelya's place. Emelya, he manages to keep up with 'em, feelin' no end jolly, singin' snatches of song to hisself, whilst them buckets waddle along, like they was so many ducks, an' walk along all by their lone selves. The folkses they meet all through the village is all agog, an' a-gapin' outer all the windys: "Lookee, now, do look! Emelya's buckets is walkin' along of their own selves, of their lone selves!"

An' he walks up to his house, an' he raises his voice:

"Ho, there, you doors! Obey the pike's command, an' by me own demand: creak, slide, by your own selves open wide! I ain't got no hankerin' to be slavin' away; I've got but one idea—for to live in this world as sweet as ever I may!"

Whereupon the doors flies ajar of their own selves, an' the buckets, soon's they had minced acrosst the threshold, took to skippin' an' trippin' inter the hut, whilst Emelya's sisters-in-law started dashin' hither an' yon, tryin' for to dodge 'em—no end skeered, they was.

"Say, what sort of come-uppance is all this, now? What sort of tomfoolery be you up to now, you fool you? How didja ever manage to have them there buckets a-walkin' about of their own selves, of their lone selves?"

"Your buckets, now," says Emelya, "they don't walk about, but mine," he says, "do that very same thing. Let the clever folk, now, bend *their* humps! Get you busy a-makin' an' a-bakin' some pancakes for me, for the work I done!"

Well, then, it weren't once an' it weren't twice that Emelya went that-a-way to the river, an' all the time his buckets was a-traispin' along of their own selves. Then, first thing you know, all the wood was out. So they ups an' asks him— Emelya's sisters-in-law, that is:

"Emelya—oh, Emelya! We be all out of cut wood. Go after wood as fast as ever you can, or else it's you yourself will be cold atop your oven."

Once more, then, without so much as one word of back talk, he gives in to 'em; out of doors he goes, with that lazy, crazy gait of his'n, an' he gives his orders:

"I," says he, "have a mortal dislike for choppin' wood. Come, now, you ax, obey the pike's command, an' by me own demand—chop away of your own self! An' as for you, you logs-out-o'-bogs, you just get along by your own selves inter the hut. I ain't wishful to be luggin' you around an' to be puttin' meself out any. Our region's rich, our region's fair, but then our sloth is wondrous rare—there's nothing with it to compare!"

That there hatchet-ax flies whizz! outer his hands, right off, then whirls up higher nor the roof an' starts in choppin' away; the doors leadin' inter the hut, inter the entry, now, flies wide open of their own selves, whilst the billets of wood ups an' begins hoppin' along; they hop about an' they flop about, like they was so many fish, or pike, or somethin'.

As for Emelya's sisters-in-law, they got skeered again over them there goin's-on, an' all 'cause they was fool women: this one hides under the table, an' that one under the chest forninst the windy—thinkin' if they was to be hit by one of them things they'd get harp an' wings! But the ax, it just keeps on heavin' away, choppin' kindlin'-wood; it made a pile so—o big—more'n a cord, I give you me word. His sisters-in-law they cuss Emelya out, an' they're madder nor hornets, an' they threaten to tell his brothers on him; but he just grins back at 'em, like he were a catfish or somethin'.

"All you got to do is get busy makin' an' bakin' me some pancakes—an' go heavy on the butter when you come to smear 'em!"—an' with that he goes into retirement atop that there oven, to sleep an' to doze an' to get ashes all over his head an' clothes.

It weren't so long thereafter that all the wood give out in the wood-pile as well. His sisters-in-law, they beset him an' they pester him, threatenin' him with his brothers: "Your brothers is comin' home soon as harvest's over, any day now, an' we'll tell 'em that you don't pay no manner of heed to us; all you do is lie there an' crush the cockroaches under you; your brothers, now, they won't spare you, lummox that you be!" Well, now, this Emelya, he were awful scary when it come to bein' punished; he were mighty afeard of fights an' sich, he were. He hopped off of that there oven purty spry, an' he put on his sheepskin coat, his wrap-rascal, you might say, belted hisself with a belt, picked up the ax out in the yard, an' stuck it in his broad girdle. His sisters-in-law, they says to him: "You ought to harness up a hoss, now, but you can't do that by your own self, seein' how feckless you be!" But he says, says he: "What would I be wantin' with a hoss, now? 'Twould only be a-tirin' the poor beast out. Why, I'm meanin' to make the sleigh go by itself, too. No sleigh would go without a hoss for you, but 'twill do that very same thing for me, see?"

He walks up to the sleigh, an' he ties the shafts back, seats hisself, an' then issues his orders: "Obey the pike's command, an' by me own demand—open ye gates by your own selves!" The gates open right quick, an' then he yells out: "As for you, you sleigh, get you a-goin', be upon your way!" Well, that there sleigh just simply flew off—no hoss ever drew it so fast as it were goin' without one! It gallops right through the town, knockin' folkses off of their feet an' ridin' 'em down. But Emelya, now, he don't give a hang, even. The people was sayin': "Oh, ah, eh! Watch that there sleigh, a-goin' along of its own self, of its lone self!"—an' was after bringin' him up short; but they had another guess comin' to 'em, for by that time there weren't nor hide nor hair, nor sight nor sound, left of him.

Then he comes to the forest, an' in that there forest the sleigh comes to a standstill. Emelya, now, he climbs down out of the sleigh, an' he takes his ax out of his belt.

"Well, now," says he, "chop away ax, all by your own self, by my, now, pike's command. As for me, I'll sit a bit, an' watch a bit, an' try to catch the louse or nit that's makin' me head itch that-a-way!"

The ax, it starts right off to chop, *clop-clop*!—an' all you can hear, both far an' near, is its keen edge a-ringin' clear through the whole forest! It chopped down as much wood as was needful, an' a little bit over, an' after that Emelya, he says: "Well, now, ye billets, all by me own demand, pile yourselves up in the sleigh! I ain't hankerin' to pile you neat; I don't think I'd find that sweet!" So the billets, they start in a-pilin' of theirselves atop one another in the sleigh, each as snug as a bug in a rug. An' that's how Emelya piled up his whole load; then he fastened it down with a rope, thrust his ax in his belt-strap, sat him down in the sleigh, an' gave his orders:

"Get you along, now, an' away, you sleigh, all by your own self!"

The sleigh dashes off once more like a swift arrow through the town; the townsmen an' the gownsmen, they caught sight of it: "Oh, ah, eh! There's that evil-doer again! What a lot of folkses he's run down!"—an' they was all for cuttin' him off, runnin' ahead on the road with clubs an' with boar-spears; only 'twere easier said nor done, for there weren't no headin' *him* off! He rode down still more folkses with his load nor he done when he'd been ridin' empty!

He drove up to his yard; his sisters-in-law, they looked out an' seen him, an' then fell to cussin' him out: "There, now, you stoopid fool! See how many innocent folkses you've run down, you lummox!" But he answers 'em back: "Well," he says, says he, "what for was they a-tryin' for to bring me up short on the Tsar's own highway, a-shovin' their-selves right under me sleigh with their cudgels an' their boar-spears?" Then he said his magic word, like the pike had taught him, an' the gates opened of their own selves before him, to oncet, an' so he rode straight inter the yard with his load. Once more, then, the billets and the logs started in to hop inter the hut; once more they frightened the wits out of Emelya's sisters-in-law with their thumpin' an' their clumpin', whilst Emelya the fool, he clambered up on that oven of his'n an' once more ordered 'em to make an' to bake pancakes for him, an' to smear 'em with butter as thick as ever they could.

Well, then, there he was, eatin' away an' eatin' away; but then he happens to cast a glance out the windy, an' what should he spy but that there's a search for him goin' on, the bailiff an' the Cossack captings bein' after wantin' to give him up to punishment for all his unholy mischief an' misdoin's. He huddled up in the darkest nook he could find, right amongst all the rubbish an' cobwebs, but, for all that, find him they did, atop that there oven of his'n.

"Get you down from off of there, Emelya," says they, "your time is come, we tell ya! What are you up to, you clown, a-ridin' honest folkses down? There, we'll take you, you fool, an' put you in the jug to cool! What d'you mean by drivin' aroun' without no hoss, disturbin' the peace an' upsettin' all an' sundry with your tarnation nonsense, throwin' folkses into conniption fits? Eh?"

So they starts in to pull him down off of that there oven, draggin' out the pest an' deprivin' him of his rest; but he got affronted at 'em, an' he says to his cudgel, that he had stood up in a nook atop his oven:

"There, now," he says, says he, "go to it, cudgel, an' knock the ee-ternal daylights out o' them!"

He just said his magic pike's-word, an' my! how that there cudgel did fly, in the twinklin' of an eye, right out of its corner, just flyin' aroun' and then settlin' down to work in real earnest on them Cossack captings and that there bailiff, now, crackin' their crowns an' thwackin' their sit-downs! They oh's an' they ah's: "What sort of a come-uppance is this—to have a cudgel lambastin' us like that?"—an' they piles out of that hut as fast as ever their laigs would take 'em. They rushes off to the head of police an' to the mounted guards: "This Emelya," says they, "he don't pay no manner of heed to us; an' as for takin' him by force, it ain't to be did, nohow! So you go by yourself, now; it's mebbe he's got more respec' for you"—but, nacherly, they never let out as much as a peep nor a goo-goo out of 'em about that there cudgel which had given them so neat an' sweet a treat.

So then all them police, an' the mounted guards, an' the very head of the police hisself, they all got together, an' the bailiff, he showed 'em where Emelya was livin', an' then they piles inter the hut, the whole herd on 'em:

"Well, now Emelya, you little fool, we're goin' for to take you with sojers; we'll make mincemeat out o' you with sabres, that we will! Climb down off of that oven, put your sheepskin jacket on you, an' off with you to the magistrate!"

But he again don't pay no sort of 'tention to 'em; the hut was *that* crowded by now, yet he just won't come along, but sits there in his nook an' sings his little song:

"Oh, you eyeses, me bright eyeses—
Emelya don't want to go to the Assizes!"

They pleads with him, all proper an' honourable; but he takes to his own ways again; again he sings about them there eyeses of his'n. Well, then, by 'n' by, when they had roused his ire again, he ups an' he says:

"By the pike's behest, an' by me own request—" an' that there cudgel of his'n was lyin' down by him all the while, mind you, atop the oven—"come, now, cudgel," says he, "an' show 'em what oak-sugar tastes like!"

That there cudgel gets up right off an' starts in tannin'

'em, goin' from head to head—the head of the head of police hisself, as well as the head of every one of them mounted guards—an' then it chased 'em all out of the hut, every man jack on 'em.

"Well, what's to be done with him now?" says the head of police. "How are we to take him now, lads?"

Well, one of the guards, he strikes on an idear—or mebbe 'twere the idear struck him, I dunno which:

"Let's take him," says he, "through a trick. Let's say that our sovereign hisself has commanded us to give you, Emelya, an invite for to call on him. He'll order all sorts of honey-cakes to be given you." (And Emelya, now, he were *that* fond of eatin' all them there cakes an' cookies, an' sich.) "He, the sovereign will feed you on 'em, now, till you won't want to eat no more."

An' that's the way they made it up amongst theirselves, an' they come to Emelya, an' they go to work on him, flatterin' his vanity an' stirrin' up his appetite an' talkin' to him with all their might. Well, then, at last he give in to 'em. "Oh, all right," says he, "I thanks you for your courtesy; get you back to your houses, an' don't be puttin' yourselves to no more worriment nor trouble. I'll ride off to him—to the sovereign, that is—of me own accord."

An' so they all left his house, an' he ups an' gives his orders to the oven: "Come, now, you oven, be off with you, by me own orders, to the Tsar hisself, right to his palace! Word of me an' you has reached the ears of the very Tsar. He, the sovereign, that is, promises for to let me have me fill of cookies, an' mebbe I ain't the lad that's fond of eatin' 'em!"

The oven begun to twist an' turn, right off, this-a-way an'

that-a-way; then it took to crashin' an' smashin', to rumblin' an' stumblin', to creakin' an' streakin', all over the hut; then it wedged its way out, somehow, through the door, though 'twere narrow, with him, with Emelya, atop, an' flew off like an arrow, whilst he sprawled hisself out, just the same like he were a-ridin' on a passenger train, with a choo-choo an' all.

He drives up to the sovereign's palace, orders the Tsar's gates to open, an' prances up atop that there oven right up to the balcony, to the grand entrance, that is, whilst he hisself is bawlin' an' caterwaulin', at the top of his lungs, for all the world to hear: " 'Oh, you eyeses, me bright eyeses!' "

The sentries come a-runnin' to him, meanin' to make him abate, to make him ashamed of hisself, but the sovereign, he heard all that there haloo-hullabaloo, an' he hisself, now, together with his daughter-heiress, steps out onto the front steps:

"What you yellin' here for," says he, "you iggamus, you? What have you come to the Tsar's mansions for," he says, "a-workin' your wonders? Why d'you come a-shovin' with your oven? Tell us who ye be—ain't you Emelya the little fool, for sure?"

Well, then, Emelya, he rises up on his oven, lifts his elf-locks outer his eyes, wipes off his snot-an'-what-not with his sleeve, an' bows him down before his sovereign's crown. "Right you be, Your Imperial Majesty; it's none other nor me," he says, says he. "The reason I come here, me sovereign an' me father, is 'cause you called me to you for to feed me cakes—an' mebbe I ain't the lad that's fond of eatin' 'em!"

"I ain't a-goin' for to be feedin' you no cakes, I ain't!"

says the sovereign to him in wrath. "I'm a-goin' to order you clapped into the jug, to oncet, that's what! I'm a-goin'," he says, "to put you under arrest!"

"An' whatever would ye be doin' such a thing as that to me for, Your Imperial Majesty?"

"Why, for this," the Tsar answers him, "that you drive about in a sleigh without no hosses to it, an' you stir up all the people, an' you have run down an' hurt a mighty heap of my subjects, that's what for! I'm a-goin' to order your head off this very minute! I'll just give the word, an' out comes the sword, an' off goes your head off of your shoulders! . . .

"An' what's furthermore," the Tsar goes on after a while, "there's an awful lot of complaints lodged against you, an' it's goin' to go ill with you on that account; I ain't," says he, "a-goin' for to pat you on the head for them there sort of disgraceful goin's-on—"

But Emelya, he strikes up his song again, 'bout "Oh, you eyeses, me bright eyeses!"—on that there oven a-sprawlin', an' that there song a-bawlin' with that ugly maw of his'n.

The sovereign, he got real wrought up then, an' all het up. He called out for his minions an' his sentinels then: "Take him, now, an' give him four-an'-twenty hours to live!" But Emelya, catchin' on as to which way things was headin', got that skeered he felt his breeches was full of somethin' else beside his laigs, an' he says as fast as ever he can:

"By the pike's command, an' by me own most humble demand, fall in love with me, you Tsar's daughter-an'-heiress; ask for to be wedded to me!"

The minions come a-runnin' toward the oven, to drag Emelya down off of there, but the Tsar's daughter, now all tears, starts to implore the sovereign, in sweet despair:

" 'Twould be better, my sovereign an' my father, if you was to execute me instead, 'cause I couldn't ever live through it if he was to come to a bad end: he's got a magic word, now! Don't you mind, now," says she, " 'cause he's got the heaves an' laigs like wheat-sheaves, an' eyes like a cockchafer, an' a nose like a wafer! Let him wipe his nose, an' once that's done, he'll pass for any king's son!"

Well, then, the sovereign, he took pity on her, on his heiress, that is. He yanked Emelya the fool aroun' by his lousy topknot, just for the looks of the thing; told him, as strict as strict could be, not to be carryin' on no more such shenanigans; with his own hands he tossed a whole pile of cookies with icin' on 'em to Emelya, where he was a-settin' atop his oven, whilst Emelya, he bowed an' bowed before him, fillin' his crop with all them goodies; then he twirled his cudgel with a shout, turned his oven right about, an' went off on that pecooliar steed, lickety-lick, headin' straight for home. He gallops, he flies, an' sings 'bout his eyes, worse nor ever before, that noisy the whole forest rung with his song!

Well, to make a long story as wide as it's long, no sooner were he out of her sight than the Tsar's daughter falls to pinin' after him an' to grievin'; she just simply couldn't get him out of her head, nohow, she had fallen *that* hard in love with him, an' all on account of that there magic pike's-word of his'n! The sovereign, he sees how she's sufferin', an' at last he turns to her an' begs her to confess everythin' to him. Well, she ups an' admits all to him:

"My sovereign, now, an' my father, I'm all wasted away, all skin an' bones, a-pinin' for my jool, for that Emelya the fool. Don't be leavin' me your domain, an' don't let me reign, but build me a family vault-crypt, if so be you don't want to marry me off to him!"

Well, an' what was the sovereign to do when he hears sich talk as that? Once more he took pity on her, an' right away he sends off envoys to that there village where Emelya was born an' grew, an' supped his stew with an old bast shoe. These envoys, they come to the village on their steeds, an' they find his place, an' they come inter his hut, an' they fall to entreatin' him:

"Emeliushka, you dear fellow, it looks like you got what you was after! You won't have to plough, an' you won't have to reap, but just stuff your guts an' catch up on your sleep. You won't have to worry 'bout cloud-bursts or drouth, but just about carryin' cakes to your mouth. Our sovereign begs for to be honoured with your company; he's after wantin' to be marryin' his daughter off to you. Wipe off your snot, curry-comb your mane, put on your best shirt, an' your breeches wide, an' we're off with you to your blushin' bride!"

But Emelya, now, what does he do but start in puttin' on airs—for, you see, they had got sweet on him, all of a sud-dint!

"I," says he, "ain't plannin' to do anythin' the way common folkses do. I stand head an' shoulders out of the common crowd. I'll ride to the palace on me oven. I ain't got no manner of use for all of your coaches an' your turn-outs. I ain't wishful for to be clamberin' down off of me oven. I've got but one idear—not to be slavin' away, but to live in this world as sweet as ever I may!"

Well, nacherly, the envoys was all rejoicin' things had

fallen out even that-a-way (the Tsar had ordered 'em not to dare show their faces again without they brought Emelya along with 'em); they give in to all his whims, an' they bow down before him, deep an' low, whilst he orders his brothers an' their women-folks to spruce theirselves up as is fittin' an' proper: "It's about time, now, you was gettin' up off of your rumps an' seein' other things besides old tree-stumps!"

But they, as if with one voice, start in yellin' an' sobbin', not bein' wishful for to be partin' with their place, an' bein' downright skeered of the whole business.

"You," they bawl at him, "will yet be the death of all of us!"

But he says right back at 'em:

"If," says he, "you don't come along nice an' quiet, I'll make you come up an' set here by main force!"

He ordered his brothers to put on their flame-coloured Sunday shirts, an' he told the women-folks to tog their-selves out in red sarafans—the little fools, now, is always fond of what's red an' bright an' strikes the sight!

Then he made the whole lot an' passel of 'em set atop the oven, an' they all looked as purty as a bunch of flowers, or somethin'; he bade 'em sit peaceful an' genteel, struck up his jolly little song ('bout his eyeses, now), an' started off on his oven. The threshold creaked, an' out they streaked!

An' out in the broad field they see a coach, right grand an' all of gold, comin' for to meet 'em: the sovereign, you see, had sent it for 'em; there was sojers standin' every-where you turned your eyes, givin' the salute an' presentin' arms, all drawn up as taut as fiddle-strings, they was, like they was on parade, or somethin'. But Emelya, now, he don't even pay no sort of 'tention to all that company.

An', once more, the oven brings him right to the Tsar's balcony.

The sovereign, he steps out:

"Emelya," says he, "have you come, now?"

"I have that—right you be! An' now, me sovereign an' me father," Emelya asks him, "what is it you'd be after wantin' with me?"

"Why," the sovereign tells him, "I'm after wantin' you 'cause you've brought me daughter low; I'm after wantin' to be marryin' you to her. Get down," says he, "off of that there oven of your'n, as fast as ever you can! An' you, our daughter, do you be bringin' him bread an' salt, for to show him our hospitality!"

Well, Emelya, of course, he gets down as fast as ever he can—that there invite was all that he'd been a-waitin' for. He bade his brothers an' their women-folks also to clamber down, to stand to one side an' not even whisper or frown. Then he kissed his sovereign's little hand, right fittin' an' proper, an' bowed his deepest respec's to his bride—even one that weren't no born fool couldn't have did it better!— partook of the bread an' salt, an' then, you understan', the whole honourable an' genteel company went all in a mob right inter the Tsar's own mansions.

There the sovereign reported hisself to the royal chaplain, biddin' him for church to be headin', to get everythin' all set for the weddin'; whilst he hisself—the Tsar, that is— brought out an image, ancient an' sanctified, an' then, wishin' 'em a long an' happy life, blessed the groom an' bride.

Then, nacherly, Emelya was took in hand, an' they wiped the nose of him, an' took him to a bath, an' took his clothes off of him, an' they rubbed an' they scrubbed all the dirt off of him, an' then they put a booful red robe onto him.

An' then, in accordance with all the laws an' rites an' ceremonies an' usages, they went an' they married him, whilst the sovereign hisself deeded half of his whole empire to Emelya the fool, right on the spot.

I, as the sayin' goes, was present at that there weddin'-feast, but can't remember any of that affair, not in the least; they treated an' regaled me so hard, 'tis true, that I can't open me eyes even now, they're *that* black an' blue!

As for Emelya, he throve with his love, an' lived happily for ever an' aye, an', both night an' day, on his soft beds of velvet lay, an' the sweetest of eats in his belly put away, an' held right tight the braids of his princess fair an' gay, an' there was but one thing that he would ever say:

"They'll get along well enough even without me—in governin' the land, that is!"

DRY VALLEY

∾ ∾

Wʜᴀᴛ ʜᴀᴅ ᴀʟᴡᴀʏs sᴛʀᴜᴄᴋ ᴜs ᴀʙᴏᴜᴛ Nᴀᴛʜᴀʟɪᴀ was her
attachment to Dry Valley.

A foster-sister to our father, growing up in the same house
with him, she had lived for all of eight years in our place at
Lunevo, had lived there as one of our kin, and not as a
former serf, a common servant. And for all of eight years,
to use her own words, she had been resting up after Dry
Valley, after that which the place had made her suffer. But
it is not in vain people say that, no matter how you feed a
wolf, he'll aye be eying the steppe. Having seen us through
the toddling stage, having seen us grow up, she had gone
back to Dry Valley anew.

I remember snatches of our childhood talks with her:

"Why, aren't you an orphan, Nathalia?"

"I am that. I take after my masters in everything. Anna
Grigorievna, your grandmother, now, she folded her little
hands in death when she was ever so young, just like my
dear father and mother done!"

"What did they die from, then?"

"Why, their time to die come—and so they ups and dies."

"No, I mean what made them die so soon?"

"Such was God's will. The masters sent my father off for

to be a soldier, on account of his misdoings; my mother didn't live to her full time on account of the masters' turkey-chicks. I, of course, can't remember—how should I?—but here's how they told it in the servants' quarters: she was the poultry-keeper, and you just couldn't count the number of turkey-chicks she had charge of. They was caught in a hail-storm whilst out on the common, and was all beat to death, every single one on 'em.—She dashed off at a run toward them, got there quick, gave one look—and the breath of life left her."

"But how is it you never married?"

"Why, my bridegroom ain't growed up yet!"

"No, do tell us, without joking!"

"Well, they do be saying that the mistress, your auntie dear, was set against me marrying. That's just why it was given out that I was a high-born miss."

"Oh, now, what sort of a high-born miss are you!"

"I am that, to a *t*," Nathalia would answer with a sly little smile which puckered up her lips into wrinkles, and then wiped her mouth with her swarthy, crone's hand. "Why, I'm a sort of an auntie to you, now. . . ."

As we were growing up, we listened ever more attentively to what was being said in our house concerning Dry Valley: that which had hitherto been incomprehensible was becoming ever more comprehensible; the strange details of life in Dry Valley were coming out ever more sharply. Who else but ourselves should have felt that Nathalia, who had passed half her days leading almost the same life as our father—who else should have felt that she was truly of kin to us, the ancient and nobly sprung Khrushchevs! And now it turned out that this gentry had driven her father into soldiering, and her mother into such fear and trembling that her heart had burst at the sight of the perished turkey-chicks!

"And, to be sure," Nathalia used to say, "what else could a body have done but drop dead from such a mishap? The masters would have packed her off to God knows where!"

And later on we found out things still stranger concerning Dry Valley: we found out that there were not, "in all Creation," folk simpler, kindlier, than the masters of Dry Valley; but we also found out that there were none "more hot-headed" than they. We found out that the old house in Dry Valley was dark and sombre; that our mad grandfather, Petr Kyrillich, had been killed in this house by his own natural son, Gervasska, a friend of our father's and cousin to Nathalia. We found out that Aunt Tonia, too, had long ago gone mad from an unhappy love-affair: she lived in one of the old servants' huts near the run-down Dry Valley estate and ecstatically played French schottisches on a pianoforte that boomed and jangled from old age. We found out that Nathalia, likewise, had been going mad at one time; that, while yet a slip of a girl, she had come to love, for all her life, our uncle Petr Petrovich, now dead, whereas he had sent her into exile to the farmstead at Little Ploughs. . . . Our absorbing dreams concerning Dry Valley could be easily understood. To us Dry Valley was only a poetical monument of the past. But what was it to Nathalia? For it was she who had said with great bitterness, as if in reply to some long-kept thought of her own:

"Why, at Dry Valley they used to sit down at table with bull-whips in their hands! It's dreadful even to think back on."

"What! With bull-whips? With dog-lashes, you mean?"

"Oh, they're all one!" said she.

"But what ever did they do that for?"

"Well, just in case of a quarrel."

"Were they always quarrelling at Dry Valley?"

"There weren't a day passed, God deliver us, but what there was a war! All hot-headed, they was—just plain gunpowder, you might say."

As for us, we simply swooned from delight at her words and exchanged enraptured looks. For a long time thereafter we pictured to ourselves the enormous garden, the enormous estate, the house with walls of oak logs, under a heavy and time-blackened roof of straw; and a dinner in the hall of this house: everybody is sitting at table, everybody is eating, throwing the bones on the floor, to the hunting-dogs; everyone is eying everyone else askance—and everyone has a dog-lash on his knees. . . . We dreamt of that golden time when we would grow up and would likewise dine with dog-lashes on *our* knees. Yet we well understood that it was not to Nathalia that these dog-lashes had afforded joy.

But, notwithstanding all this, she left Lunevo for Dry Valley, for the well-spring of her dark recollections. She had neither a nook of her own nor any near of kin there; and in Dry Valley she worked not for Aunt Tonia, who had long ago ceased to be her mistress, but for Claudia Markovna, the widow of the late Petr Petrovich. But then, Nathalia could not live without that very homestead.

"What can a body do? It's a matter of habit," she would say unassumingly. "Where the needle goes, now, the thread is bound to follow, I guess. The place of your birth is the place of your worth. . . ."

Nor was she the only one who was afflicted with an attachment for Dry Valley. And, besides, this was hardly an attachment, but rather something far deeper, far stronger. God, what passionate lovers of recollections, what ardent partisans of Dry Valley, were all the others of our servants as well! And that goes without saying for our aunt Tonia, for our father.

Aunt Tonia passed her days in a hut, in utter poverty. Dry Valley had bereft her of happiness, and of reason, and of human semblance. Yet, despite all the persuasions of our father, she would never even entertain the idea of abandoning the nest she had been born in, of settling in Lunevo.

"Why, I'd rather break stones in the mountain quarries!" she was wont to say.

Our father was a man without a care in the world; for him, it seemed, there existed no attachments whatsoever. But a profound melancholy sounded in his stories of Dry Valley as well. It was already a long, long time ago that we had migrated from Dry Valley to Lunevo, which was a country-seat situated amid fields, and belonging to our great-aunt, Olga Kyrillovna. Yet he complained about his life almost to his very end:

"There's only one Khrushchev now left in the whole world—only one! And even that one is not at Dry Valley!"

True, it would not infrequently happen that right after such words he would fall into deep thought as he looked out of the window, out on a field, and would suddenly smile mockingly as he took his guitar down from the wall.

"Oh, Dry Valley is a fine place, too—may it perish from off the face of the earth!" he would add with the same sincerity with which he had been speaking just the minute before.

But his soul, as well, was a Dry Valley soul: a soul over which recollections had an inordinately great sway, the sway of the steppe, of its sluggish ways, of that ancient domesticity which blended into one the village, the domestics, and the manor-house of Dry Valley. True, we Khrushchevs are of a noble race, inscribed in the sixth Book of Heraldry, and there were among our legendary ancestors many renowned men of ancient Lithuanian blood, as well as many Tatar princelings, whose breed would more than once tell in us. But then, the blood of the Khrushchevs had been mingling with the blood of the serfs and of the village from time out of mind. Who had given life to Petr Kyrillich? Traditions speak with different tongues concerning this. Who was the sire of Gervasska, his slayer? From our earliest years we had heard that it was Petr Kyrillich himself. Whence was derived so sharp a dissimilarity in the characters of our father and our uncle? There is a speech of many tongues concerning this also. For was not Nathalia foster-sister to our father? Had he not exchanged crucifixes with Gervasska? It's long, long since time for the Khrushchevs to be reckoned as of kin to their domestics and their village!

My sister and I, too, lived for long in this yearning for Dry Valley, in its seductiveness. The domestics, the village, and the manor-house at Dry Valley made up one family. This family had been ruled even by our forebears. And a thing like that is long felt, even by posterity. The life of a family, of a line, of a clan, is deep, knotty, mysterious— quite often it is a fearsome thing. But in its dark depths, as well as in its traditions, its past, lies such a family's very strength. In written and other memorials Dry Valley is no richer than a Bashkir steppe. In Russia the place of these is taken by tradition. And tradition, as well as song, is a poisonous drug for the Slavic soul! Our former serfs, earnest sluggards and dreamers, all of them—where else could they ease their soul if not in our house?

Our father remained as the sole representative of the masters of Dry Valley. And the first language in which we began to speak was that of Dry Valley. The first tales, the first songs that stirred us were also those of Dry Valley, told by Nathalia, by our father. Yes—and could anybody else have sung as did our father, who had been taught the art by the serfs, about his "mistress true and fair, with such a sprightly, queenly air"? Could anybody else have sung this song with such insouciant sadness, with such kindly reproachfulness, with such weak-willed soulfulness? Could anybody else have told a tale the way Nathalia did? And who was nearer and dearer to us than the mujiks of Dry Valley?

Dissensions, quarrels—there you have what the Khrush-chevs have been famed for, time out of mind, like every family that has been long and closely living together. And at the time of our childhood there occurred such a quarrel between Dry Valley and Lunevo that for almost ten years Father would not set foot across the threshold of the house where he had been born. Thus it came about that we had not so much as a good look at Dry Valley during our child-hood; we were there but once, and that in passing, on a journey to Zadonsk. But then, dreams are, at times, far more powerful than reality, and, dimly but ineradicably, there were impressed upon our memories a long summer day, certain undulating fields, and an abandoned high road, which had enchanted us with its vast vista and with the hollow-trunked willows which had survived here and there near it; we retained a memory of a beehive on one of these willows, growing far back from the road amid the fields of grain—a beehive left to the will of God amid fields flanking an abandoned road; we retained a memory of a wide turn by an upward-sloping field, of a few poverty-stricken, chimneyless huts overlooking an enormous, barren common, and of the yellowness of stony gullies beyond the huts, and of the whiteness of the shingle and the rubble at the bottom of these gullies. . . .

The first event which horrified us had likewise to do with Dry Valley: it was the murder of Grandfather by Gervasska. And, as we listened to the tale of this murder, we had an endless vision of these yellow gullies, retreating somewhere into the distance. It seemed to us all the time that it must have been through these very gullies that Gervasska had fled after having done his horrid deed, and then "plunged out of sight, like a stone to the bottom of the sea."

The mujiks of Dry Valley called at Lunevo not at all with the same ends in view as did the Dry Valley domestics, but about "gettin' a bit more ground, like"; but they, too, entered our house as if they had been born in it. They would bow from the waist before my father, would kiss his hand, and then, with a backward toss of their hair, would kiss him, as well as Nathalia and ourselves, on the lips, and each of us thrice. They would bring, by way of presents, honey, eggs, home-spun towels. And we, who had grown up amid fields, who were sensitive to smells, and no less avid for them than for songs and traditions—we retained forever in our memories that peculiar, pleasant odour, somehow reminiscent of flax, of which we became aware whenever we kissed the Dry Valley folk. We retained, as well, a memory of their presents, redolent of the old village amid the steppes: the honey smelt of blossoming buckwheat, and rotting hives of oak; the towels, of little outlying barns and huts innocent of chimneys, dating back to the times of our grandfather. . . .

The mujiks of Dry Valley did not tell any stories—and, besides, what tales had they to tell? There were even no traditions existing among them. Their graves are nameless, while their lives are so much alike, so meagre and so vestigeless! Inasmuch as the fruits of their labours and their cares were bread alone—the most realistic kind of bread, the kind you eat. They digged them ponds in the stony bed of the little Stone River, which had long since gone dry, and whose dry bed had come to be dignified by the name of Dry Valley. But ponds are, after all, nothing much to be relied upon: they *will* dry up. They builded them dwellings. But their dwellings are not long-enduring: the least bit of a spark, and they burn down to fine ashes. . . . What was it, then, that drew all of us (and Nathalia most of all) even to the barren common, to the huts and the gullies, to the ruined estate of Dry Valley? Was it aught else but this ancient domesticity, this our blood-kindred to the desolate lure of the steppe?

II

Nurses, old servants, are usually dignified by the use of their patronymics. She was always called only by her first name: at first by the familiar diminutive, Natashka, and later on, Nathalia. She did not look like a nurse—from her cradle to her grave she remained a true peasant woman. Yes, and Dry Valley, in its turn, had but little about it of that which is usually ascribed, in stories, to the nests of the landed gentry.

It was only in our late adolescence that it befell us to set foot in that homestead which had given birth to the soul of Nathalia, which had dominated her whole life—the homestead of which we had heard so much.

I remember the occasion just as though it were but yesterday. There had come a cloud-burst, with deafening peals of thunder and blindingly quick, fiery serpents of lightning, just toward evening, as we were driving up to Dry Valley. A dark-lilac cloud had careened heavily toward the northwest, majestically screening half the sky ahead of us. Flatly, sharply, and deathly white, the plain of grain-fields showed palely green below the enormous background of this cloud. The low, wet grass on the high-road was vivid and extraordinarily fresh; the horses, wet and somehow instantaneously grown gaunt, splashed along through the indigo-hued mire; the tarantass swished, moistly. And suddenly, just at the turn of the road into Dry Valley, amid the fields of tall, wet rye, we caught sight of a tall and exceedingly odd figure in dressing-gown and cowl; we could not determine whether this scarecrow was an old man or an old woman; it was beating a piebald muley-cow with an old, dry branch.

On our approach the branch began to work faster, and the cow, clumsily switching its tail, blundered out on the road, while the old scarecrow (we could by now see that it was a woman), shouting something, started walking toward the tarantass, and, having approached, drew her pale face toward us. Looking with fear into her dark, insane eyes, feeling her sharp, chill nose touching our noses, and becoming aware of her strong hut-odour, we exchanged kisses with her. Was this not Baba Yaga herself, that old hag, that old witch of the fairy-tale? However, there was a cowl, made out of some filthy rag, sticking up on the head of this Baba Yaga; her robe, torn, and wet to the waist, was put on right over her naked body, hardly concealing her gaunt breasts; she was shouting, just as if we were deaf, just as if it were her purpose to start a ferocious barrage of abuse; and by this shouting of hers, as well as all the other details, we gathered that this was Aunt Tonia.

Claudia Petrovna, too, began to shout—gaily, however, and as rapturously as a boarding-school miss. She was a fat little, short little woman, with a grey little tuft on her chin, with little eyes that were extraordinarily alive. Sitting by the open window of the big house with two great entrances, knitting away at a cotton sock, and with her spectacles raised to her forehead, she was watching the common, which had run over into the courtyard.

Nathalia, tiny, sunburned, in half-boots of felt, in a red woollen skirt and a grey blouse with a broad V at her dark, wrinkled neck—Nathalia bowed low, with a soft smile, as she stood near the entrance to the right. As I glimpsed this neck of hers, her thin collar-bone, her wearily sad eyes, I remember I reflected: "It was she who grew up together with our father; a long, long time ago, but precisely here, where of our grandfather's house of oaken timbers, a house that had burned several times, there has been left only this poor-looking habitation, while of the garden there are left only growths of shrubs and a few old birches and poplars, and of the offices and servants' quarters, only a hut, a granary, a barn, and an ice-house grown over with wormwood and bracken. . . ."

We smelt chips and charcoal burning under a samovar; there was a deluge of questions; there began to appear, from century-old what-nots, little crystal jam-dishes, gold tea-spoons worn down to the thinness of a maple-leaf, sugar cookies, saved against the arrival of guests. And while the conversation was coming to a glow (a conversation of intensified amicability, after the long quarrel), we went off rambling through the darkening chambers, seeking the balcony, which was also an exit into the garden.

Everything was blackened by time, plain, crude, in these empty, low-ceiled chambers, still adhering to the same arrangement as in grandfather's day, although made over from what remained of those same rooms in which he had dwelt. In one corner of the butler's pantry a large image of St. Mercurius of Smolensk showed darkly—he whose iron sandals and helmet are preserved on a solea in the ancient cathedral at Smolensk. We had heard that Mercurius had been a doughty wight, who had been called to save the Smolensk region from the Tatars by the voice of an icon of the Mother of God, the icon of Œdigytria the

Guider. Having overwhelmed the Tatars, the saint had
fallen asleep and had been beheaded by his foes. Thereupon, having taken his head in his hands, he had come to
the gates of the city, that he might make known what had
befallen.—And one felt eerie when looking at the penny
woodcut depiction of a headless man, holding in one hand
a deathly-bluish head in a helmet, and in the other the
icon of The Guider—when looking at this cherished image
of Grandfather's, which had gone through several dreadful
conflagrations and had split in the fire. It was thickly bound
in silver, and on its reverse side guarded the genealogy of
the Khrushchevs, inscribed with tildes.

As if in keeping with this image, heavy iron catches were
fastened to the heavy leaves of the door, on both top and
bottom. The floor-boards in the dining-room were inordinately wide, dark, and slippery; the windows were small,
with frames that went up and down. Through this room, a
diminished double of that same one where the Khrushchevs
used to sit down at table with bull-whips in their hands,
we passed into the parlour. Here, opposite the door of the
balcony, had on a time stood the pianoforte on which Aunt
Tonia had played when she had been enamoured of
Voitkevich, who was an officer in the army and a comrade
of Petr Petrovich's. And farther on gaped doors leading
into the lounging-room, and another, a corner room; in
these, on a time, my grandfather had had his quarters.

The evening, as well as the day, was a murky one. Among
the clouds, beyond the garden whose trees had almost all
been chopped down, beyond the half-empty threshing-barn
and the silvery poplars, heat-lightnings were flaring, mo-
mentarily revealing cloud-capped, rosily aureate moun-

tains. The cloud-burst had probably missed the Troshin forest, which showed darkly far beyond the garden, on the slope of the hills beyond the gullies. From thence was borne to us the crisp, warm smell of oaks, which blended with the smell of verdure, with the moist, gentle breeze which occasionally ran through the tips of the birches (all that was left of a ruined garden-walk), through the high nettles, the quitch-grass, and the bushes around the balcony. And the deep quiet of evening, of the steppe, of the depths of Russia, reigned over everything.

"Come and have your tea," a low voice called us back.

It was Nathalia, participant in and witness of all this life, its chief narratrix; while behind her, watching attentively with her insane eyes, somewhat stooping, gliding decorously over the dark, smooth floor, moved her erstwhile mistress, Aunt Tonia. She had not taken off her cowl; but, instead of a robe, she now had on an old-fashioned dress of barége, and a silk shawl of a faded gold tint was thrown over her shoulders.

"*Où êtes-vous, mes enfants?*" she was shouting, with a genteel smile, and her voice, clear and cutting, like that of a parrot, rang out strangely in the empty, black chambers. . . .

III

Even as there was an enchantment about Nathalia, about her peasant simplicity, about all her lovely and pitiful soul, born of Dry Valley, so was there an enchantment about the ruined estate at Dry Valley itself.

There was a scent of jasmine in the old parlour with its warped floor-boards. The balcony, rotted and greyish blue from time (we had to leap down from it, owing to the absence of steps), was sunk in nettles, elder bushes, and priest's-cap. On hot days, when the baking sun was right over the balcony, when its sagging French window was open, and the joyous reflection of the panes was transmitted to the tarnished oval mirror which hung on the wall opposite the French window—on such days we were constantly recalling Aunt Tonia's pianoforte, which at one time had stood under this mirror. At one time she had played on it, following the yellowed pieces of music, with titles all in scrolls, the while *he* had stood behind her, frowning, with his left hand firmly against his hip, his jaws firmly clenched. Marvellous butterflies, in tiny smocks of dazzlingly gay cotton prints, and in Japanese raiment, and in shawls of black-and-lilac velvet, would flutter into the parlour. And one evening, just before his departure, he had, in a fit of vexation, slammed his palm down on one of them, as it was quiveringly settling down to rest on the lid of the pianoforte. All that was left of it was a little silvery dust. But when the wenches who had been cleaning up wiped off this dust a few days later, Aunt Tonia had hysterics. . . .

From the parlour we would go out on the balcony, sit down on its sun-warmed boards, and meditate, on and on.— The wind, running through the garden, brought to us the silken rustling of the birches with their satiny-white trunks, maculated with black, and their wide-flung green branches; the wind, soughing and rustling, came running from the fields, and a glaucous-golden oriole would emit its raucous and joyous cry, darting like a wedge over the white flowers, in pursuit of the chattering jackdaws that, with their numerous kindred, used to inhabit the ruined chimneys and dark garrets, where there was an odour of old bricks, and the golden light fell in streaks through the skylights upon mounds of violet-grey ashes. The wind would die away; the bees crawled sleepily over the flowers near the balcony, consummating their leisurely task, and all one could hear amid the stillness was the even murmur, flowing like a ceaseless drizzle, of the silvery leafage of the poplars. . . .

We rambled through the garden; we penetrated into the jungle of the border hedges. There, amid these hedges, which blended with the grain-fields, in the ancestral bath-house, with its ceiling fallen through (the same bath-house where Nathalia had secreted a small mirror she had purloined from Petr Petrovich), lived white bunnies. How softly they hopped out on to the threshold, how oddly, wiggling their whiskers and split lips, they squinted their eyes, goggling and set far apart, at the tall cotton-thistles, at the bushes of henbane, and the thick growths of nettles that stifled the blackthorn and the small cherry orchard!

And in the half-open threshing-barn there lived a great horned owl. He perched on a cross-beam, choosing as dusky a place as possible, with his ears pricked up, with his yellow, unseeing pupils popping out, and he looked savage, fiendish. The sun was sinking far beyond the garden, into the sea of grain; evening was advancing, peaceful and clear; a cuckoo was cuckooing in the Troshin forest; somewhere over the meadows the pipes of old Stepa, the shepherd, resounded plaintively. . . . The horned owl perched on, biding the coming of night. At night everything slept in the fields and the village and the manor-house. But the horned owl kept on hooting and weeping. On noiseless wings he would swoop around the threshing-barn and over the garden, fly up to Aunt Tonia's hut, sink gently to its roof, and then emit a painful cry. Aunt would wake up on her bench near the oven.

"Most sweet Jesus, have mercy upon me!" she would whisper, sighing.

The flies droned sleepily and discontentedly on the ceiling of the hot, dark hut. Not a night passed but something would turn up to disturb their slumbers. Now it would be a cow, scratching its side against the wall of the hut; now a rat would scamper over the jerkily jangling keys of the pianoforte, and, losing its footing, would tumble with a crash among the shards of crockery and other broken-up things which Aunt used to pile so carefully in a corner; now the old black tom-cat would come home late from traipsing around somewhere and would lazily beg to be let into the hut; or else this same horned owl would come a-flying, prophesying misfortune with its cries. And Aunt, overcoming her sleepiness, brushing away the flies which in the darkness crawled into her eyes, got up, groped along the benches, banged the door open, and, stepping out on the threshold, would, at a guess, send a rolling-pin whizzing at the starry sky. The horned owl, rustlingly catching his wings against the thatch, would dart off the roof and fall low somewhere into the darkness. He almost touched the ground, smoothly volplaned to the threshing-barn, and then, rocketing upward, would come to rest on its ridge. And his wail would again come floating to the manor-house. He perched there, as if recollecting something, and then would suddenly emit a scream of astonishment; would fall silent, and then unexpectedly launch into hysterical hoots, laughter, and squeals; again he would fall silent, and then break into moans, snivellings, and sobs. . . .

And the nights were dark, warm, with lilac-hued cloudlets, and calm,—calm. . . . The lisping of the drowsy poplars drowsily ran and streamed on. Heat-lightning would warily flicker over the dark Troshin woods, and there was ever the sun-warmed, crisp odour of oak-trees. Near the woods, above the plain of oats, against a sky-glade among the clouds, Scorpio, of a sepulchral mountain-blue, glowed as a silver triangle.

We returned to the manor-house late. Having breathed our fill of the dew, of the freshness of the steppe, of the field flowers and grasses, we carefully climbed up on the porch and stepped into the dark entry. And frequently we found Nathalia at prayer before the image of St. Mercurius. Barefooted, diminutive, with her arms crossed on her breast, she stood before him, whispering something, crossing herself, bowing low to him, who was invisible in the darkness. And she did all this as simply as though she were chatting with someone near and dear to her, and as simple, kindly, and benign as herself.

"Nathalia?" we would call to her softly.

"Yes, it's me," she would respond, softly and simply, interrupting her devotions.

"How is it you're not sleeping yet?"

"Why, I guess I'll catch up on my sleep in the grave. . . ."

We would sit down on the locker near the window-sill and would open the window; she remained standing, with her arms crossed on her breast. The heat-lightning flickered mysteriously, lighting up the dark chambers; a quail was drumming somewhere far off, out in the dewy steppe. With a warning uneasiness an awakened duck would quack on the pond. . . .

"Were you out for a stroll?"

"We were."

"Oh, well—you're young yet! Why, we used to stroll all night through, the same way. . . . One glow would drive us out; another would drive us in. . . ."

"You used to live well before, didn't you?"

"We did that."

And a long silence would ensue.

"Why does that horned owl cry so, nursie?" my sister would ask.

"There's nor rhyme nor reason to his crying. There's no getting rid of him! If only somebody would fire a gun to frighten him off! The way things are, a body gets to feeling downright eerie, always thinking mebbe its cries bode some ill. Why, that owl is forever frightening the young lady. And, mind you, she could easy be frightened to death!"

"Tell us, how did she begin to ail?"

"Why, you know how it is—tears, tears all the time, and longing. . . . Then she took to praying. . . . And, on top of that, she grew meaner and meaner to us maids, and ever more angry toward her brothers. . . ."

And, recalling the dog-lashes, we would ask:

"Then that means they weren't getting along well with one another?"

" 'Well' is hardly the word for it! And especially after she was took sick, now, and your grandfather died, and the young masters took a holt of the reins, and the late Petr

Petrovich went and got married. All hot-headed, they was—just plain gunpowder, you might say!"

"And did they flog the servants often?"

"Why, there wasn't any such ways in our household. Just think of how I had misbehaved! And yet all that happened in the end was that Petr Petrovich ordered them to crop my hair real close with the sheep-shears, to put a threadbare shift of striped ticking on me, and to send me off to a far-off farm."

"And just what had been your fault?"

But the answer which followed was far from always direct and prompt. At times Nathalia would tell her story with amazing directness and thoroughness; but at others she would falter, pondering over something; then she would emit ever so slight a sigh, and, by her voice (since we could not see her face in the dark), we gathered that she was sadly smiling.

"Why, my fault lay in just that I— For I've already told you. . . . Young and foolish, that's what I was. 'Alack and alas, a sweet nightingale in a garden sang; 'tis an old, old tale. . . .' And, naturally, I being a girl at that time—"

My sister would ask her kindly:

"Come, nursie, say that poem to the very end—do!"

"This is no poem, but a song. . . . And, besides, I couldn't recall it now."

"That's not so—that's not so!"

"Oh, well, if you like—" And, in a patter, she would finish: " 'Ah, woe—' I mean to say: 'Alack and alas, a sweet nightingale in a garden sang; 'tis an old, old tale! Dark the night; his song is a sweet heart-ache, and a silly lass tosses wide awake. . . .' "

Mustering up her courage, my sister would ask:

"And were you very much in love with uncle?"

And Nathalia would whisper, dully and briefly:

"Very much so."

"Do you always remember him in your prayers?"

"Always."

"Is it true what they say—that you fainted away when you were being carried off to Little Ploughs?"

"I fainted dead away. We girls working in the house was awful delicate. We was no end chicken-hearted and touchy when it come to being punished. . . . After all, you couldn't liken us to the commoner of our fellow-servants! When Evsenii Bodulya drove off with me, I became all dazed from grief and fear. . . . As we was going through the town, I almost stifled, I was that unused to the air there. But as soon as we got out into the real steppe, why, I got to feeling so tender, and so sorry for myself!—There were an officer that looked like *him* dashing along toward us—and I just let a scream out of me and keeled over like I was dead! But when I come to myself, I just lay there in the cart and I thinks to myself: 'I feel fine, now; just like I were in the Kingdom of Heaven itself!' "

"Was our uncle stern?"

"God save us from such another!"

"But still, wasn't it Auntie who was the most self-willed of them all?"

"She were that,—she were just that! I'm telling you, now: they even brought her to a holy man. . . . We went through an awful lot with her! She ought to be living and enjoying herself, right proper; but no, she turned stubborn and proud, and so she got cracked. . . . How this

Voitkevich gentleman used to love her, now! But there, it weren't no use!"

"Well, and what about Grandpa?"

"And what could I say about him? He were sort of feeble-minded, he were. And, of course, he had his crotchets as well. They was all hot-headed in them days. But then, the former masters, now, didn't look down on our sort. There was times when your papa dear would punish Gervasska at dinner-time—and Gervasska sure had it coming to him!—but, come evening, you'd see the two of them in the servants' quarters, raising Cain together and thrumming away on their balalaikas—"

"But tell us—was this Voitkevich good-looking?"

Nathalia would become thoughtful. Then:

"No, I wouldn't want to tell a lie," she would answer; "he were something like a Kalmuck. And yet he were serious and would get whatever he were after. He was for-ever reading poems to her—forever frightening her, now: 'I'm going to die, you'll see, and will come after you—' "

"Yes, but didn't Grandfather, too, go mad because of love?"

"It were on account of your grandmother. That's another matter altogether, miss. And, besides, our house itself was gloomy; none too cheerful, God be with it! You just listen to my foolish speech, if it please you. . . ."

And, in an unhurried whisper, Nathalia would launch into a long, long narrative.

There were in this narrative jests, reservations, evasions; there were animation, pensiveness, unusual simplicity. But, side by side with all this, there were other things: a mys-terious air, a stern and canorous half-whisper. But the prevalent element was a certain sadness of long standing. And everything was permeated with a feeling of an ancient faith in predestination, with a feeling of a never-voiced, vague, yet constant self-suggestion that every one—every one!—of us must take one role or another upon himself, in accordance with one dispensation of fate or another.

IV

If one is to believe traditions, our great-grandsire, a man of means, had migrated from Kursk to Dry Valley only toward the end of his days; he had no liking for our localities, for their desolate spots, their forests. Why, there even came to be a proverb that "the forests were everywhere in the old days." People who had to make their way over our roads some two hundred years back had to make their way through thick forests. Stony River, as well as those uplands through which it ran, and the village and the estate, and the knolly fields all around—they all lost themselves in the forest.

However, things had no longer been so in Grandfather's time. In Grandfather's time the landscape was a different one: there was a spaciousness, half-pertaining to the steppe; there were denuded mountain-slopes; there were rye, oats, and buckwheat in the fields, and, by the high-road, infrequent hollow-trunked willows; while over the rise of Dry Valley there was only white flint to be seen. All that was left of the forests was but the single Troshin grove. But the garden had, of course, been a marvellous one. There had been a broad avenue of seventy spreading birches; clumps of cherry-trees, swamped in nettles; impassable thickets of raspberry bushes, acacias, lilacs; and, near where the borders of the garden verged with the grain-fields, well-nigh a whole grove of silvery poplars. The house was thatched with straw, but so thick, dark-hued, and impenetrable that no roof-iron could compare with it. And the house faced a courtyard, along the sides of which stretched the longest of offices and of servants' quarters, each building having several additions, while beyond the courtyard spread an endless green common, and the seigniorial village was scattered wide—a village large, poor, and care-free.

"It took entirely after its masters!" Nathalia used to say. "The masters, they was care-free, too: not at all good managers, nor greedy. Semion Kyrillich, that was brother to your grandpa, he divided up with us, taking for hisself what was bigger and better, which was their father's estate nigh the capital; as for us, all we got was Little Ploughs, Dry Valley, and four hundred souls thrown in. And of these four hundred, now, well-nigh half run off . . ."

Our grandfather, Petr Kyrillich, had died when he was about five-and-forty. Our father would often say that Grandfather had gone mad when a suddenly risen hurricane had sent a whole downpour of apples upon him as he lay asleep on a rug under an apple-tree in the garden. But in the servants' quarters, according to the words of Nathalia, Grandfather's feeble-mindedness was explained differently: they said that Petr Kyrillich had begun to fail through melancholy soon after the death of Grandmother, who had been a beauty; they said that a great storm had also swept over Dry Valley just before evening of the day she died, and that the hurricane which, together with a black cloud, had swooped down upon the sleeping Petr Kyrillich, had really staggered him with the idea that his own death was

214

approaching. And so Petr Kyrillich—a stoop-shouldered, brown-haired man, with dark, solicitously kind eyes, who resembled Aunt Tonia a little—had finished his days in harmless lunacy. The Khrushchevs, according to Nathalia's words, had never known what to do with their money, and so now, in morocco half-boots and a gay Tatar kaftan (short, and fastened with hooks), he roamed all over the house, preoccupied and noiseless, and, looking over his shoulder, shoved gold pieces into the cracks of the oak timbers.

"I'm just putting that by for little Tonia's dowry," he would mutter whenever they caught him at it. "It's safer this way, my friends—much safer. But, after all, let it be as you wish; if you don't want me to do it, I won't. . . ."

And later he would do the same thing all over again. And if it were not that, he would take to shifting about the ponderous furniture in the dining-room or in the parlour; he was forever expecting someone to arrive, although his neighbours practically never visited Dry Valley. Or else he would complain that he was hungry and would concoct a cold mess for himself of bread, scallions, and bread-cider; he clumsily pounded and brayed the scallions in a wooden bowl, crumbled bread therein, poured in thick, foaming bread-cider, and sprinkled in so much salt that the mess would turn out to be bitter, and eating it would be too much for him.

But when, after dinner, life in the manor-house would become dormant, all having scattered to their favourite nooks and dozed off for long, long naps, the poor lonely fellow, who slept little even at night, was absolutely at a loss as to what to do with himself. And, having found the loneliness beyond his endurance, he would take to peeping into the bedrooms, into the entries, into the maids' rooms, and cautiously calling the sleepers:

"Are you asleep, Arcasha?—Are you asleep, Toniusha? . . ."

And, receiving an angry and loud response: "Do get away from me, Papa dear!"—he would offer a hasty reassurance:

"There, sleep, sleep, my soul—I'm not going to wake you!"

And he would again be on his way, avoiding only the butler's pantry, inasmuch as the flunkeys were an exceedingly rude race; but ten minutes later he would bob up on the same threshold anew, and, anew, with still greater caution, would call out, inventing the pretext that somebody had just driven through the village with jingle-bells that sounded like those of the stage-coach— "Could it possibly be Petie coming home on leave from his regiment?"—or else saying that a fearful cloud, full of hail-stones, was gathering.

"He, the darling old fellow, were very much afeard of a thunder-storm, now," Nathalia would tell us. "I was still a bare-headed slip of a girl then, but I remember it yet, for all that. Our house was all black, somehow. . . . None too cheerful, God be with it! And a day in summer is as long as a year. There was that many servants nobody knew what to do with 'em—of flunkeys alone there was five. . . . You know how things are: after dinner the young masters would retire for a rest, and, following their example, we their faithful louts would do the same. The wenches would go off to the maids' quarters; after dinner they would rattle

their lace-bobbins and their spindles a bit for the looks of
the thing, would scatter feathers and down all through the
chambers (we was forever stuffing feather-beds), and then
go off in a doze wherever they happened to be.

"As for the flunkeys, now—why, they was altogether too
brazen; they just used to sit in their big room, braiding
whips just to show off, weaving quail-nets, or thrumming
away on their balalaikas, and a lot they had to care or grieve
about! They'd stuff their guts with a lot of dried oat-meal
and hasty pudding and then go to sleep. And at such a time
Petr Kyrillich, he'd better not go near them—especially
Gervasska. 'I say, my good fellows! Are you all asleep?'
But Gervasska, he'd lift up his head from the bin he was
lying on and ask: 'And how would you like for me to fill
the seat of your breeches with nettles, right now?'—'Why,
whom are you saying that to, loafer that you are?'—'I was
talking to the hobgoblin, sir, in me sleep . . .'

"And so that's why Petr Kyrillich used to go to our
rooms, for the most part: 'Arcasha, are you asleep?—
Natka, are you asleep? . . .' And you'd jump up, all
a-tremble. . . . But he'd say: 'There, sleep, sleep, my soul
—I'm not going to wake you.' And again he'd take to pacing the dining-room, the parlour, and be looking out of the
windows, out into the garden, all the time; mebbe there was
a cloud to be seen. And thunder-storms, truth to tell, used
to gather ever so often in the old days. Then, too, the
thunder-storms was great ones. Just as soon as afternoon
was come, the orioles would start in their screaming, and
little clouds would start crawling up from beyant the garden. It would get all dark within the house; the witch-grass
and the thick nettles would start in a'rustling; the turkey-

hens and their chicks would hide theirselves under the balcony. . . . It were downright eerie and would put a body in the dumps!

"As for the old man, he'd sigh, cross hisself, and be all a-flutter to light a wax taper in front of the holy images and to hang up the sanctified towel he'd got from *his* late father —I was deathly afeard of that there towel. . . . Or else he'd chuck the scissors out of the window. That were first and foremost, them scissors; a very good thing, that, to ward off the lightning. You'd get burned right up to your waist when they made you clamber, after it was all over, after them scissors, right in amongst all them nettles, now, and they burning the very life out of you. We had a whole thick forest of 'em, a-growing and a-flourishing!"

Things had been jollier in the Dry Valley home when the French tutors were living there: at first a certain Louis Ivannovich, a fellow in the widest of pantaloons, which narrowed down at the ankles, with long moustaches and dreamy blue eyes, who combed his hair from one ear to the other to mask the bald patch on the crown of his head; and, later, an elderly, eternally chilled Mlle Suzie. Yes, things were jollier when one could hear through all the rooms the thunderous voice of Louis Ivannovich yelling at Arcasha: "Go 'way and nevaire rrreturrrn!"—when one could hear in the class-room: *"Maître corbeau sur un arbre perché!"* and when Aunt Tonia, then a little girl, was doing her exercises on the pianoforte. For eight years these French people lived on at Dry Valley, remaining there so that Petr Kyrillich might not feel lonely or bored, remaining even after the children were taken to the capital city of the province; they left the house only just prior to the return

218

of the youngsters for their third vacation. When this vacation was over, Petr Kyrillich no longer sent either Arcasha
or little Tonia anywhere; it was enough, in his opinion, to
send off only Petie. And the children were left for all time
both without instruction and without supervision.—Nathalia used to say:

"I, now, was the youngest of them all. Well, Gervasska
and your papa dear, now, was almost of the same years and
therefore was the closest of friends and chums. Only it's the
truth they say: A wolf is no kinsman to a steed. They got
to be friends, now; they swore to be friends for all eternity;
they even exchanged their crucifixes. But Gervasska in a
short while ups and does something; he well-nigh drownded
your papa dear in the pond! All scabby he were, this
Gervasska, yet already a master hand at schemes that
should have made him a convict. 'Well, now,' says he once
to the young master, 'when you grow up, are you goin' for
to flog me?'—'I am that!'—'Oh, no, you ain't!'—'What
d'you mean, I ain't?'—'Oh, nothin'!'—and this is what he
thought up: we had a barrel standing above the ponds, just
on the very slope of the hill; so what does he do but make
a note of it and then sics on Arcad Petrovich to climb inside
of it and dasts him to roll down the hill in it. 'You'll be the
first, young master, to scoot down the hill, and then it'll be
my turn. . . .' Well, now, the young master he just goes
and listens to him: he climbs in, shoves off, and down the
hill he goes thundering, right into the water! My, how he
did go! Mother of God and Queen of Heaven! All you could
see was the dust whirling along like a pillar! Thanks be,
there turned out to be some shepherds near by. . . ."

As long as the French people lived on in the house at Dry

Valley, the house had kept an inhabited appearance. In Grandmother's day there had yet been in it masters and managers, and such things as authority and submission, and reception-rooms and rooms for the family, and week-days and holy days. An appearance of all this persisted even when the French people had lived there. But they went away, and the house was left entirely without managers. While the children had been small, the first place was seemingly occupied by Petr Kyrillich. But what could he do? Who was master over whom: he over the domestics, or the domestics over him? The pianoforte was closed down; the cloth vanished from the oak table—they dined without any table-cover, and whenever they could; there was no passing through the entries on account of the borzoi wolf-hounds. Things so fell out that there was never a soul to concern itself with keeping the place clean, and the dark, timbered walls, the dark, heavy doors and lintels, the old holy images, whose penny-woodcut countenances covered a whole corner in the dining-room—all these things turned black, speedily and altogether. Of nights—especially during a thunder-storm, when the garden rioted under the rain, and the visages of the painted saints in the dining-room were momently lit up, and the rosily golden, quivering sky would be revealed, would fling itself wide open over the garden, and then, amid the darkness, the peals of thunder split the air—of nights one felt afraid in the house. And in the day-time the house was drowsy, deserted, and filled with tedium.

With the years Petr Kyrillich grew weaker and weaker, was becoming ever more imperceptible; the decrepit Darya Ustinovna, Grandfather's foster-mother, was the official chatelaine. But her authority was almost on a par with his;

while Demian, the overseer, did not interfere in the management of the household: all he knew was the husbandry of the field, occasionally saying with a lazy mockery: "Oh, well, I don't take any advantage of my masters. . . ." Our father, who was a youth at the time, had other things on his mind besides Dry Valley: his crazes were hunting, the balalaika, his love for Gervasska, who was numbered among the flunkeys, but who actually disappeared for days at a time with Father on certain swamps, or in the carriage-shed, studying the fine points of the balalaika and the shepherd's pipes.

"We all used to know," Nathalia would say, "that the house was for them only a place to sleep in. And if they wasn't sleeping in the house, then it meant they was either in the village or in the carriage-shed or else out hunting: in the winter it was hares; in the autumn, foxes; in the summer, quail, duck, or else bustard; they'd sit them down in a racing-cart, sling their light guns over their shoulders, call out for the bitch Dianka, and off they went, with God's blessing: now it would be Middle Hill; on the morrow it would be them Meshcherskia swamps; the day after it would be the steppes for them. And always with that there Gervasska. That lad were the head and front in everything, yet he made out like it were the young master who were dragging him on to everything. Arcad Petrovich loved him, who were his enemy, as if he was truly a brother to him, but he, this Gervasska, the further things went, the more he made sport of the young master, and that more and more cruelly. Arcad Petrovich might say: 'Well, now, Gervassii, let's have a go at the balalaikas! Teach me how to play *Beautiful the Sunset over the Dark Grove*, for God's sake!'

But Gervasska, he'd just look at him, let the smoke out through his nose, and then say, with a sort of little sneering smile on him: 'You've got to kiss me hand first.' The young master, he'd turn all white, jump up from his place, and slap Gervasska's cheek for him, but the other would only toss his head and turn still blacker, frowning like he were a bandit or something. 'Stand up, you good-for-naught!' Gervasska would stand up, stretching hisself like he were a borzoi, the drugget breeches on him hanging all loose. He don't say a word. 'Ask my forgiveness!'—'My fault. sir.'—But the young master, he's like to choke, and he don't know what more to say. 'You'd better be saying "sir"!' he's shouting. 'I,' he says, 'am trying to be treating you like an equal, good-for-naught that you be; I,' he says, 'think at times I wouldn't begrudge giving up my soul for you. . . . But you—what are you up to? Are you angering me on purpose?'

"It's a curious thing," Nathalia would add, "it was Gervasska who used to make sport of the young master and your grandfather, and lord it over them, whereas the young lady used to do them very things to me. . . . The young master (and, truth to tell, your grandfather hisself, as well) thought the world and all of Gervasska, and I felt the same way about the young lady. . . . That is, as soon as I was come back from Little Ploughs and had come a little to my senses after my misbehaviour. . . ."

V

It was after Grandfather's death that they used to sit down at table armed with dog-lashes—after the flight of Gervasska and the marriage of Petr Petrovich; after Aunt

Tonia, having become cracked, had consecrated herself as a bride of the Most Sweet Jesus, and after Nathalia had come back from those same Little Ploughs. And the reason for Aunt Tonia's having become cracked, and for Nathalia's banishment to Little Ploughs, had been love.

The tedious, dull times of Grandfather were replaced by the times of the young master. Petr Petrovich (who had, unexpectedly to all, resigned from his regiment) returned to Dry Valley. And his coming proved the ruination both of Nathalia and of Aunt Tonia.

They both fell in love—and never noticed how they had come to do so.

It had seemed to them, at first, that life had simply become a blither affair. They had come to feel for the first time that they were young girls, and had given themselves up to the charm of this sensation.

Petr Petrovich had at first given a new turn to life in Dry Valley,—a turn festive and seigniorial. He arrived with his crony, Voitkevich; he brought a cook with him— a clean-shaven alcoholic, who eyed askance and with disdain the jelly-forms, nicked and turned green, and the crude knives and forks. Petr Petrovich wanted to show himself before his crony as hospitable, generous, rich—and went about it clumsily, boyishly. Yes, and he *was* almost a boy, very delicate and handsome in looks, but harsh and cruel by nature; a boy daring and self-assured, but easily confused, and that almost to tears, and then long harbouring a secret malice against the one who had caused his confusion.

"I remember, Brother Arcadii," said he on the very first day of his stay in Dry Valley, "I remember we used to have some madeira in our cellar that was not at all bad. . . ."

Grandfather turned red and wanted to say something, but could not summon up enough courage and only started to tug at the bosom of his short Tatar kaftan. Arcadii Petrovich was astonished.

"What madeira?"

But Gervasska gave Petr Petrovich a brazen look and fleered.

"You've forgotten, sir, if you please," said he to Arcadii Petrovich, without even trying to conceal his mockery, "that, truth to tell, we had so much of that there madeira that we didn't know what to do with it. But us servants has managed to get rid of it. 'Tis a wine for the masters' table, but we, being fools, used to drink it in place of bread-cider."

"What's all this?" Petr Petrovich raised his voice, a dark flush, peculiarly his own, mantling his cheeks. "Keep still, you!"

Grandfather rapturously chimed in:

"That's right, that's right, Petie! Serve him out again!" he cried out joyously, in his piping voice, and almost burst into tears. "You simply can't imagine how he makes naught of me! I've already more than once thought of stealing up on him and bashing his head in with a brass pestle! Honest to God, that's what I've thought of doing! Some day I'll stick a dagger in his ribs!"

But Gervasska did not lose his presence of mind even at this point. "I've heard, sir, that there's a heavy penalty for that sort of thing," he retorted, frowning. "And then I, too, have an idea always popping into my head: it's high time for the old master to be going to the Kingdom of Heaven!"

Petr Petrovich used to say that after such an unexpectedly impertinent answer he had restrained himself only
because a stranger was present. He said but one thing to
Gervasska: "Get out of here this minute!" But afterwards
he had become actually ashamed of his hot-headedness,
and, hastily apologizing before Voitkevich, with a smile
raised to him those charming eyes which all those who knew
Petr Petrovich could not forget for a long while.

Nathalia, too, could not forget those eyes—for all too
long a while.

Her happiness was unusually brief, and who could have
thought that it would terminate in a journey to Little
Ploughs—the most remarkable event in her whole life?

The farmstead of Little Ploughs has survived even to
this day, although it has long since passed into the hands
of a merchant from Tambov. It consists of an elongated
hut, a storehouse, the long crane of a water-well, and a
threshing-floor, surrounded by melon-patches. The farmstead had been like that even in Grandfather's day; however, even the town lying between it and Dry Valley has
changed but little.

And Natashka's misdeed had consisted in her having
stolen, altogether unexpectedly even to herself, a little fold-
ing silver-framed mirror belonging to Petr Petrovich.

She had caught a glimpse of this mirror and had been so
taken by its beauty (as, however, she was by all things else
that appertained to Petr Petrovich) that she had not been
able to withstand the temptation. And for several days,
until the mirror was missed, she lived in a stunned state,
overwhelmed by her crime, under the witching spell of her
dreadful secret and her treasure, as if she were the heroine

of the fairy-tale concerning the Little Crimson Flower. Whenever she lay down to sleep she prayed to God that the night might pass as quickly as possible, and that, as quickly as possible, the morning might come. There was a gala mood in the house, which had taken on new life, had become filled with something new, something wondrous, upon the coming of the young master, as handsome as Adonis, dandified in dress, pomatumed, with a high red collar to the coat of his uniform, with a face swarthy, but as delicate as that of a miss.

There was a gala mood even in the entrance hall, where Natashka used to sleep, and where, at dawn, springing down from the coffer that was her bed, she at once recalled that there was joy in this world, because standing near the door and waiting to be cleaned was a pair of boots, so small and light that they were fit to be worn by any king's son. And the most frightening and festal thing of all lay beyond the garden, in the abandoned bath-house, where the small double mirror in its silver frame was hidden—beyond the garden, whither, while all were yet asleep, Natashka sped secretly through the dew-covered thickets, that she might gloat over the possession of her treasure, might bring it out on the threshold, open it in the hot morning sun, gaze at herself till her head swam, and then hide it, secrete it again, and again speed home, to wait all morning upon him whom she dared not even raise her eyes to and for whose sake, in an insane hope of proving to his liking, she used to look so long in the mirror.

But the fairy-tale of the Little Scarlet Flower had come to a speedy end—an exceedingly speedy end. It ended in such disgrace and shame as there was no name for, as

Natashka thought, inasmuch as the most secretly cherished things she had borne within her soul became understood by all. It ended with none other than Petr Petrovich himself ordering her to have her hair cropped, so as to make her homely—her, who used to prim herself, used to blacken her eye-brows with stibium before the little mirror, having created some sort of a sweet secret, some unparalleled intimacy between herself and it.

He himself had discovered her crime and had transformed it into a simple theft, the silly prank of a little serving-wench, who, in a threadbare shift of striped ticking, with a face swollen from tears, was, in the presence of all the servants, put in a dung-cart and, disgraced, suddenly torn away from all that was near and dear to her, was driven off to some unknown, fearsome farmstead, into the distant prospects of the steppe. She already knew that there, on the farm, she would have to watch the chicks, the turkeys, and the melon-patches; there she would be baked brown by the sun, forgotten by the whole world; there, out on the steppe, the days would be as long as years, when the horizons sink in the shimmering mirage, and everything is so still, so sultry, that one feels like sleeping the sleep of the dead the livelong day, were one not compelled to listen to the subdued crackling of peas parched by the sun in their pods, to the housewifely fussing of the brood-hens in the hot earth, to the turkeys exchanging peacefully sad gobbles—were one not compelled to watch for the shadow, weirdly swooping downward, of a chicken-hawk and to leap up and scare him off with a high-pitched, long-drawn-out *shoo—oo!* . . .

There, on the farm, what would she not have to endure

from the old peasant woman alone who had been given the power of life and death over her and who was probably already awaiting her victim with impatience! Natashka had but one advantage over those who are being carted off to the scaffold: the possibility of strangling herself. And that was the only thing that sustained her during her journey to the place of her banishment—of course a perpetual banishment, as she supposed.

En route, from one end of the district to the other, what had she not seen! However, her mind was taken up with other things. She thought (or rather felt) but one thing: life was at an end. Her crime and disgrace were too great for her to hope for a return to life. As yet there remained near her a man she knew well—Evsei Bodulya. But what would happen when he would hand her over into the hands of that old peasant witch and, after sleeping over, would go off in the morning, abandoning her forever in a strange place?

After having wept her fill she had felt hungry, and Evsei, to her wonder, regarded this as a very simple matter and, as they had a bite, talked with her just as if nothing whatsoever had happened. And later on she had fallen asleep, and when she awoke, they were already in the town. And the town struck her only by its tedium, dry air, and sultriness, and also by a something vaguely frightening, depressing, like a dream which one could not relate.

All that remained in her memory of this day was that it was very hot in the steppe in the summertime, that there was nothing in the world as endless as a summer day or as long as a high-road. There also remained in her memory an impression that there were spots in the streets of the town

paved with cobble-stones over which the cart rattled most
oddly; that, from afar, the town smelt of iron roofs, while
in the middle of the square where they halted to rest and
bait their horse, near the sheds of the slap-bang eating-
places (which sheds were empty because it was toward
evening), the smells were those of dust, of pitch, and of
rotting hay, wisps of which, trodden into the horse-manure,
always remain wherever the mujiks may have put up.

Evsei unharnessed the horse and let it feed from a bag
that rested on the cart, shoved the cap, in which he had been
sweltering, on the nape of his neck, wiped his sweat with
his sleeve, and, all black from the baking sun, went off to a
cook-shop. He gave exceedingly strict orders to Natashka
to keep her eyes peeled, and, if anything happened, to yell
so's the whole square might hear on 't. And Natashka sat
there without stirring, without taking her eyes off the
cupola of the cathedral (which at that time had just been
built)—a cupola that glowed like an enormous silver star
somewhere far beyond the houses. She sat there until Evsei,
still chewing and by now grown cheerful, had returned and,
holding a loaf of bread under his arm, began putting the
horse back in the shafts.

"Me an' you, queenie, is a bit late!" he was muttering
animatedly, but one could not tell whether he were addressing the horse or Natashka. "Oh, well, guess they won't kill
us for it! Guess we ain't goin' to no fire—I ain't a-goin' to
break me neck goin' back, neither; I thinks more of the
master's hoss, brother, than I does of your damned mug,"
he was saying, this time apostrophizing the overseer at Dry
Valley. "Look at him openin' his mug: 'I'll have you look
sharp! In case anythin' goes wrong, I'll fix you so's you

won't be able to sit down for a month of Sundays. . . .'
'Aaah,' thinks I, an' I got my bellyful of mistreatment right
there an' then! You take the masters, now, an' even they
ain't never took me breeches down yet. So where do you
come in, you low-down, ornery houn'?—'Look sharp!' But
why should I look sharp? Guess I ain't worse off for brains
nor you be! If I feel like it, I won't come back at all, at all;
I'll get the wench to where she's goin', an' then cross meself,
an' that's the last they'll ever see of me. . . . Why, I do be
wonderin' at this wench, now—what's the fool grievin'
about? Ain't the world wide enough? Let some carters with
oxen pass by the farm, or certain of the little ancients
amongst the pilgrims, an' just say the word, an' in a minute
you'll find yourself beyant Rostov, the father of all cities—
Let 'em go an' look for you then!"

And the thought of "I'll strangle myself!" was replaced
in the cropped head of Natashka by the thought of flight.
The cart began to creak and sway. Evsei lapsed into silence
and led the horse off to a well in the middle of the market-
place. The sun was setting beyond a great monastery garden, in the direction they had come from, and the windows
in the yellow jail which stood opposite the monastery,
across the way, gleamed with gold. And the sight of the
jail aroused the thought of flight still more. "There, escaped
folk manage to get along too! Only, they do be saying that
the holy little ancients scald with boiling milk the eyes of
the wenches and lads they steal, and then palm them off as
poor little unfortunates, to make kindly folk shell out;
whilst the carters carry them off to the very sea and sell
them to the Nogai Tatars. . . . Things so fall out, too,
that the masters catch their runaways, forge leg-irons on to

them, and put them in jail. . . . But I guess them prisons, as Gervasska says, is full of your own kind, and not of cattle!"

But the windows of the jail were dimming; her thoughts were becoming confused. No, running away was still more frightful than strangling oneself! Evsei, too, had fallen silent, had sobered up.

"We're a bit late, lassie," he was saying, by now uneasily, jumping up and perching sideways on the edge of the cart.

And the cart, getting out on the paved highway, again began to jolt, to jar, and to rattle sharply over the cobble stones.—"Ah, the best thing of all, now, would be to turn the cart back!" Natashka half-thought, half-felt. To turn it back, to gallop all the way to Dry Valley, and to fall down at the feet of her masters! But Evsei was urging his horse on. The cathedral no longer seemed a silver star beyond the houses. Ahead lay a white, barren street, the white, cobble-paved roadway, white houses; and all this terminated in the enormous white cathedral under its new cupola of white tin, and the sky over it had become a wan blue, and arid. . . . But there, at home, at this time the dew was already falling, the garden was fragrant with freshness, there was a pleasant odour issuing from the warm kitchen; far beyond the cultivated plains, beyond the silvery poplars on the boundaries of the garden, beyond the time-worn bath-house, so sacred to her, the evening glow was burning out, while the doors of the parlour were open on the balcony, the scarlet light of the glow mingling with the dusk in the corners of the room. . . .

And the young lady of the house, with a sallow-swarthy

complexion and dark eyes, who resembled both Grand-father and Petr Petrovich, was every minute adjusting the sleeves of her light loose-fitting dress of orange silk, intently following the notes as she sat with her back to the evening glow, and, as she struck the yellowed keys, filling the parlour with the triumphantly canorous, delectably despairing strains of Oghinski's *Polonaise* and apparently paying no attention whatsoever to the military officer standing behind her: thickset, dark-visaged, with his left arm akimbo, and in grim concentration watching her agile hands. . . .

"She's got her man, and I have mine," Natashka used to half-think, half-feel on such evenings, and, the heart swooning within her, would run off into the chill, dewy garden, clambering deep into the wilderness of nettles and the acridly smelling damp burdocks, and then stand there, awaiting that which could never befall: that the young master, Petr Petrovich, might come down from the balcony, walk along the garden-path, catch sight of her, and, suddenly turning aside, approach her with rapid strides, while she, from terror and happiness, let not a single sound escape her. . . .

But the cart rattled onward. All around her was the town, sultry and stinking—the same town she had hitherto pictured to herself as something enchanted. And Natashka, with a sickly wonder, gazed at the well-dressed populace pacing to and fro over the flagstones near the houses, near the gates and the shops with open doors— "And what ever made Evsei travel this way?" she was thinking. "How did he ever pluck up the courage to go rattling through here with his cart?"

But they passed the white cathedral, started going toward the shallow river down dusty hill-sides, rutted and pitted, past sooty smithies, past the tumbledown hovels of the local citizenry. . . . Again came the familiar odours of sun-warmed, fresh water, of slime, of the evening freshness of the fields. The first light glimmered in the distance on a hill, in a lonely little house near a turnpike.—And now they had come entirely out into the open, had crossed a bridge, and come up to the turnpike—and their eyes beheld the stone-paved, deserted road, showing dimly white and running away into the endless distance, into the indigo-blue of the fresh night over the steppe. The horse struck a jog-trot and, after passing the turnpike, fell into a steady walk. And again one could hear that at night all is quiet, exceedingly quiet, upon earth and in the sky—save for a jingle-bell sobbing somewhere far away. It sobbed ever more audibly, ever more resoundingly, and finally blended with the well-timed beats of a troika, with the rhythmic rumble of wheels running and approaching over the paved high-road. The troika was driven by a young stage-driver (free, and not a serf); while in his half-covered carriage there was sitting an army officer, his chin buried in the collar of his hooded uniform overcoat. As he came up with the cart, he raised his head for an instant—and suddenly Natashka caught sight of his red collar, his black moustache, his youthful eyes, which were flashing under a casque that was somewhat like a bucket. She cried out and keeled over in a dead faint.

An insane thought had flared up in her head that this was Petr Petrovich, and, by that pain and tenderness which went like lightning through her susceptible, lowly heart, she had suddenly comprehended what she had been deprived of: of being near him.—Evsei made a dash for the travelling-jug and began dashing water over her cropped, lolling head.

Thereupon she was brought to by an attack of nausea and quickly put her head over the side of the cart. Evsei supported her clammy forehead with the palm of his hand.—And then, relieved, chilled, with the collar of her blouse sopping wet, she lay on her back and contemplated the stars. The thoroughly frightened Evsei kept silent, thinking that she had fallen asleep; he merely shook his head from time to time and occasionally (and hopefully) urged on his horse. The cart shook and ran on and on. But to the little wench it seemed that she was without a body, that now all she had left was her soul. And this soul felt "like it were in the Kingdom of Heaven itself."

A little scarlet flower, grown in faery gardens, was this love of hers. But into the steppe, into a wilderness still more primeval than the wilderness of Dry Valley, did she betake this her love, in order that there, in quietude and loneliness, she might overcome its first sweet and searing torments, and then for a long time, forever, till the headstone would be put over her grave, bury it deep within the depths of her Dry Valley soul. . . .

VI

Love in Dry Valley was of an extraordinary nature. Extraordinary, too, was hatred.

Grandfather, who had perished just as ludicrously as his slayer, just as all those in Dry Valley were perishing, was killed in the same year that Nathalia was exiled. On the Feast of the Intercession of the Holy Virgin, which was a high holiday in Dry Valley, Petr Petrovich had invited a lot of guests and was very much excited: would the leader of the local nobility keep the promise he had given to attend? Grandfather, too, was joyously excited—no one knew over what.—The leader came, and the dinner was a glorious success. It was both noisy and jolly—Grandfather felt the gayest of all.

Early on the morning of the 2nd of October (the very next day) he was found on the floor of the parlour, dead.

In resigning from active service Petr Petrovich did not conceal the fact that he was sacrificing himself for the sake of saving the honour of the Khrushchevs, the ancestral nest and the ancestral estate. He did not conceal the fact that he would have to take the management of that estate, "willy-nilly," into his own hands. He would also have to form acquaintanceships, so that he might associate with the more enlightened and useful among the noblemen of the district, and simply to keep up his relations with the others.

And, in the beginning, he carried out all this punctiliously: he paid visits even to all the small landowners, even down to the small farm of his aunt, Olga Kyrillovna, a monstrously fat old woman who suffered from sleeping-sickness and who cleaned her teeth with snuff. . . . By fall no one any longer wondered that Petr Petrovich was managing the estate autocratically. And, too, by now his appearance was no longer merely that of a young Adonis of an officer who had come home on leave, but that of a proprietor, of a young landowner. Whenever he became confused now, the flush that mantled his cheeks was no longer

as deep as on former occasions. He took good care of his
person, had filled out, wore expensive Tatar jackets; he
indulged himself in red Tatar slippers for his small feet;
his small hands he adorned with turquoise rings. His lovely
eyes proved to be, to the wonder of all, not black, but hazel,
as befits a man with a dark complexion. Arcadii Petrovich,
for some reason, felt embarrassed about looking into these
eyes, was always at a loss about a topic of conversation with
him, yielded to Petr Petrovich in everything at first, and,
for days at a stretch, was away hunting.

On the Feast of the Intercession Petr Petrovich had
wanted to charm every single one of his guests by his open-
handed hospitality, and also to show that none other than
he was the first personage in the house. But Grandfather was
dreadfully in the way. Grandfather was blissfully happy,
but tactless, garrulous, and pitiful, in his small velvet cap
which had been blessed by contact with the bones of a
saint, and in his new, inordinately wide, blue Cossack coat,
made by the household tailor. Grandfather, too, had
imagined himself an open-handedly hospitable host, and
bustled about from early morning, contriving some silly
ceremony out of the reception of the guests. One of the
leaves of the door from the entrance hall into the dining-
room was never opened. He himself moved back the metal
catches at the top and bottom of this leaf, himself moving
up a chair, and, all shaking, climbing up on it to reach the
upper catch. And when he had thrown both leaves of the
door open at last, he stationed himself on the threshold and,
taking advantage of the silence of Petr Petrovich, who was
almost fainting from humiliation and resentment, but who
had determined to endure everything in patience, did not

leave his place until the last guest had arrived. He did not take his eyes off the front entrance, and they had to open that door as well; this too, it appeared, was demanded by some old custom. In his excitement he shifted from foot to foot at his post; but whenever he caught sight of a guest entering, he would dash forward to meet him, hurriedly execute an old-fashioned scrape, hop upward a little, crossing his legs like a dancing master, deliver a low bow, and, spluttering in his agitation, say to each guest, even to those whom he did not know:

"Oh, how glad I am—how glad to see you! It's a long time since you've dropped in on me! Step in, do—step in!"

Petr Petrovich was also infuriated because Grandfather, for some reason, informed each and every guest of little Tonia's departure to Lunevo, to Olga Kyrillovna's: "To-nechka got sick from loneliness; she's gone off to her dear aunt for the whole autumn."

What were the guests to think after such unsolicited announcements? For the episode with Voitkevich was, of course, already known to all and sundry. Voitkevich may possibly have really had serious intentions, what with his enigmatic sighs whenever he was in Tonechka's vicinity, playing piano duets with her, reading Pushkin to her in a subterranean voice, or else reciting to her with morose pensiveness: "Thou art betrothed to one dead by holy words that thou hast said. . . ."

Yet Tonechka would flare up in fury at his every attempt, even the most innocent, to express his feelings—such as offering her a flower, for instance; and Voitkevich had suddenly gone away. But when he was gone, Tonechka took to having sleepless nights, to sitting by an open window

237

in the dark, just as though awaiting a certain time, known only to herself, to break into loud sobbing and thus awaken Petr Petrovich. For a long time he would lie with clenched teeth, listening to her sobs, and to the broken, drowsy murmur of the poplars beyond the windows, in the dark garden: a murmur like the sound of a never-ceasing drizzle. Then he would go to calm her. The maids, too, with sleep-laden faces, went to calm her as well; occasionally Grandfather would also come running in alarm. Thereupon Tonechka would start in stamping her feet, shrieking as she did so:

"Get away from me—you're my bitter enemies, all of you!" And the thing would wind up with hideous vituperation—almost a brawl.

"But do understand—do understand," Petr Petrovich would hiss in fury, after driving the maids and Grandfather out of the room, slamming the door to, and grasping the hasp hard and fast, "do understand, you viper—what will people imagine?"

"Oh!" Tonechka would squeal out in a frenzy. "Papa dear, he's yelling all over the place that I have a big belly!"

And, clutching his head, Petr Petrovich would dash out of her room.

On the Feast of the Intercession, too, he had more than once felt like clutching his head. Gervasska, likewise, worried him: what if he should say something impertinent if Petr Petrovich were not careful of what *he* said?

Gervasska had shot up fearfully. Huge, ungainly, yet the most striking, the most intelligent among the servants, he, too, was togged out in a blue Cossack coat, loose, baggy trousers of the same colour, and soft, heelless boots of goatskin. A kerchief of lilac-coloured woollen yarn was tied about his thin, dark neck. His black, dry, coarse hair he had combed back with a parting on one side, but had refused to have his hair clipped short in the back, and merely had it cut evenly all around. He had nothing to shave— there were only two or three scanty and coarse curls showing black on his chin and near the corners of his great mouth, of which it was said: "His mouth goes from ear to ear, an' it buttons in the rear." Lanky-legged, very broad in his bony, flat chest, with a small head and deep eye-sockets, with thin, ash-blue lips, and large, bluish teeth, he, this ancient Aryan, this Parsee of Dry Valley, had already received his nickname: The Borzoi. On seeing him bare his teeth, on hearing his occasional little coughs, many thought: "Oh, but you're going to croak soon, Borzoi!" But aloud they dignified this milksop by calling him by his full name and patronymic, Gervassii Aphanassievich— a dignity not extended to the other servants.

The masters, as well, feared him. The masters had the same quirks in their make-up as the servants did: they had either to command or to fear. To the wonder of the domestics, Gervasska had nothing whatsoever comin' to him for his impertinent answer to Grandfather on the day of Petr Petrovich's arrival. Arcadii Petrovich had said to Gervasska, succinctly: "You're absolutely an animal, brother!" To which he had received an answer that was likewise exceedingly succinct: "I can't stand him, sir!" But it had been Gervasska himself who had come to Petr Petrovich; he stopped on the threshold, and, as was his way, slouching back in a free and easy manner on his legs (which were disproportionately long as compared with his torso, and which were clad in the loosest of belled trousers), and with his left knee projecting angularly, made a request to be flogged.

"I'm entirely too rude and hot-headed a fellow, sir," he had said indifferently, his dark eyes sparkling.

And Petr Petrovich had sensed a hint in the word "hot-headed" and took water.

"There's plenty of time for that, my dear fellow—plenty of time!" he raised his voice with assumed sternness. "Get out of here! I can't bear the sight of anybody as impertinent as you. . . ."

Gervasska remained standing and kept silent. Then he said:

"Very well, if such be your will."

He stood yet awhile longer, twisting the coarse hair on his upper lip, moved his livid jaws like a dog, without his face expressing any emotion whatsoever, and then walked out. Since that time he had become firmly convinced of the advantage of this expedient: of expressing nothing on his face and being as succinct as possible in his answers. As for Petr Petrovich, he began avoiding not only having any conversation with him, but even looking him in the eyes.

Just as indifferently, just as enigmatically, did Gervasska conduct himself on the Feast of the Intercession. Everybody had run his or her feet off in getting ready for the holiday, giving and receiving instructions, scolding, arguing, scrubbing floors, cleaning the dark, heavy silver of the icons with chalk-paste that turned blue as one cleaned, kicking out the dogs that kept on creeping into the entries, worrying that the gelatine would not jellify, that there would be a shortage of forks, that the turnovers and faggots would be overdone. Gervasska alone fleered calmly and kept on saying to Casimir, the frantic alcoholic chef:

"Take it easy, father deacon, or else your under-cassock will bu'st."

"See that you don't get drunk," Petr Petrovich, stirred up over the uncertainty of the coming of the guest of honour, had absent-mindedly said to Gervasska.

"I ain't never drunk a drop in all me born days," Gervasska had let drop in answer, as if to an equal. "Drink don't interest me."

And later, in the presence of all the guests, Petr Petrovich had yelled all over the house, even ingratiatingly:

"Gervassii Aphanassievich! Don't you go and get lost now, please! Without you I'd be like a man without hands."

While Gervasska, in the politest manner possible, and with dignity, had responded:

"Don't put yourself out, sir, if you please. I wouldn't dast leave the room."

He waited on the guests as never before. He fully justified the words of Petr Petrovich, who said to the guests in his hearing:

"You can't even imagine to what an extent this dunderhead is impertinent! But he is positively a genius! He has hands of gold!"

How could Petr Petrovich have possibly even supposed that he was dropping into the cup the one drop that would make it overflow? Grandfather heard Petr Petrovich's words; the old man began to tug at the breast of his Cossack coat and suddenly called out to the leader of the nobility, across the whole table:

"Your Excellency! Extend your helping hand to us! I

come to you as to a father with a complaint against this my servant! This one, this one—this Gervassii Aphanassievich Kulikov! He makes naught of me at every step! He, and none other—"

He was cut short, reasoned with, calmed down. Grandfather had been stirred to tears, but everybody had fallen to calming him down so unanimously, and with such respectfulness (somewhat mocking, of course), that he gave in and once more felt himself childishly happy. Gervasska stood at attention near the wall, with downcast eyes and with his head turned slightly to one side. Grandfather could see that this giant had too small a head, that it would be still smaller if it were to be clipped, that the nape of his neck was ridged, and that there was a particularly great amount of hair precisely at the back of his neck—coarse, black hair, roughly hacked, as if with a hatchet, and forming a protrusion over his thin neck. From sunburn, from the winds of the hunting-fields, Gervasska's dark face was scaling in spots, and bore pale-lilac blotches. And Grandfather, in fear and alarm, cast occasional glances at Gervasska, but nevertheless shouted joyously to his guests:

"Very well, I forgive him! Only, because of that, I shan't let you go for three whole days, my dear guests! I shan't let you go, not for anything! But especially I beg of you not to go away before evening. When it gets on toward evening, I'm not myself; there's such a sadness falls upon me, and such eeriness!—There are little clouds rolling up. . . . Two more of Boney's mounseers were caught in the Troshin woods, they say. . . . I'm bound to die in the evening, sure as fate. . . . Remember my words! It was Martin Zadeka, the soothsayer, who foretold me that, himself. . . ."

But it was early in the morning that he died.

He had had his own way, after all; a great many people had remained, "for his sake," to sleep over. All evening they drank tea. There was an awesome quantity of jam, and that of all different sorts, so that one could always walk up and try a little of this and then walk up again and try a little of that. Then a great number of card-tables were placed about, and so many spermaceti candles were lit that they were reflected in all the mirrors, and there was an aureate glow, as in a church, throughout the rooms, filled with the fumes of fragrant Zhukovski Latakia and with hubbub and conversation. But the main thing was that many *did* remain to stay overnight. And therefore there was not only a new day of merriment ahead, but there were also great cares and worries—for, had it not been for him, for Petr Kyrillich, the holiday would never have come off so well, there would never have been so animated and so rich a dinner!

"Yes, yes," Grandfather was thinking excitedly that night, after he had taken off his Cossack coat and was standing in his bedroom before a prie-dieu, before the waxen tapers burning on it, contemplating the blackened image of Mercurius, that holy man, "yes, yes—death is cruel to a sinner. . . . Let not the sun go down upon your wrath!"

But at this point he recalled that he had wanted to think upon something else. With his back hunched, and whispering the fiftieth Psalm, he paced through the room, snuffed the incense cone that looked something like a little nun (it was smouldering on his little night-table), picked up the Psalter, and, opening it, with a deep, happy sigh lifted up his eyes anew to the headless saint. And suddenly he struck upon that which he had wanted to think about, and a smile lit up his face:

"Yes, yes—'When the old man is alive, folks are fain to kill him off; when the old man is gone, they would fain buy him back!'"

Afraid of oversleeping, and of overlooking some instruction or other, he hardly slept at all. But early in the morning, when that peculiar quiet which follows only gala occasions still reigned throughout the rooms, still untidied and redolent of tobacco, he went cautiously, in his bare feet, into the parlour, solicitously picked up several bits of chalk which had been dropped near the unfolded tables with their green-cloth tops, and ah'd faintly as he caught a glimpse of the garden beyond the glass doors—of the bright sheen of a chill, azure sky—of the morning hoar-frost which covered with its silver the floor and the railing of the balcony—of the brown leaves among the denuded thickets under the balcony. He opened the door and sniffed the air: there was still an acrid and spirituous odour of autumnal corruption emanating from the bushes, but this odour was becoming lost amid a wintry freshness. The sun, which had barely appeared beyond the village, lit up the tree-tops of the picturesque garden-path—the tops of the half-denuded birches, white-trunked and spattered with fine, flaked gold—and there was a lovely, joyous tone of elusive lilac about these white-and-gold tree-tops, showing clearly against the azure of the sky. A dog ran past in the cold shadow of the balcony, crunching over the grass, which was frost-bitten and looked just as if it had been sprinkled with salt. This crunching reminded him that winter was not so far off, and, with an agreeable shudder of his shoulders, Grandfather stepped back into the room and, with bated breath, started to shift about and to place back the heavy furniture, which emitted a low growl as it was shoved over the floor. From time to time he glanced at the mirror, wherein the sky was reflected. Suddenly Gervasska entered, inaudibly and quickly: without his Cossack coat, sleepy, and "as bad-tempered as the Devil," as he himself happened to relate afterwards.

He entered and sternly called out in a whisper:

"Not so much noise, you! What are you shovin' your nose for into work that ain't yourn?"

Grandfather lifted up his excited face and, with the same tenderness which had never forsaken him all day yesterday and all of last night, answered, likewise in a whisper:

"There, you see what sort of a fellow you are, Gervassii! I forgave you yesterday, but you, instead of being grateful to your master—"

"I'm sick an' tired of you, you old slobberin' fool!" Gervasska cut him short. "Get out of me way!"

Grandfather looked with fright at the back of Gervasska's head, now still more prominent above his thin neck, which was sticking up out of the open collar of his white shirt. But he flared up and blocked with his body the folding-table which he wanted to drag into a corner.

"You get out of my way!" he cried out in a low voice, after an instant's thought. "It's you who ought to be making way for the master—you'll bring me to sticking a dagger in your ribs yet!"

"Ah!" said Gervasska in vexation, with a gleam of his teeth, and struck him in the chest with the back of his hand.

Grandfather slipped on the smooth oaken floor, threw up his arms—and struck one of his temples right against a sharp corner of the table.

On catching sight of the blood, and of Grandfather's eyes, with their pupils senselessly diverging, and of the gaping mouth, Gervasska, without himself knowing why he was doing it, tore off Grandfather's still warm chest a little golden image and a scapulary on a soiled, worn cord . . . looked over his shoulder, and then tore Grandmother's wedding ring off the dead man's little finger. . . . Then, inaudibly and quickly, he went out of the parlour— and became a needle in a haystack.

The only living person among all the Dry Valley folk who saw him after that was Nathalia.

VII

While Nathalia was living in Little Ploughs, two more great events had taken place in Dry Valley. One was Petr Petrovich's marriage; the other, the departure of the two brothers as volunteers in the Crimean campaign.

She came back only after two years; everybody had forgotten all about her. And, having come back, she did not recognize Dry Valley, even as Dry Valley failed to recognize her.

On that summer evening when the cart, sent from the masters' manor-house, had come creaking up to the hut on the farm, and Natashka had jumped out on the threshold, Evsei Bodulya had cried out in wonder:

"Come, can it really be you, Natashka?"

"Why, and who else should it be?" Natashka had answered, with a barely perceptible smile. And Evsei had shaken his head.

"You sure has lost a great deal of your good looks!"

And yet she had merely become unlike her former self. From a cropped, round-faced, and clear-eyed slip of a girl she had become transformed into a short but graceful lass, rather thin, but not at all sickly, and reserved in asking or answering questions. She was barefooted, in a length of checked woollen material wrapped around her by way of a skirt, and in an embroidered blouse; although she had her head covered with a dark kerchief, after the way of the peasant women in our region, she was a trifle swarthy from the sun, and her face was covered with tiny freckles, the colour of millet. But to Evsei, a true son of Dry Valley, the dark kerchief and the tan and the freckles all seemed ugly, of course. Yes, and she herself supposed that they were just that. However, anybody might have noticed, by that slight smile with which she had said: "Why, and who else should it be?" that she was proud of the changes which had taken place in her, and that she was apparently even pleased at being homely.

On the way to Dry Valley Evsei said:

"There, now, lass, you've become fit to be a bride. D'you want to get married, now?"

She merely tossed and shook her head.

"No, Uncle Evsei—I'll never marry."

"An' whatsomever may the reason for that be?" asked Evsei—and even took the pipe out of his mouth. And unhurriedly, half in jest and half in earnest, she explained that it weren't everybody, now, that could get married; she'd sure enough be put to waiting on the young mistress— whilst the young mistress had given herself to God, and therefore wouldn't let her get married; and, besides, she, Nathalia, had dreamt dreams that was all too plain, and that more nor once—

"Well, an' just what was it you dreamt?" asked Evsei.

"Why, just this and that—mere trifles," she answered him. "Gervasska, he frightened me no end at the time Petr Kyrillich come to die. He told me a lot of news, and I got to thinking— Well, and that's how I come to have the dreams."

"But is it really the truth, now, that this here Gervasska stopped over for a midday bite at your place?"

Natashka pondered awhile.

"He did that. He comes and he says: 'I'm come to you from the masters on important business; only let me have a little somethin' to eat first.' Well, we set out a meal for him, like we would for any wayfarer. Well, when he'd eaten his fill, he walks out of the hut and tips me a wink. I ran out—and, just round a corner of the hut, he made a clean breast of everything to me, and then went on his way."

"But how is it you didn't call out for the people in charge?"

"That's easier said nor done. He threatened to kill me. Ordered me not to say anything before dinner-time. But to the old man and woman he said: 'I'm goin' to get me some sleep under the storehouse. . . .'"

All the domestics in Dry Valley regarded her with great curiosity; her friends and coevals in the maids' room pestered her with questions. But she answered her friends as briefly as ever, and just as though she were admiring from the side a certain role she had taken upon herself.

"I've had a good time," she kept on repeating.

While once, in the tone of a pilgrim woman, she had said:

"There's a plenty of all things at the Lord God's. I've had a good time."

And simply, without any shilly-shallyings, she stepped into the working, everyday life of Dry Valley, as though not at all surprised that there was no Grandfather, that the young masters had gone off to war as volunteers, that the young lady had become touched and was roaming all over the house, following in Grandfather's footsteps, that Dry Valley was being managed by a new mistress, who was a stranger to everybody,—small, plump, very lively, pregnant, who had come out of a Moscow finishing school and had at one time been governess with the masters of Chirkizovo, but who now used to speak of Petr Petrovich as Petrusha.

She had once called out at dinner: "Do call this—what d'you call her?—Natashka!"

And Natashka had entered, quickly and inaudibly, crossed herself, made a bow toward the corner where the holy images were, then to the lady and the young lady of the house, and stood waiting for interrogations and orders. Of course it was only the lady of the house who interrogated her; the young lady, who had shot up exceedingly and had become very thin and whose nose had grown still sharper, did not let even so much as a word drop as she fixedly and dully regarded Nathalia. And it was the mistress who had assigned Nathalia to attend the young lady. And Nathalia had made a curtsy and simply said:

"I'm at your service."

The young lady, regarding Nathalia just as attentively and indifferently as before, had suddenly pounced upon her on the evening of the same day, and, with her eyes crossed from fury, had cruelly and with delight yanked and torn Nathalia's hair because she had been clumsy in pulling off one of the young lady's stockings. Natashka began crying like a child, yet let everything pass without a word. But when she had gone into the maids' room and had sat down on a chest, she even smiled through the tears that hung on her eyelashes, as she picked the torn clusters out of her hair.

"My, but she's mean as mean!" said she. "I'm going to have a hard time with her."

The young lady, when she awoke the next morning, lay abed for a long time, while Natashka stood near the threshold and, with head bowed, watched out of one corner of her eye the pale face of her mistress.

"Well, what did you see in your dreams?" the young mistress asked her at last, just as apathetically as if someone else were talking for her. Nathalia answered:

"Nothing, it seems."

And thereupon the young lady, just as precipitately as the day before, jumped out of bed, insanely let her cup fly at Nathalia, tea and all, and, falling on the bed and screaming, burst into bitter tears. Natashka managed to dodge the cup, and soon learned to dodge with extraordinary nimbleness. It turned out that the young lady would occasionally retort to those stupid serving-wenches who answered her question concerning their dreams with: "We ain't seen nothin'," by screaming: "Well, then, cook up some lie or other!" But since Natashka was not mistress of the art of lying, she had to develop another ability within her: that of dodging things.

Finally they brought a man of medicine for the young mistress. The man of medicine learnedly diagnosed her ailment as "pulmonary ossification," and prescribed a mountain of pills, a sea of black drops. Apprehensive of being poisoned, Tonia compelled Natashka to sample all these pills and drops, and, without demur, sample them all she did, one after the other. She had learned soon after her coming that the young lady had longed for her arrival as one benighted longs for the "light of day." It was none other than Tonia who had recalled her existence, had strained and strained her eyes watching for the cart to come from Little Ploughs, had ardently assured all and sundry that she would get entirely well, would be freed of every ache and yearning, just as soon as Natashka would return from banishment. Natashka had returned—and was met with utter indifference.

But: weren't the young lady's tears the tears of bitter disenchantment? Wasn't the cruel notion of compelling Nathalia to sample the medicines really a fierce avidity to get well? Natashka's heart gave a throb when she realized all this. She went out into the corridor, sat down on a coffer, and again began to weep. She wept softly, enjoying her tears; for long stretches at a time she stared fixedly through her tears at a point somewhere in the distance. She was doing just what other peasant women do on such occasions, yet her thoughts were of the little mirror, of her departure for Little Ploughs, of all she had lived through there—and once more her face would become distorted like a child's, and she would fall to wailing, but barely audibly.

"Well, now, do you feel better?" the young mistress had asked her on one occasion as she had entered with swollen eyes.

"Better, miss," Natashka had said in a whisper, although, on account of the medicines, her heart would be stilled every now and then and her head was turning; and, walking up to the young lady, she had kissed her hand warmly.

And, for a long while thereafter, she walked about with drooping eyelashes, afraid to lift up her eyes at the young lady, touched by pity both for her mistress and for her own loneliness.

"Oo-ooh, you tuft-headed snake-in-the-grass!" Soloshka, one of her fellow-maids, had once yelled at her—Soloshka, who more often than anybody else had tried to become Nathalia's confidante in all her secrets and emotions, yet was forever running her head against Nathalia's brief, simple answers, precluding any of the charm of girlish friendship.

Natashka had smiled sadly.

"Oh, well," she had answered thoughtfully, "you're right, at that. Tell me who your friends are, and I'll tell you who you be.—There are times when I don't grieve as much after my father and my mother as I do after them tuft-head country folks of mine at Little Ploughs. . . ."

But she had hardly told the truth. She could not forget Little Ploughs; she could have told with rapture of many things concerning the place, had it not been for the role she had taken upon herself. Yet she had never really considered "them tuft-head country folks" as dear to her as her father and mother.

At Little Ploughs she had not at first considered as at all significant any of the new things surrounding her. She and Evsei had arrived toward morning, and on that morning the only things that had struck her as odd were that the hut was very long and very white, visible from afar among the surrounding plains; that the tuft-head woman who was stoking up the oven greeted them hospitably, while her tuft-head husband paid no attention to Evsei's talk. Evsei jabbered away with never a rest: about the masters, and about the Dry Valley overseer, and about the heat during their journey, and about what he had eaten in the town, and about Petr Petrovich—and, as a matter of course, about the affair of the little mirror, while Sharyi, the tuft-head mujik, or The Badger, as he was called in Dry Valley, had merely tossed his head from time to time, and, when Evsei had fallen quiet at last, suddenly glanced at him absent-mindedly, and most gaily began to sing *Blizzard Whirl, Blizzard Swirl* in a nasal whine. . . .

Then, little by little, she began coming to herself and to be wonderstruck by Little Ploughs, to find ever more charm in the place and an ever-greater dissimilarity to Dry Valley. What was the hut of the tuft-heads alone worth, with its whiteness, its well-made, evenly cut thatch of reeds! How rich the orderliness of this hut's interior as compared with the slovenly poverty of the Dry Valley dwellings! What costly tinsel images hung in one corner of this house—what wondrous paper flowers surrounded them—how beautifully the gaily broidered towels hung above them showed! And what about the flowered cloth on the table? And the dove-grey pots and pipkins, ranged row on row on the shelves near the oven?

But most amazing of all were her hosts. In just what way they were amazing she could not altogether understand, but she constantly felt that they were. Never yet had she seen any mujiks as neat, placid, and orderly as Sharyi. He was not tall; his head tapered to a wedge, and the thick, strong silver of its hair was clipped; he was clean-shaven, save for his moustaches, also silvery, and narrow, like a Tatar's; his face and neck were black from sunburn, and all in deep wrinkles—but these, too, were somehow orderly, well defined, and, for some reason or other, called for. His walk was awkward, since he wore heavy boots; his breeches, of coarse white linen, were stuck into these boots, and into his breeches he tucked his shirt of the same material, roomy under the arm-pits, with a turned-down collar. As he walked, he stooped over a little. But neither this mannerism, nor his wrinkles, nor his grey hair, made him look aged. There was none of our Dry Valley weariness, nor of its sluggishness, about his face. His small eyes had a sharp and slyly mocking look. He reminded Natashka of an old Serbian who had once come wandering into Dry Valley with a boy who scraped on a fiddle.

As for his tuft-head yoke-mate, Marina—she had been nicknamed The Spear by the Dry Valley folk. Stately was this tall, fifty-year-old woman. Her face, with its broad cheek-bones, was rather coarse, yet almost good-looking because of its straightforwardness and the austere liveliness of her eyes: one could not determine whether they were agate or amber-grey, since they were as chatoyant as a cat's. A yellowish tan covered evenly her smooth skin, so different from the skins of the Dry Valley dwellers. A large black-and-gold, red-dotted kerchief rested in a high turban on her head; by way of a skirt she had a black, narrow length of woollen material closely enveloping her elongated, almost maidenly contours and sharply setting off the whiteness of her blouse. She shod her stockingless feet in shoes with metal-tipped heels; her bare calves were thin, but rounded out; from the sun they had become like polished yellow-brown wood. And when at times she would sing at her work, contracting her eyebrows, in a strong, chesty voice, the song concerning the siege of Pochaev town by the unbelievers:

> When the even-glow began
> And lit all Pochaev town—

and of how the Mother of God had herself "come for to deliver" the town's holy monastery—when she sang, there was in her voice so much of hopelessness, of ululation, of something churchly, yet, at the same time, so much of grandeur, of power, of menace, that Natashka, in eerie ecstasy, did not take her eyes off the singer.

This tuft-head couple had no children; Natashka was an orphan; and, had she been living in a Dry Valley household, she would have been called an adopted daughter and, at times, a thief; now they would have pitied her, now made her life miserable with recriminations. But these tuft-heads were almost cold to her, yet equable in their treatment of her, not at all inquisitive, and none too talkative.

In the autumn the country-wives and wenches of Kaluga were drafted for the reaping and the threshing; these women were dubbed "fly-aparts," because of their loose and motley sarafans. At such times the farm was a noisy place; there was a never-stilled din of talk. But Nathalia kept aloof from the fly-aparts; they had the repute of being loose, of having the pox; they were amply-bosomed, brazen, and saucy; they cursed atrociously and with gusto, bywords and pithy sayings simply pouring out of them; they mounted horses astride, like any mujik; they galloped along as if Old Nick himself were after them.

Had Nathalia's mode of life been an accustomed one, her grief would have become dissipated in frank confessions, in tears and songs. But then, her songs did not jibe with the songs of the others. The fly-aparts would lead off their songs in their coarse voices and then swell out in an inordinately close and stentorian chorus, with yells and whistling. All Sharyi would sing were things that were mocking and made you dance. While Marina in her songs— even the love-songs!—was austere, proud, and pensively sombre:

> On the dam I willows planted,
> And they sway—

she would narrate in a plaintive, drawling recitative, and then add, lowering her voice, decisively and hopelessly:

> And the one I came to love—
> My own dear, my own love—
> Is gone away. . . .

But what songs did Natashka know? What had remained in Dry Valley of Slavic song, which had degenerated there,

had there become as shallow as a stream in dry weather?
Only plaints against fate, against father and mother, because " 'gainst my will they are marryin' me, givin' me up
to—" a cruel father-in-law, or a cruel mother-in-law, or
cruel sisters-in-law. . . . Or else there were timorous reproaches to one who had whispered all sorts of sweet things
into a fair one's ears and then had forsaken the owner
thereof, up to them in trouble:

> Weren't it only yesterday, before one an' all,
> That your own dear you did poor me call?

And so in solitude, in the wilderness, she had drained,
slowly, the first bitter-sweet venom of unrequited love, had
overcome, through suffering, her shame, her jealousy, her
fearful and endearing dreams, which had often come to
her of nights, her unfulfillable reveries and expectations,
which had long haunted her in the silent days of the steppe.
Often a searing feeling of the wrong done her was replaced
in her heart by tenderness—her passion and despair by
resignation, by a desire for a life near *him* (though most
unassuming, most unobtrusive), for a love forever hidden
from all, and expecting nothing, demanding nothing.

The tidings, the news which reached her from Dry Valley,
would sober her up. But if there were no tidings for a long
time, if there were no feeling of the everyday life of Dry
Valley, Dry Valley would begin to seem so lovely, so desired, that at times she had not strength enough to endure
her loneliness and sorrow. . . . Suddenly Gervasska had
appeared. Hurriedly, abruptly he had flung out to her all
the news of Dry Valley; within half an hour he had told
her what another could not have told in even a day—up

to and including his "shoving" Grandfather to his death. And then he had said firmly:

"Well, and now good-bye forever!"

Burning her through and through with his huge eyes as she stood there overwhelmed, he called out as he set foot on the highway:

"And it's high time you knocked all that foolishness out of your head! He's like to marry any day, any minute now, whilst you ain't good enough to be his mistress, even.— Come to your senses!"

And come to her senses she did. She lived through the dreadful news, became her own self—and came to her senses.

After that the days began to drag one after the other, evenly, tediously, like those pilgrim women who kept on trudging over the paved road that ran past the farm, and, as they paused for a rest, held long conversations with her, teaching her patience and trustfulness in the Lord God, whose name was pronounced stolidly, piteously; but, above all, they taught her one rule: not to think.

"Whether we think or whether we don't, things ain't a-goin' to come out our way," the pilgrim women would say as they retied their bast slippers, puckering up their tortured faces and looking into the distance of the steppe with eyes of exhaustion. "There's a plenty of all things at the Lord God's. . . . Pluck a few scallions for us, lassie, when nobody's lookin'. . . ."

While others, as is their way, even sought to frighten her with her sins, with the other world; they held forth a promise of calamities and perils still worse than those of the present. And once Nathalia happened to dream two

258

dreadful dreams, almost directly one after the other. She was forever thinking of Dry Valley—it was rather hard not to think of it at first! She thought of her young mistress, of Grandfather, of her own future; she was trying to foretell whether she would marry, and, if she did, when and whom. . . . On one occasion her thoughts so imperceptibly passed into a dream that, with perfect clearness, she saw that the time was just before the evening of a sultry, dusty, disquietingly windy day, and that she was hastening to a pond with buckets. . . . And suddenly she sees on a hillside a hideous, large-headed dwarf, a mujik in troddendown boots, hatless, with red elf-locks, all ruffled by the wind, in an unbelted shirt, fiery-red and fluttering. "Gaffer!" she called out in alarm and terror. "Why, is there a fire somewhere?"—"Everything's goin' to be blown down to the last stick right away!" the dwarf made answer, likewise in a shout that was muffled by the scorching wind. "There's a cloud comin' the like of which you never heard tell of! An' don't even dare think of gettin' married! . . ."

As for the other dream, it was still more frightful: she seemed to be standing, at noonday, in a hot, empty hut, which somebody had barred on the outside. She was wellnigh swooning, awaiting something to befall—and then, from behind the oven, there jumped out an enormous, grey he-goat. He got up on his hind legs and went straight for her—obscenely excited, with his eyes, which were burning like coals, joyously insane and imploring. "I'm your bridegroom!" he cried out in a human voice, running up to her quickly and awkwardly, with a quick patter of his small hind hoofs, and, at full speed, falling on her breast with his front ones. . . .

When, after such dreams, she would leap up on her bed in the entry, she all but died from the palpitation of her heart, from her fear of the dark, and from the thought that she had never a soul whom she might come running to.

"Lord Jesus!" she would whisper in a patter. "Mother of God, Queen of Heaven, and all ye sainted martyrs of God!" But, since all the sainted martyrs appeared to her brown-hued and headless, like St. Mercurius, she would feel still more terrified.

And when she came to thinking over her dreams, she'd start getting it into her head that her years as a young girl were at an end, that her destiny had already been determined (it was not for nothing that something extraordinary had befallen her: her love for the young master!), that some other trials were awaiting her, that she must emulate the self-restraint of the tuft-head couple, and the simplicity and resignation of the pilgrim women. And, since all natives of Dry Valley are aye fond of playing parts, of hypnotizing themselves with the ineluctability of that which apparently has to be, although they themselves invent the latter, Natashka consequently assumed a part as well.

VIII

She could hardly stand on her feet from joy when, on the eve of St. Peter's Day, having jumped out on the threshold, she understood that Bodulya had come to fetch her, as she caught sight of the dust-covered, ramshackle cart from Dry Valley; as she caught sight of the torn hat on Bodulya's shaggy head, of his tangled, sun-faded beard, his face, tired and excited, ill-favoured and aged before its time, its features even somehow incomprehensibly lowly and disproportionate. She caught sight, too, of a hound she knew well, likewise shaggy, bearing a certain resemblance not only to Bodulya but to all of Dry Valley; this hound was of a dull grey along his spine, while from the front his chest and thick-furred neck seemed just as if they had been smoked through and through by the smoke of a chimneyless hut.

But Bodulya had voiced his surprise—and she had become self-possessed, had felt an access of pride, and had entered into her part.

On the way home Bodulya had jabbered away about whatever happened to pop into his head. He spoke of the Crimean War, now seemingly rejoicing over it, now deploring it, and Natashka would say reasoningly:

"Well, now, it seems like them French mounseers has to be brought up short. . . ."

The entire long day *en route* to Dry Valley passed in an uncanny sensation of gazing with new eyes upon old, familiar things, of reliving, as she neared her native region, her former self, of noticing changes, of recognizing the people she met.

At the turn of the highway into Dry Valley, on the fallow lands grown over with goldilocks, a two-year-old colt was romping; an urchin, with one bare foot holding down a rope halter, was hugging the colt's neck and striving to throw his other foot over the colt's back; the animal would not submit, however, running about and jolting the urchin. And Natashka became joyously excited as she recognized the lad.

They came upon Nazarushka, the centenarian gaffer, who

no longer sat in his empty cart like a mujik, squatting on
his heels, but like a country-wife, with the legs stretched
out; his shoulders were hunched up high, tensely and
weakly, his eyes were colourless and pitifully mournful;
"there weren't enough of him left to put in a coffin, even,
he were that wasted away"; he had no head-covering, and
was clad in a long, worn-out shirt, all leaden-hued from
his constantly lying atop the oven. And again her heart
gave a start: she recalled how, three years back, Arcadii
Petrovich, the best-natured and lightest-hearted of men,
had wanted to flog this same Nazarushka, who had been
caught red-handed stealing a wisp of a radish out of the
truck-garden, and how, almost dead with fright, he had
wept in the midst of his fellow-servants, who had surrounded him and were laughing and shouting:

" 'Tain't no use, Gran'pa—you sure will have to take
your breeches down! There ain't no gettin' out of it!"

And how her heart had begun to thump when she caught
sight of the common, of the string of huts, and the estate
itself: the garden, the high roof of the house, the rear walls
of the servants' quarters, of the storehouses, of the stables!
A field of yellow rye, choked with corn-flowers, came up
to these very walls, up to the quitch-grass and the cotton-
thistles. Somebody's white, brown-spotted calf was deep
among the oats, stripping and munching their clusters. All
the surroundings were peaceful, simple, usual; it was only
in her mind that everything was becoming even more unusual, ever more disquieting: in her mind, which had become altogether confused when the cart started rolling
briskly through the yard, with borzois showing whitely
here and there, as headstones show in a country church-

yard—when, after two years of living in a hut, she had first entered the cool house, so familiarly smelling of wax candles, of lime blossoms, of pantry odours, of Arcadii Petrovich's Cossack saddle, thrown down on a bench in the entry, of quail cages, now empty and hung over a window—and when she had timidly glanced up at St. Mercurius, who had been shifted out of Grandfather's bedroom into a corner of the entry. . . .

As of yore, the sombre dining-room was gaily lit by the sun, shining from the garden into the little windows. A chick, which for some unknown reason had got into the house, was emitting orphaned peeps as it wandered through the parlour. Lime blossoms were drying on the sun-warmed, brightly lit window-sills and giving forth a sweet fragrance. . . . It seemed as if all the things from of old which surrounded her now had taken on a new youth, as they always do in houses where there has been a recent death. In everything—everything!—and especially in the scent of the lime blossoms, she felt a part of her own soul, her childhood, her adolescence, her first love. And she felt pity for those who had grown up, who had died, who had changed. The lads and lasses of her own age had grown up. Many old men and women, whose heads nodded from decrepitude and who had occasionally looked out dully on God's world from the thresholds of the servants' quarters, had forever vanished out of that world. Daria Justinovna had vanished. Grandfather had vanished, who had feared death so, like a child, who had thought that death would overcome him slowly, preparing him for the final dreadful hour, and who had been mown down so unexpectedly, with such lightning speed, by its scythe.

And one could not believe that he no longer was, that it was precisely he who had crumbled to dust under the mound of a grave near the church in the Chirkizovo hamlet. One could not believe that this black, gaunt, sharp-nosed woman, now apathetic, now frenzied, now uneasily talkative and as frank with Nathalia as with an equal, and now pulling out handfuls of that same Nathalia's hair—one could not believe that this woman was the young lady Tonechka. One could not understand why the house was run by some Claudia Markovna or other—a little shrill-tongued woman with a tiny black moustache. . . . Once Natashka had timidly peeped into her bedroom, had caught a glimpse of the fateful little mirror—and had felt in her heart a sweet surging of all her former fears, joys, tenderness, expectation of shame and happiness, the odour of dew-covered burdocks under an evening glow. . . . But she drove deep within the secret places of her heart all her emotions, all her inclinations, and was ever taming, ever calming herself with the words of the pilgrim women, which words seemed to her the pinnacle of wisdom: "There's a plenty of all things at the Lord God's. . . ."

The old, old blood of Dry Valley was flowing in her veins! There was all too little flavour in the bread she ate, grown on the clayey soil surrounding Dry Valley. There was all too little savour in the water she drank, drawn from those ponds which her grandsires had dug in the bed of the dried river. Neither of the bastinado nor the rack was she afraid; the only thing she was afraid of was to be made a laughing-stock. Exhausting workdays did not frighten her; what frightened her was the unusual. Not even death held any terror for her; but she was thrown into trepidation

by dreams, the darkness of night, storm, thunder—and fire.
She bore within her, like a babe under the heart, a dim
expectancy of some inevitable calamities or other. . . .

This expectancy aged her. Then, too, she was incessantly
assuring herself that her youth had passed and was seeking confirmation of that belief in everything. And not even
a year had gone by since her return to Dry Valley when
there was not a trace left of that youthful feeling with
which she had once more set foot across the threshold of its
house.

Claudia Markovna was duly confined. Theodosia, the
poultry-keeper, was elevated to nursedom. And Theodosia,
who was still a young woman, donned the dark dress of
an old woman and became filled with humility and the
fear of God. The new Khrushchev was as yet barely able to
goggle his milk-sodden, meaningless little eyes; he dribbled
saliva in bubbles; overcome by the weight of his head, he
helplessly slumped forward, and bawled ferociously. And
yet he was already styled the young master; ancient, ancient
bits of baby talk were already heard issuing from the
nursery:

"There he is, there he is, that old boogy-mans with hims
big sack! Hey, there, boogy-mans—'tain't no use your
comin' to us—we ain't a-goin' to let you have the young
master! He ain't a-goin' to cry no more! . . ."

And Natashka followed Theodosia's example, consider-
ing herself a nurse also: the nurse and crony of her ailing
young mistress.

Olga Kyrillovna died that winter, and Natashka managed
to beg permission to go to the funeral with the old women
who were rounding out their old days in the servants'

quarters. At Lunevo, after the burial, she went through the ritual of eating shredded wheat and honey, which mess inspired her with aversion by its insipid and mawkish taste, and, upon returning to Dry Valley, told with touched emotion that the late mistress had "looked that natural, like she were alive," although even the old women could not pluck up enough courage to look at the coffin with that monstrous body.

And in the spring they imported a wizard from the Chermashnyi settlement for the young mistress: the celebrated Clim Erokhin, a comely, rich freeholder, with a hoary beard, with hoary, curly locks, parted in the middle; a very capable husbandman, usually very simple in his speech, but who became transformed into a magus by the bedside of the ailing. His clothing was remarkably sturdy and neat: an iron-drab coat, cut in at the waist and with long, belled skirts, a red sash, and strong, well-sewn boots. Crafty and keen were his small eyes; piously did they seek the holy images; carefully, with his well-built torso bent ever so slightly, would he enter the house; he started the conversation in a business-like manner. At first he spoke about the crops, about the rainfall and the drought; then he would drink tea,—leisurely, daintily; then he would again cross himself, and then (and only after all that) would inquire about the ailing person:

"It's sundown . . . gettin' dark . . . it's time," he would say with a mysterious air.

The young mistress was having the ague; she was on the verge of rolling off the bed to the floor in convulsions as, sitting in her bedroom at dusk, she waited for Clim to appear on the threshold. Nathalia, who was standing near her, was also enveloped in eerie fear from head to foot. The entire house was falling quiet; even the lady of the house herself was packing her room full of serving-wenches and talking in whispers. None durst light even a single candle; not a single voice durst raise itself. The merry Soloshka, who was doing sentry-go in the corridor near the young lady's door, in case Clim should call out or have some order to give—Soloshka felt things growing dark before her eyes, while her heart was thumping in her throat. And now he was going past her, untying, as he went, a small handkerchief with certain bits of shamanistic bones. Then, amid the graveyard silence, she heard his loud, odd voice resounding in the bedroom:

"Arise, bondswoman of God!"

Next his hoary head appeared out of the half-closed door.

"A board!" he let drop in a lifeless voice.

And the young lady, with her eyes popping out from terror, and her whole body grown as cold as a corpse, was made to stand upon this board, which was placed on the floor. It was so dark by now that Nathalia could barely distinguish Clim's face. And suddenly he was launching into his incantation, in a strange voice that somehow seemed to come from a distance:

"Philat shall arise . . . and shall the windows open . . . and throw the doors ajar . . . and call out and say: 'Come, pining—come, yearning! . . .'"

"Come, pining—come, yearning!" he was now calling out, with sudden power and awesome authority. "Pining, disappear—into woods dark, drear; thou art not wanted here! Out upon the ocean, where the sea-mew flies"—he

had by now fallen to muttering, in a muffled, sinister patter
—"out upon the wide sea Rowdy Isle doth rise. . . . There
an old bitch lies, with grey fur and eyes. . . ."

And Nathalia felt that there were not, and that there
could not be, any words more terrible than these, which
at once carried all her soul somewhere to the marge of
a wild, faery, primevally barbarous world. And one could
not but believe in their potency, just as Clim himself could
not but believe in it—Clim, who at times wrought downright miracles with those whom malady possessed; the same
Clim who was saying, as he sat in the entry after his spell
of witch-doctoring, mopping his sweating forehead with a
handkerchief and again beginning on the tea:

"Well, now, there's still two more sundowns to go. . . .
Mebbe, if God so wills, she'll get to feelin' summat easier.
. . . Did you sow buckwheat this season, ma'am? They
do be sayin' buckwheat's comin' up fine this year—fine as
fine can be!"

They were expecting the masters to come back from
Crimea that summer. But Arcadii Petrovich sent a reg-
istered letter with a new demand for money, and the news
that they could not return before the beginning of autumn,
by reason of Petr Petrovich's wound—a minor wound, but
one that required rest. Danilovna, the Sibyl of Chirkizovo,
had someone sent to her, to ask if this trouble would end
well. Danilovna went off into a dance and fell to clicking
her fingers, which, of course, signified: It would that. And
the mistress was reassured.

As for the young lady and Nathalia, they had troubles
of their own to think of. The young lady had felt eased-up
at first. But toward the end of midsummer her trouble

started all over again; again came the pining, and such a fear of thunder-storms, of conflagrations, and of something else, which she was keeping secret within her, that she had other things on her mind besides her brothers. And Nathalia got into the same frame of mind concerning them. Although she remembered to pray for Petr Petrovich's health in every prayer of hers (just as afterwards, throughout her life to her very grave, she used to pray for the repose of his soul), the young mistress was, nevertheless, the nearest of all to her by now. And her young mistress was infecting her ever more and more with her fears, expectations of calamities, and with that which she was keeping a secret.

And that summer was a sultry, dusty, windy one, with thunder-storms an everyday occurrence. Dark, disquieting rumours were circulating among the common folk: about some new war or other, about certain uprisings and conflagrations. Some were sayin' that, any minute now, all the mujiks would be allowed to go free, whilst others was sayin' just the opposite: startin' in with autumn, all the mujiks was goin' to be took an' made into clean-shaven recruities—every mother's son on 'em. And, as is ever the way in troublous times, vagabonds, fey folk, and monks sprang up in incomputable numbers. And the young mistress all but had fist-fights with the mistress, all on their account, furnishing them with bread and eggs.

One of these visitors was Dronya—lanky, red-haired, inordinately ragged. He was simply a drunkard, but played the little innocent. He'd walk through the yard toward the house in such deep thought that he knocked his head against walls and leapt away with a joyous face after every such collision.

"My little birdies!" he would cry out in a falsetto, hopping about, distorting his whole body, and especially his right arm, making something in the nature of a shield against the sun out of it. "My little birdies are off—they're off, flyin' through the heavens!"

And Nathalia, following the example of all peasant women, watched him as one is supposed to watch the lesser folk of God: stolidly and pityingly. As for the young lady, she would make a dash for the window, and, with tears, would shout in a piteous voice:

"Dronya, thou most worthy man of God, pray to God for me, sinner that I be!"

And at this shout Natashka's eyes would become staring from dread suppositions.

Another visitor was Timosha Klichinsky, of the Klichino settlement: small, womanishly fat, with big breasts, with the face of a squint-eyed baby that had grown daft and asthmatic from its corpulence, yellow of hair, in a blouse of white calico and short, small breeches. As he neared the front steps, he walked hastily, taking small steps and walking on the toes of his swollen feet, and his narrow little eyes had such a look as if he had just scrambled out of deep water or had just saved himself from almost inescapable peril.

"Troubbel!" he would mumble, gasping. "Troubbel. . . ."

They would calm him down, feed him, and await some word or exploit from him. But he said nothing, breathing hard through his nose and greedily smacking his lips. And having done with smacking his lips, he again tossed his sack over his shoulders and uneasily sought his staff.

"But when are you coming again?" the young mistress would call after him. And he would answer also by calling out, in an incongruously high alto, for some reason confusing her patronymic:

" 'Bout Holy Week—'bout Holy Week, Lukianovna!"

And the young mistress wailed piteously after him, by now in a tone that was near to confession:

"Holy man of God! Pray to God for me, sinner that I be!"

And the others present crossed themselves and sighed, inasmuch as there really were tidings of calamities coming from everywhere, almost every day—tidings of thunderstorms and conflagrations. And the ancient fear of fire was constantly growing in Dry Valley. Just as soon as the sandy-yellow sea of ripening grain would begin to dim under a cloud gathering at the back of the estate—just as soon as the first gust of wind swirled up over the common, and a distant thunder-peal rumbled by heavily—the country-wives rushed to bring the small, dark panels of the icons out on their thresholds, and to get ready pots of milk, which, as everybody knows, quenches a fire the fastest of all. And in the manor-house the scissors went flying out of the window into the nettles; the sanctified towel, of fearful potency, was taken out; the window-curtains were drawn; wax candles were lit with trembling hands. . . .

Even the lady of the house became infected with fear—and one could not tell whether this were a pretence or if she were in downright earnest. Formerly she used to say that a thunder-storm was "a phenomenon of nature." Now she, too, would make the sign of the cross and shut her eyes tight, crying out at every lightning-flash, and, in order to

increase her own fright as well as the fright of those surrounding her, she was forever talking about a certain unusual thunder-storm which had broken out in the year 1771,
in Tyrol, and which had killed one hundred and eleven
people, all at one fell swoop. And those who heard her
caught up the refrain and hastened to tell their own stories:
now about the willow by the highway, burned to ashes by
lightning; now about a peasant woman who had been
stunned by thunder, just the other day, at Chirkizovo;
now about a certain troika, so deafened by a thunder-peal
while travelling that all the three horses had fallen on their
knees.

Finally a certain Iushka attached himself to these vigils—
"a monk who had transgressed," as he styled himself.

IX

By birth Iushka was a mujik. However, he'd never
done an honest day's work in all his life, but lived wherever
God might send him, paying for the hospitality extended
to him with stories about his utter idleness and about his
"transgression." "I'm a mujik, brother, yet smart, an', to
top it all off, I also look like a hunch-back," he used to
say. "So why should I work?"

And, true enough, his gaze was like that of a hunch-
back: caustic and clever. He had no hair growing on his
face; his shoulders, because of rachitis of the thoracic cavity,
he held raised; he gnawed his finger-nails; his fingers, with
which he was every minute tossing back his long, bronze-
red hair, were thin and strong. To till the soil had seemed
to him "unseemly an' boresome." And so he'd gone to the

abbey at Kiev, had "grown up a bit there," and had been expelled for his "transgression." Then, having reasoned out that to pretend to be a pilgrim to holy places, a man seeking salvation for his soul, was an old dodge and, on top of that, might turn out an unprofitable one, he tried to pretend something else: without taking off his cassock, he began to boast openly of his idleness and lewdness, to smoke and to drink as much as he could (he never grew drunk), to jeer and mock at the abbey, and to explain, with the aid of the most indecent gestures and bodily movements, for just what reason he had been driven out of that abbey.

"Well, you know how it is," he would tell the mujiks, winking, "you know—right off they took an' chucked this slave of God right out on his ear, for that same thing. An' so I ups an' starts rollin' home, to my own region. . . . I'll manage to get along, now!"

And he was right: get along he did. And White Russia, his home region, received him no less hospitably, shameless sinner that he was, than she did those who sought salvation for their souls: it gave him food and drink, put him up for the night, listened to him with rapture.

"And so you just took a vow never to work?" the mujiks would ask him, their eyes glistening in anticipation of his caustic franknesses.

"The Devil alone could make me work now!" Iushka would respond. "I'm spoilt, brother, that's what! I'm more ruttish nor the goat we had in the abbey. You take these same wenches, now (I wouldn't want the grown women, not if you was to give 'em to me for nothin'); they fear me

273

like death, an' yet they love me. Oh, well, I'm not so bad meself! I mayn't have no fancy feathers on me, but me bones is trim!"

Having bobbed up at the Dry Valley estate, he, like one who knew his way about, went straight into the house—into the entry, where Natashka was sitting on a bench, humming to herself: "I, a maiden young, as I swept the hut, found me something sweet." Catching sight of him, she jumped up in terror.

"Why, and who are you?" she cried out.

"A man," Iushka answered, quickly looking her over from head to foot. "Tell your missus I'm here."

"Who is it?" the mistress as well called out from the dining-room.

But Iushka reassured her in a moment; he told her he was an erstwhile monk and no desertin' soldier, as she had probably thought; that he was returnin' to his birthplace, an' that he begged that he be searched first an' then be allowed to stay overnight, to rest up a bit, like. And he so impressed the mistress with his straightforwardness that the very next day he was able to shift himself to the footmen's quarters and become absolutely one of the household. Thunder-storm followed thunder-storm, but he indefatigably entertained his hostesses with stories; he struck upon the idea of boarding up the skylights in order to safeguard the roof from lightnings; he ran out on the steps during the most fearful thunder-claps, in order to demonstrate how little they were to be feared; he helped the serving-wenches to prepare and bring in the samovars.

The wenches eyed him askance, feeling his quick, lecherous glances upon them, but they laughed at his jests, while

Natashka, whom he had already more than once stopped in the dark corridor with a quick whisper: "I've fallen in love with you, wench!" durst not lift up her eyes to him. He was both repulsive to her because of the smell of atrocious tobacco which had permeated his whole cassock, and frightful . . . frightful.

She already knew to a certainty what would befall. She used to sleep alone in the corridor, near the door of her young lady's bedroom, and Iushka had already told her curtly: "I'll come. You may slit my throat, but I'll come. But if you start screamin', I'll burn the house down to the ground, an' all of you with it. . . ." But what deprived her of strength most of all was the consciousness that something *inevitable* was being consummated, that the realization of her fearful dream was at hand, that evidently it had been written down for her since birth that she was to perish with her young mistress.

By now all understood that the Devil himself came to dwell in the house of nights. All understood exactly what it was (outside of thunder-storms and conflagrations) that was driving the young mistress out of her mind, that compelled her to moan delectably and wildly in her sleep, only to leap up thereafter with such horrible screams that the most deafening peals of thunder were as nothing compared with them. She screamed:

"The Serpent of Eden, of Jerusalem, is strangling me!"

And who else should this Serpent be save the Fiend, save that grey he-goat that enters the rooms of women and maids of nights? And is there anything in the world more fearful than his visitations in the dark, on inclement nights with never-silenced peals of thunder, and with reflections of the lightnings upon the black icons? That passion, that lust with which the fly-by-night vagabond whispered to Natashka were also not human; how, then, could one offer resistance to them? Thinking of her fateful, her inevitable hour as she sat on her horse-blanket, spread on the floor in the corridor, and gazing intently into the darkness with a pounding heart, hearkening to every crackling and rustling in the sleeping house, even the least, she was already feeling the first attacks of that painful ailment which for a long time tortured her afterwards: her foot would suddenly begin to itch, a sharp, pricking spasm would pass through it, bending, twisting all the toes toward the sole—and then, excruciatingly, voluptuously twisting the sinews, ran over the legs, over the whole body, up to the very gullet, until there was a moment when she wanted to cry out, and that still more frenziedly, still more delectably and agonizingly, than the young mistress did. . . .

And the inevitable was consummated. Iushka came—precisely on that fearful night that marked the end of summer, on the night before the Day of Elijah the Dispenser, that ancient fire-darter. There was no thunder on that night, and there was no sleep for Natashka. She dozed off—and suddenly became wide awake, as if from a jolt. It was the very dead of night—she understood this with her insanely pounding heart. She leapt up and looked at one end of the corridor, then the other: on all sides the sky, silent, full of fire and mysteries, was flaring up, catching on flame, quivering, and blinding one with its golden and wan-blue heat-lightning. The entry was momently turning as light as day. She started running—and stopped as if she were rooted to the spot; the aspen timbers which had

long been lying in the yard under the window showed blindingly white whenever the heat-lightning flared. She wanted
to go into the dining-room. There one window was raised;
one could hear the even noise of the garden. The room was
still darker than the entry, but the fiery light flickered
still more vividly outside all the panes; everything would
be flooded with darkness, only, the next moment, to start
quivering again, to burst into flame, now here, now there—
and the whole garden, with its lace-work of tree-tops, its
spectres of pale-green birches and poplars, would tremble,
grow, and appear in silhouette against the enormous horizon, now golden, now pale violet.

" 'Out upon the wide sea Rowdy Isle doth rise . . .' "
she fell to whispering. " 'There an old bitch lies, with grey
fur and eyes. . . .' "

And no sooner had she uttered these primitively awesome
words than, turning around, she caught sight of Iushka,
who, with shoulders hunched up, was standing two paces
away from her. A flash of heat-lightning lit up his face—
pale, with the eyes like black rings. Inaudibly he ran up
to her, quickly clasped her around the waist with his long
arms—and, crushing her, with a single swing threw her first
on her knees, then flat on her back, on the cold floor of the
entry. . . .

Iushka came to her on the following night as well. He
came also many other nights—and she, losing consciousness
from horror and aversion, submissively gave herself up to
him. She durst not even think of resisting him, nor of
imploring protection from her mistresses or the domestics,
just as her young lady durst not resist the devil who, of
nights, took his delight in her, and just as (so they say)

even Grandmother herself, an imperious belle, durst not resist her house-serf Tkach, a desperate good-for-naught and a thief, who was at long last sent off to Siberia, as a settler. . . . Finally Natashka palled upon Iushka; Dry Valley, too, palled upon him, and he vanished suddenly, even as he had suddenly appeared.

A month after his vanishing Nathalia felt that she was going to be a mother. And in September, on the day following the return of the young masters from the war, the manor-house at Dry Valley caught on fire and blazed long and fearfully: her other dream had been fulfilled as well. It caught on fire at dusk, during a downpour, from a bolt of lightning—from a golden ball, which, as Soloshka said, had leapt out of the stove in Grandfather's bedroom and had gone dashing, bouncing through all the rooms. As for Nathalia, who, upon catching sight of the smoke and fire, had started running with all her might from the bath-house (the bath-house, where she passed whole days and nights in tears)—Nathalia told afterwards that in the garden she had run up against someone clad in a red, close-fitting kaftan and a high Cossack cap with gold braid; he, too, was running with all *his* might through the wet bushes and burdocks. Whether all this had really happened or had been merely an illusory image, Nathalia could not vouch. The only well-authenticated thing is that the terror which had overwhelmed her had also freed her from the child she had been expecting.

And from that autumn she had faded. Her life entered that everyday rut which she did not get out of until her very end. Aunt Tonia was taken to the bones of a saint at Voronezh. After that the Devil no longer dared approach her, and she calmed down, beginning to live like everybody else. The disorder of her mind and soul told only in the glitter of her wild eyes, in her extreme slovenliness, in a furious irritability, and in a mood of depression whenever the weather was bad.

Nathalia, too, had been with her at the visit to the saint's bones, and she, too, had attained during this journey to tranquillity, to a solution of all that had already seemed inescapable. Into what trembling she used to be thrown by the mere thought of her meeting with Petr Petrovich! No matter how she steeled herself in preparation for it, it was beyond her power to imagine that meeting calmly. And what of Iushka—what of her disgrace, her ruin! But the very uniqueness of this ruin, the unusual depth of her sufferings, that element of the fatal which was present in her misfortune (why, it was not in vain that the horror of the fire had well-nigh coincided with it!), and the pilgrimage to the sainted martyr's shrine—all these had given her the right to look simply and calmly into the eyes not only of all those surrounding her, but even those of Petr Petrovich. God himself had marked her and her young mistress with His baleful finger; were *they* the ones to fear people? As a black little nun, as a meek and simple servant, light and pure, just as if she had already taken the viaticum—thus did she re-enter the house at Dry Valley upon her return from Voronezh; unwaveringly did she approach to kiss Petr Petrovich's hand. And for but an instant did her heart quiver—youthfully, tenderly, like a young girl's—when her lips touched his small, swarthy hand with its turquoise ring. . . .

Things dropped back to their everyday routine in Dry

Valley. Definite rumours concerning the emancipation of
the serfs arrived, and even evoked alarm among both the
household servants and the people in the village. What
lay ahead of them—something worse, perhaps? It's easy
enough to say: Start living a new life! The masters, too,
were faced with living a new life, and yet they hadn't known
how to live even in the old way. . . . Grandfather's death;
then the war, and the comet, which latter threw the whole
country into terror; next the burning of the manor-house,
and after that the rumours concerning emancipation: all
these had rapidly changed the faces and the souls of the
masters, had deprived them of their youth, their insou-
ciance, their former fits of flaring up and cooling down, but
did give them ill nature, tedium, hard fault-finding with
one another. "Squabbles," as our father used to put it,
sprang up; things reached the dog-lashes-at-table stage. . . .

Need began to remind them of the insistent necessity of
mending, somehow or other, their affairs, which had been
thoroughly spoiled by the Crimean War, by the fire, by
debts. And in the management of the estate the brothers
only interfered with each other. One (Petr Petrovich) was
absurdly greedy, stern, and suspicious; the other (Arcadii
Petrovich) was absurdly generous, kind-hearted, and trust-
ful. Having patched up an agreement, of sorts, between
them, they decided upon an enterprise which was bound
to bring in a big return. They mortgaged the estate and
bought about three hundred underfed, gaunt horses; they
collected them through almost the whole district, with the
help of a certain gypsy by the name of Ilya Samsonov.
Their intention was to feed the crow-baits up during the
winter and to sell them at a profit in the spring. But, after

having consumed an enormous quantity of flour and straw, the horses (almost all of them, one after the other) dropped dead toward the spring. . . .

And the discord between the brothers kept on growing and growing. At times things reached such a pass that they grabbed their knives and guns. And no one knows what the end of all this would have been had not a new calamity descended upon Dry Valley.

One winter day, in the fourth year after his return from the Crimea, Petr Petrovich went off to Lunevo, where he had a mistress. He lived for two days on the farm; all the time there he drank, and was tipsy even when he started for home. It was snowing very hard; the open sleigh, covered with a rug, was harnessed with two horses, but Petr Petrovich gave orders to unharness the off-horse, a young, hot-blooded animal that sank up to its belly in the porous snow, and to tie it behind the sleigh, while he himself lay down to sleep, with his head toward it. Dusk—misty, leaden-hued—was coming on. And, as he was falling off to sleep, Petr Petrovich called out to Evsei Bodulya (whom he frequently took with him instead of the regular coachman, Vasska the Cossack, being afraid that Vasska would do away with him, since all the domestics were incensed against him because of floggings)—Petr Petrovich called out: "Get along with you!" and kicked Evsei in the back. And the shaft-horse, a powerful bay, already wet, steaming, and with his milt clacking, dashed off with them over the snow-filled, "hard-sleddin'" road, into the dark turbidity of the desert plain, toward the ever-deepening, frowning winter night. . . .

But at midnight, when everybody at Dry Valley was

already dead asleep, someone knocked in quick alarm at a window of the entry where Nathalia slept. She jumped down from her bench and, barefooted, ran out on the front steps. Near the steps, showing dimly and darkly, stood the open sleigh, the horses, and Evsei, who was holding a whip.

"Trouble, lass—trouble!" he began to mumble, in a muffled voice—oddly, as if it were all a dream. "The master's been killed . . . by the off-horse. . . . It ran too fast, slipped up on its haunches, an' struck him with one of its fore hoofs as it were tryin' to get up. . . . Crushed his whole face in. . . . He's already beginnin' to get cold. . . . 'Tweren't me that done it—'tweren't me, s'help me Christ, 'tweren't me!"

Coming down the steps without a word, her bare feet sinking in the snow, Nathalia walked up to the open sleigh, crossed herself, sank to her knees, clasped the icy, bloodied head to her, and fell to kissing it and screaming, so that she could be heard all over the estate, in a wildly joyous scream, strangling from her sobs and her laughter.

X

Whenever it befell us to rest after cities in the quiet and poverty-stricken wilderness of Dry Valley, Nathalia would relate to us, anew and anew, the tale of her perished life. And at times her eyes would darken, would become fixed, her voice passing into a stern, measured half-whisper. And there was forever coming to my recollection the crude image of the saint which had hung in a corner of the entry in our old house. Beheaded, the saint had come to his fellow-

townsmen, bringing his lifeless head in his hands as witness
to his story. . . .

Even those few material traces of the past which we had
on a time found in Dry Valley were vanishing by now. Our
sires and grandsires had left us no portraits, no letters—
not even the simple appurtenances of their daily existence.
And whatever little there had been had all perished in the
fire. For a long time there had been standing in the entry
a certain trunk, bound with hair-sealskin, worn bald in
some spots and with tatters that had turned as hard as
wood; it had been bound therewith a century ago, this
trunk of Grandfather's, made of curly Karelian birch,
and with drawers that could be pulled out. It had been
stuffed chock-full of charred French vocabularies, and with
churchly books that were unbelievably soiled and covered
with wax-candle drippings. Subsequently this trunk, too,
had vanished. The ponderous furniture that had stood in
the dining-room and the parlour vanished as well or got
broken. . . The house was becoming ramshackle, settling
more and more into the ground. All those long years which
has passed over it since the time of the last events told of
here had been for it the years of a lingering death. . . .
And its past was becoming ever more legendary.

The Dry Valley folk grew amid a life that was dull,
sombre, but still a life that was intricate, that had a semblance of a settled existence and of well-being. To judge
by the inertia of this existence, to judge by the adherence
of the Dry Valley folk to that existence, one might have
thought that there would never be an end to it. But they,
these descendants of the steppe nomads, were submissive,

weak, "no end chicken-hearted and touchy when it come to being punished"! And, as under a plough furrowing a field the small hummocks over the underground passages and burrows of the hamsters disappear, one after the other, without leaving a trace, even so did the Dry Valley nests disappear before our eyes, rapidly and leaving never a trace. And the dwellers in those nests perished, scattered; as for those that had survived, somehow or other, they, also somehow or other, were dragging out the remnant of their days. And we had come not upon a social order, not upon life, but merely upon recollections of both, upon a half-wild simplicity of existence.

Ever more rarely with the years did we visit our steppe region. And ever more unkindred was it becoming to us, ever more faintly did we feel our tie with that mode of life and that class whence we had issued. Many of our clan are illustrious and of ancient lineage (even as our branch is). The chronicles cite our names; our ancestors were not only royal dapifers, and leaders in battle, and "men of high rank," but the nearest of fellow-champions, and even of kin, to the tsars. And, had they called themselves knights, had those of our branch been born a little more toward the west, how steadfastly we would speak of them, how long we would still maintain our position! A descendant of the knights could not say that within half a century a whole class had well-nigh vanished from off the face of the earth; that so many of us had degenerated, had gone out of our minds, had laid violent hands upon ourselves, had drunk ourselves to ruin, had sunk and simply become lost somewhere in the shuffle! Such a descendant could not confess, as I am confessing, that we have not even the least definite idea of the life not only of our remote ancestors, but actually of that of our great-grandsires; he could not confess that with every day it is becoming ever more difficult for us to imagine even that which occurred only half a century ago!

That place where the Lunevo estate had stood has long since been ploughed and sown, just as the ground has been ploughed and sown on the sites of many other estates as well. Dry Valley still held on, somehow or other. But, after having cut down the last birches in the garden, after having disposed, in parcels, of almost all the arable land, even its owner, the son of Petr Petrovich, forsook the old place; he went to work, becoming a conductor on a railroad. And the old women who dwelt in Dry Valley—Claudia Markovna, Aunt Tonia, Nathalia—were drearily dragging out their last years. Spring changed to summer, summer to autumn, autumn to winter. . . . They had lost count of these changes. They lived by and in recollections, dreams, quarrels, cares for their daily bread. In the summer those places where the estate had of yore spread wide were sunk deep in fields of rye belonging to the mujiks. The house they surrounded had become visible from afar. The brushwood (all that was left of the garden) had become such a wilderness that the quail called near the very balcony. But summer wasn't so bad! "Summer is paradise for us!" the old women used to say. It was the rainy autumns and the snowy winters that were long and hard in Dry Valley. Cold and hunger reigned then in the empty, decaying house. It was drifted over by blizzards, penetrated through and through by the piercing, frosty Sarmatian wind. As for heating, the house was heated very rarely. Of evenings a small tin lamp shed its meagre light through the windows of the mistress's

chamber—the only habitable one. The mistress, with her
eye-glasses on, wearing a short sheepskin coat and felt
boots, knit away at a stocking, bending toward the little
lamp. Nathalia dozed on the cold ledge of the oven. And
the young mistress, looking like a Siberian shaman, sat in
her hut and puffed on a pipe. When Aunt was not on the
outs with Claudia Markovna, the latter would put her little
lamp, not on the table, but on the window-sill. And Aunt
Tonia sat in the strange, faint half-light which fell from the
house into the interior of her icy hut, cluttered up with the
broken pieces of old furniture, piled with shards of broken
dishes, encumbered with the old pianoforte, which had
slumped over on its side. So icy was this hut that the hens,
toward the care of which all of Aunt Tonia's forces were
directed, used to have their feet frozen as they passed the
night on these shards and broken pieces of furniture. . . .

But now the Dry Valley estate is altogether empty. All
those mentioned in this chronicle have died, and so have
all their neighbours, all their coevals. And at times one
thinks: "Come, now—*have* they ever really lived in this
world?"

Only when visiting country churchyards does one feel
that all this has actually happened; one feels even an eerie
nearness to these people. But even to feel this one has to
make an effort; one has to sit, to ponder, over the grave of
a kinsman—that is, if one can but find it. It is a shameful
thing to say, but it cannot be concealed: we do not know
the graves of Grandfather, of Grandmother, of Petr Petrovich. All we know is that their place is near the altar
of the little old church in the Chirkizovo hamlet. There is

no getting through to this church in the winter-time: it is surrounded by waist-high snow-drifts, out of which a cross sticks up here and there, or the top of a bare bush, or even some single, scraggly twig.

On a summer day you drive through a hot, quiet, and empty village street, hitch your horse near the church enclosure, beyond which the fir-trees stand in a dark-green wall, baking in the heat of the sun. Beyond the wicket, open all the way, beyond the white church with its rusty cupola, is a whole grove of low, many-branched elms, ash-trees, osiers; shade and coolness are everywhere. One wanders for a long time along bushes, along hummocks and pits covered with thin churchyard grass, along stone plates, porous from the rains and snows, grown over with black, powdery moss, almost sunk into the ground. . . . Here are two or three monuments of iron. But whose are they? So greenish-aureate have they become that the inscriptions upon them can no longer be read.

Under what hummocks, then, are the bones of Grandmother, of Grandfather? Why, God alone knows! One is aware of but one thing: they are here somewhere, near at hand. And one sits and ponders, making an effort to picture these Khrushchevs, forgotten of all men. And their times begin to seem now infinitely distant, now ever so near. Thereupon, with joy, one says to oneself: "This isn't hard to imagine—it isn't! One must but remember that this gilded cross, leaning askew against the blue summer sky, was the same in their times as it is now. . . . That the rye was just as yellow, and ripening in just the same way in the fields, deserted and sultry, while here were shade, coolness, bushes . . . and amid the bushes, there had been ambling and grazing an old, white nag, just like the one I am seeing now, with shedding, age-green withers, and rosy, splitting hoofs. . . ."

TRANSLATOR'S NOTES

⌣ ⌣

The Elaghin Affair
  Quand même pour toujours!: If so, then for always.
  Krassinski, Count Sigismund Napoleon (March 19, 1812, Paris—March 24, 1859, Paris). Famous Polish poet, novelist, and patriot. His poems, *The Undivine Comedy, Iridion, Summer Night,* and others, are attempts, in poetical form, to solve philosophical and social problems. There was also another Krassinski, Valerian, likewise a count (1780?–1855), a historian, who lived in England in 1855.
  Bashkirtseva, Marie Constantinova (November 23, 1860–October 31, 1884), young and beautiful, talented as an artist, and friend of many celebrities, including Guy de Maupassant, with whom she corresponded as an *inconnue;* best known for her diaries, translated into French, German, and English, but only in "edited" versions.—Marie Vetser, Baroness; young and beautiful; beloved of Rudolph von Habsburg, who killed her (January 1889) and then committed suicide, in despair over his father's orders to break off the liaison.
  Pani is Polish for "Lady," "Madam."
  "If it were done . . . then 'twere well it were done quickly!"—from the beginning of Macbeth's speech as he

enters, Act I, Scene vii.

The Elaghin Affair is dated: Maritime Alps, 1925.

The Bride

Title changed by author. Original title: *Casimir Stanislavovich.*

The Café Philipov was celebrated, among other things, for the delectable Philipovskiya *piroʒhki:* baked dumplings with meat filling, the dough something like that of crullers, but ever so much more savoury.

There is (or was) a Tverskaya Street in Moscow, as well as a Tverskoi Boulevard.

Braga is mead; *Praga* is, of course, Prague.

Wind-broken horses emit a roaring, or bellowing sound, on the run.

The story is dated 1916.

The Mordvinian Sarafan

A sarafan is a loose sleeveless garment, usually worn by Russian peasant women. Sometimes it is a dress, put on over the head; sometimes a long smock, open in front, as in the case of the "fly-aparts" in *Dry Valley.*

The Mordva, or Mordvinians, are a Finnish-Ugrian agricultural race in the central Volga region; in antiquity they were warlike, and at one time formed an independent princedom. They are professing Christians, but not hopelessly so, being rather addicted to pagan rites and customs, such as sacrifice of animals and the like. A Mordvinian sarafan, therefore, would be something particularly vivid and heathenish.

Dated: Maritime Alps, 1925.

A Creepy Story
  Dated: Paris, 1926.

Temir Aksak Khan
  Dated: Paris, 1921.

The Scream
  In this story, as well as in *The Third Cock-Crow,* I am
indebted to the able seamanship of Captain W. H. Yost, Jr.,
who has read these stories in proof.
  Dated: 1911.

The Star of Love
  The Midnight Glow, or Midnight Star: the Morning
Star; in this case Venus, although Jupiter, Mars, and
Saturn also bear the name of the Morning Star.
  Since dialect is employed in the original, I have not hes-
itated to employ dialect in translation. The same holds
true of other stories in this collection where dialect is used,
since it is part of my creed that to lovelify original dialect
into lavender scented (and hued) English is unfair not only
to the author and reader, but to the translator as well, and,
in general, though a prevalent practice, is also a pernicious
one.
  Dated: Paris, 1921.

Transfiguration

  Compare this vigil with that in Gogol's immortal *Viy,* in
Evenings on a Farm near Dikanka.
  Dated: Paris, 1921.

The Cricket

A coffin-nail is, of course, any cigarette, but generally an atrocious one. Bunin uses a word which implies that it was actually rolled from a piece of newspaper. I did not use the British term "gasper," since (if I may be permitted to obtrude an opinion) I have generally found that British slang, when it is not effete or downright silly (its main characteristics) is lacking in vigour, in vividness, and, above all, in poetry.

Dated: Capri, 1911.

Long, Long Ago

Ivan Ivannich's full name is Ivan Ivannovich Ivanov, and he is, it need hardly be added, brother to the John Smiths and the Jean Durants of this world.

Arbat Street was one of the most ancient in Moscow. The name is derived from *arba*, the Tatar word for "cart." There was also an Arbat Square. The past tense is used advisedly, since the names may have been changed.

Dated: Amboise, 1922.

Cicadas

This meditation, or self-analysis, or confession of an author's faith (call it what you will; it can hardly be called a story) is one of Bunin's best things, and, to me, the finest piece in the present collection. *Cicadas* belongs in the same category with Poe's *Eureka* as a poem in prose.

"And I gave my heart . . . therewith." *Ecclesiastes*, i, 13. "Lo . . . many inventions." *Eccles.*, vii, 29. "Be not . . . over-wise." *Eccles.*, vii, 16. "There is no remembrance . . . come after." *Eccles.*, i, 11. "The dead know not . . .

under the sun." *Eccles.*, ix, 5–6. "I made me great works . . . orchards." *Eccles.*, ii, 4–5. "I got me . . . maidens." *Eccles.*, ii, 7. "I gathered . . . provinces." *Eccles.*, ii, 8. "What profit . . . sun?" *Eccles.*, i, 3. "For unto whomsoever . . . the more." *St. Luke*, xii, 48.

"Taste thereof . . . and ye shall be as God." Here Bunin's text has been followed. *Genesis*, iii, 5 reads: "Eat thereof . . . and ye shall be as gods."

"God is in heaven, and we upon earth." *Ecclesiastes*, v, 2 reads: ". . . thou upon earth."

"Tasting thereof, we increase cognition, consciousness,— that is, sorrow." This, obviously, derives from *Ecclesiastes*, i, 18: "For in much wisdom is much grief: and he that increaseth knowledge increaseth sorrow."

"The fool . . . flesh." *Eccles.*, iv, 5. "He that observeth . . . reap." *Eccles.*, xi, 4.

"Vanity of vanities . . . sun?" *Eccles.*, i, 2. "The sleep . . . sweet." *Eccles.*, v, 12. "There is nothing . . . labour." *Eccles.*, ii, 24. "Go thy way . . . heart." *Eccles.*, ix, 7.

"Sun, stand thou still!" *Joshua*, x, 12.

"Night unto night showeth knowledge." *Psalm*, xix, 2. The Russian reads "transmits knowledge."

Maya, in Hindu mythology, is both Mother of the World, the embodied active will of the Creator; and also Illusion, in the form of a heavenly maiden, replacing Nescience.

Cicadas is dated: Maritime Alps, 1925, and, I believe, was written in a single day (or night).

The Night of Denial

Mara, in Hindu mythology, is the ruling spirit of evil; the Tempter.

". . . a divine node, a high . . . protuberance." This is most perceptible in a large, greystone head of Buddha of the T'ang period. See Plate II, article "Buddha and Buddhism," *Encyclopædia Britannica*, 14th edition.

This story is dated: Paris, 1921.

The Third Cock-Crow

Sinope: a seaport town in Asiatic Turkey; capital of the ancient kingdom of Pontus. On the 30th of November 1853 Phoca was evidently on the side of the Russians, when Admiral Nachimov overwhelmed Osman Pasha's whole fleet at Sinope.—Phoca is Nicephorus, and, while his story is quite as smug, it is not altogether as vomitory as other hagiologies. Nicephorus dwelt in Antioch, under Valerian and Galienus. He belonged to the laity, but led an edifying life. When his estranged bosom crony, "the priest Sapritius," in spite of having made an Uncle Tom speech from his rack, apostatized at the last moment to escape being decollated for the Faith, Nicephorus, to atone for Sapritius (who was still obdurate about forgiving Nicephorus for a spat the two had had), went to the block in his friend's place, thus receiving "the crown of martyrdom, which Sapritius had so wantonly cast from him."

Pontos (from the Greek, signifying the open sea) is the Black Sea.

The Third Cock-Crow is dated 1917.

Of Emelya the Fool, and of How He Turned Out to be the Wisest of All

Emelya is apparently elder brother to the folk-zany of Russia, Ivannushka the Little Fool, who is neither so foolish as Simple Simon nor so cunning as Tyl Eulenspiegel, nor so witty as Hojja.—According to Bunin's own opinion, this story is "utterly untranslatable into any language." If any academic language of the Ph. D.'s is meant, I agree with the author heartily. Yet I do not believe it untranslatable into any living tongue that has a vulgate to correspond with the racy, picturesque, tangy speech of the original. At least I could not resist the attempt to translate it.

The story is dated: Paris, 1921.

Dry Valley

The title is a literal translation of *Soukhodol*. The author's explanation of the name's derivation from a dried river-bed has been incorporated in the story.

Maître corbeau sun un arbre perché would mean, in any good schoolboy translation: Master Crow upon a tree perched. *Ou êtes-vous, mes enfants?*: Where are you, my children?

A tarantass is a low, four-wheeled carriage, resting on two long, springy poles. A samovar is a self-cooking tea-urn. A balalaika is a species of mandolin, triangular, and in all sizes, from one as small as a ukulele to one as big as a bull-fiddle. A troika is a team of three horses, harnessed abreast. A kaftan is a robe. A borzoi is a wolf-hound.

"Faggots" is British for meat-cakes. The Russian is *khvorosti*, which has the same curious double-meaning of meat-cakes and of firewood.

A solea is a raised part of the floor in a Greek (or even Latin) church, between choir and presbytery, or ambo and sanctuary, usually occupied by relics or things of that sort.

Tildes: an unavoidable precise term; diacritical signs

(such as the $\tilde{}$ mark over *n* in Spanish); used for contractions in Church Slavonic.

Skull-caps sanctified by contact with the bones of saints and martyrs were worn to ward off, or even to allay, headaches, and were also considered a sovereign remedy against all sorts of maladies.

Dyed-in-the-wool Russians (the smokers, of course) do not sigh for anything in vanished Russia so much as they do for the superb, fragrant, unbelievably fine Latakia grown and processed on the Zhukovski tobacco-plantations. Even the worst sort (IV) was infinitely better (so they mourn) than the finest mixture from a Fifth Avenue or a Regent Street tobacconist's. . . .

"Let not the sun go down upon your wrath."—*Ephesians,* iv, 26. "Death is cruel to a sinner." Literal translation. The author believes it to be a churchly saying, but not in the Bible. The nearest Biblical equivalent I have been able to find is "The sting of death is sin"—*I Corinthians,* xv, 56. Any information would be appreciated.

Grandfather's pupils diverged senselessly after Gervasska "shoved" him to his death; Aunt Tonia's eyes were crossed in a fit of fury. . . . The author used a word which could mean either "cross-eyed" or "wall-eyed." I have therefore consulted Dr. Martin Cohen, the eminent eye-specialist, and am indebted to his opinions, which I hope I have given correctly: After a violent or accidental death the cadaver generally has diverging pupils; the eyes of a person in a raptus are most likely to be crossed.

"Tuft-heads": The Great Russians thus dubbed the Little Russians, who had (the men, at least) *khokhli*—forelocks or tufts—the rest of the head being shaven: a custom

borrowed from the Tatars, who grew these hirsute adornments so that Mohammed might have something to grab
hold of when it came to lugging the true believers into paradise. The Little Russians retaliated by derisively calling the
Great Russians *katzapi:* literally "goat-like," because of
their addiction to beards. (Cf. Prof. A. Beardsley's *Influence of Hirsute Adornments upon the Growth of Civili-
zation in Europe* (London, 1853), Vol. III, p. 576.

Dry Valley is dated 1911.

The photograph used as a frontispiece belongs to the
period when most of the stories in this collection were
written.

The texts used have been specially corrected and emended
by the author.

B. G. G.

New York City
Spring–Summer, 1934